THE DARK SIDE OF TOWN

THE DARK SIDE OF TOWN

A FIA McKEE MYSTERY

Sasscer Hill

Minotaur Books
New York

THE DARK SIDE OF TOWN. Copyright © 2018 by Sasscer Hill. All rights reserved. Printed in the United States of America. For information, address St. Martin's Press, 175 Fifth Avenue, New York, N.Y. 10010.

www.minotaurbooks.com

Designed by Omar Chapa

Library of Congress Cataloging-in-Publication Data

Names: Hill, Sasscer, author.
Title: The dark side of town / Sasscer Hill.
Description: First edition. | New York : Minotaur Books, [2018] | Series: A Fia McKee Mystery
Identifiers: LCCN 2017045714 | ISBN 9781250097019 (hardcover) | ISBN 9781250097026 (ebook)
Subjects: LCSH: Thoroughbred Racing Protective Bureau—Fiction. | Government investigators—Fiction.| Undercover operations—Fiction. | Women detectives—Fiction. | Horse racing—Fiction. |GSAFD: Mystery fiction.
Classification: LCC PS3608.I43773 D37 2018 | DDC 813/.6—dc23
LC record available at https:lccn.loc.gov/2017045714

Our books may be purchased in bulk for promotional, educational, or business use. Please contact your local bookseller or the Macmillan Corporate and Premium Sales Department at 1-800-221-7945, extension 5442, or by email at MacmillanSpecialMarkets@macmillan.com.

First Edition: April 2018

10 9 8 7 6 5 4 3 2 1

This novel is dedicated to the memory
of the "iron racehorse,"
the courageous and speedy Thoroughbred:
For Love and Honor.

ACKNOWLEDGMENTS

From law enforcement, my thanks to R. George (Bob) Clark, former New York State Trooper, whose familiarity with upstate New York was invaluable. And a most grateful thanks to Scott Silveri, former Chief of Police, Thibodaux Police Department, Thibodaux, Louisiana, who was always ready and willing to answer my questions about police methodology.

From the Thoroughbred Racing Protective Bureau, my thanks to James Gowan, former Vice President, and J. Curtis Linnell, Vice President of Wagering Analysis and Operations.

From the racing world, I'd like to thank racehorse trainer and consultant David Earl Williams, M.S., Ph.D.

As always, my thanks to my critique group, Mary Beth Gibson, Steve Gordy, and Bettie Williams. Couldn't do it without you guys.

Many thanks to my excellent agent, Ann Collette, and my terrific Minotaur editor, Hannah Braaten.

THE DARK SIDE
OF TOWN

1

Dense fog enveloped the backstretch at Saratoga Race Course that morning, leaving the Oklahoma Training Track virtually invisible. Still, I could smell its sandy dirt and sense the expanse of the mile oval stretching away from me.

Jogging the gravel path that paralleled the track, I shoved my hands deeper into the pockets of my jacket, hugging the black denim tighter around my rib cage against the dawn chill.

Out on the dirt, the pounding of hooves drew closer, the sound muffled in the moisture-laden air. Beyond the rail, the horses flying past me were ill-defined, almost ghostly.

The sudden, deafening crack of a handgun was neither muffled nor poorly defined. My years as a Baltimore street cop left no doubt as to what I had heard. I stood still, eyes and ears straining.

Ahead, someone screamed, "Oh, my God!"

I raced forward. The high-pitched wails of the woman grew louder. As I drew close, I could make out her thin body and pale face staring at a form splayed on the ground at her feet. The acrid scent of gunpowder floated past me. The coppery stench of blood was unmistakable.

I closed the distance between us. "Hey," I said, heading off her next cry. "Maybe you should step back. You don't want to mess up the scene, right?"

Though she'd stopped screaming, she didn't seem to hear me. She stared at the figure on the ground, her body shaking. I stared, too. Male, the back of his head blown out, his hand still clutching a revolver. Suicide?

The woman moaned. I could almost see another scream rising in her throat. "Do you have a phone?" I asked, trying to distract her. "Hey, look at me!"

She did, her eyes huge and round.

"Do you know him?"

"I, no. I mean, I've seen him before. At the track."

Gently, I grasped her arm. "Come on. Don't look at him. We need to get help. Do you have a phone?" I asked again.

She nodded numbly.

"Okay, good. Call 911."

I had almost pulled my own cell to make the call before I'd stopped. Though no longer a street cop, I was working undercover and needed to keep a low profile.

As the woman talked to the dispatcher, she grew more focused, giving her name, saying a man had been shot—or maybe had shot himself—at the Oklahoma Training Track just inside the East Avenue entrance to Saratoga's backstretch.

"No," I heard her say, "I ran over here when I heard the gun go off, and I saw—"

The dispatcher must have sensed her rising hysteria and said something to divert it. As they are trained to do, he kept his witness on the phone.

The mist began to break up and rise toward the treetops and spires crowning the historic wooden barns to my right. I eased away from the woman, stepped into a lingering column of fog, and glanced back. Good, I could barely see her. I shouldn't be involved here, so I double-timed it toward my original destination, the barn where I worked as a hot walker.

In the distance, a police siren wailed. The sound drew closer as I hurried away.

Later that morning, I led a hot, sweating racehorse named Bionic along my barn's dusty aisle and listened for more gossip about the shooting everyone was saying was a suicide. The guy had apparently been an apprentice jockey from South America, only no one knew much about him. They said he'd just arrived from Ecuador, or Chile, or maybe Uruguay.

"Whoa back," I called to Becky Joe, the groom who led her horse behind me.

I stopped Bionic to allow him a few sips of water, and as he sank his lips into the bucket hanging from the shedrow rail, I rolled back his cooler sheet to see if his reddish-brown coat was drying out. Thirsty, he sucked up the water until I pulled him away. He was still too hot to drink much, and I rolled the sheet back over his neck so the cool air hitting his wet coat wouldn't cause muscle cramping.

I glanced back at Becky Joe Benson. Maybe sixty, she was short, wore high-heeled cowboy boots, and a brown suede Stetson years past its glory days. I turned back and headed down the shedrow with Becky Joe behind. At this track, the two of us were nobodies, yet we led a couple of horses worth hundreds of thousands of dollars.

This was my first time in Saratoga. I'd been on the job at this barn a week and hadn't figured Becky Joe out yet. She had a drinking problem, used to be a jockey, then was an unsuccessful trainer, and had fallen down the ranks to groom. But she was smart and unquestionably well educated. No doubt she had a story. Everyone at the racetrack did.

Her filly was further along in the cooling process than my colt. She was dried out enough that Becky Joe had already removed her sheet. When I glanced back, Becky Joe let the filly empty her water bucket, then led the horse into a stall to see if she wanted to pee.

I walked on, passing equine heads that peered over stall gates or snatched bites of hay from the nets fastened outside their stalls. The sharp tang of liniment stung my nose, and somewhere, a metal-shod hoof struck the wood inside one of the stalls that had been there since 1863. Many legends had raced at Saratoga.

I tried to concentrate on these things, but my mind wanted to play games with me, flitting back to the acrid odor of burnt gunpowder and the metallic reek of blood. The image of the jockey's blown-out head, the terrible smell of death. What darkness had made him give up on life?

Turning the corner at the end of the aisle, I was so lost in my thoughts, I almost ran into Stevie Davis. Skinny and young, Stevie might reach five foot three, if his socks were thick enough. During the few days I'd worked at Saratoga, the gaunt lines on the kid's face seemed to have increased. It made no sense to me. His frame was so scrawny, he didn't need to starve himself to make jockey weight. Something else was eating him.

Catching my eye, the seventeen-year-old did an about-face and walked alongside me and Bionic. "Fay, you hear about that guy that shot himself?"

I almost corrected him, since my real name is Fia McKee. But at Saratoga Race Course that summer I needed people to believe

I was Fay Mason. Using aliases for undercover work in the past, I'd found it safer to stick with my own initials.

"It's all they've talked about all morning," I said. "Why do you think he did it?"

"I don't know. Whole thing creeps me out." But his lips curved upward and the troubled look in his eyes receded a moment as he smiled at me. He was a good-looking kid, with light brown hair, clear, intelligent eyes, and a honed face with good bones. Still, he carried worry lines that shouldn't be there. Stevie was the stable jockey for the Saratoga trainer I'd been sent to investigate, a thug named Marzio (a.k.a. Mars) Pizutti.

As we walked on, I could smell Bionic's sweat, hear the breath blowing from his nostrils, and see where the flesh immediately above his eye was slightly sunken with exhaustion. His bright reddish-brown coat was offset by jet-black legs, mane, and tail, the classic markings of a blood bay.

"He doing okay?" Stevie asked, staring at the horse. "He's supposed to race in a few weeks, and I'll get the call."

"Pizutti knows more about that than me," I said.

Stevie had just worked the colt five-eighths of a mile, and Bionic's cardiovascular system was not recovering as quickly as Pizutti probably wanted. Personally, I thought the horse would have been better off working three-eighths with a gallop out at whatever speed he was comfortable with. But as a lowly hot walker, my opinion was irrelevant.

At the end of the shedrow, Pizutti—cocky, rotund, and egotistical—emerged from his office.

I thought I heard Stevie say, "Oh, shit," under his breath. As much as I disliked what I knew about Pizutti, I had to admit he had an uncanny connection with his horses. He had a soft round face, was a little jowly beneath his chin, and his expression, as usual, was bland, making me wonder what it was about the man that made Stevie so uncomfortable. Pizutti glanced at Bionic, then flicked his gaze over at me.

"Hey, what's your name again?"

"Fay," I said.

"Yeah, right. Let me see that horse."

"Yes, sir." *You'd think the guy would know his horse's name.* I hadn't spoken to him much in the few days I'd been here. Mostly he'd fired off instructions and I'd nodded and gotten on with it.

I led the big colt to him, and stopped. Stevie edged away and stood against the wall as Pizutti placed his palm on Bionic's chest to see how much dampness and heat remained.

Pizutti glanced at me. "I tell you what, Fay. It's kinda like a fine line, you know? Too much or too little. I think he maybe did too much today." He pursed his lips as if annoyed with himself. "Keep him going, okay?"

"Yes, sir." I could smell stale beer on him.

"Hey," he said, "I keep telling you. Lose the 'sir' stuff. Call me Mars. Right?"

His voice held a whining quality, the volume always soft, like maybe he'd been unhappy as a kid and hadn't wanted to draw attention to himself.

"Okay, Mars," I said.

I clucked to Bionic and moved forward. Stevie started to follow.

"Hey," Mars said, crooking a finger at the kid, "wait up. Need to talk to you 'bout something."

While the jockey paused, I headed down the shedrow with Bionic, thinking how my work for the Thoroughbred Racing Protective Bureau (TRPB), sometimes placed me in risky situations. I believed in the agency's mission to protect the integrity of horse racing, but with the immense sums of money involved and the endless cash pouring into online betting outlets, we fought an uphill battle. The lowlifes that would do anything for money were never far away.

This big picture didn't affect me emotionally. A jockey eating his gun did. And smaller things struck a heartstring, too. Like the haunted eyes of Stevie Davis, or the game-on face of a racehorse determined to annihilate his competitors. The exalted, shouting bettor trading high fives with his buddies because he'd won, or the slumped shoulders and frightened face of a man who just bet borrowed money and lost. That's the stuff that touches my soul.

Bionic snorted as a calico stable cat darted across the aisle in front of the colt's hooves. The horse stopped, lowered his head, and blew gently on the cat. She arched her back and bumped it against the horse's nose before streaking into a stall.

I clucked to my horse, and as we moved on, I considered my personal goal—protecting the people and animals that make racing such a phenomenal sport. And they needed protecting from Mars Pizutti.

The guy was backed by powerful people, and his horses won a lot of races. Too many races. He'd had numerous infractions and suspensions. He'd filed false times for works and managed to place fictional ones in the *Daily Racing Form,* leaving the bettors to believe the horse was less talented and capable of winning than he actually was. He used body-building anabolic steroids like stanozolol and anti-inflammatory corticosteroids like prednisone.

The New York Racing Association (NYRA) had difficulty regulating steroids as they are naturally occurring and are present in low levels in most horses. Current regulations allowed for the presence of steroids like stanozolol and anti-inflammatory corticosteroids like prednisone if the horse was on the vet's list.

This prohibited the horse from racing until the high levels dropped to natural levels.

But Pizutti was a magician at keeping those levels on the edge between legal and illegal. When he did get caught, he'd always gotten off with a fine and been back in his barn within days.

The NYRA had finally suffered enough and had solicited the TRPB to plant an agent in Pizutti's barn.

As a hot walker, I was almost invisible as I led horses each morning. No one would notice me watching, listening, or using my cell phone to record and photograph the goings-on in the trainer's barn.

By now, Bionic and I had walked past the long row of stalls on the rear side of the barn and turned the corner back to Pizutti's side. The trainer was talking to Stevie at the far end of the aisle. The jockey had his arms crossed over his chest, and though I was still thirty stalls away, his stance appeared defensive.

Since Bionic had been the last horse out on the course that day, it was now late in the morning. Much of the help had finished up and headed to the track kitchen for lunch, leaving the barn quiet, the morning bustle noticeably subdued.

Two stalls down, Becky Joe stepped onto the shedrow holding a tote stuffed with grooming tools, hoof picks, a bottle of liniment, and rolls of Vetrap. Her other hand held a tub of poultice. Apparently, she'd just finished "doing up" her filly's legs.

As she stopped and waited for me and Bionic to go by, I heard raised voices. A quick look ahead showed Stevie shaking his head.

"Been in that boy's shoes," Becky Joe muttered. "Didn't like it then, don't like seeing it now."

"What's going on?" I asked.

She stared at her scuffed leather boots. "Couldn't say."

I walked on, growing close enough to hear Stevie's next words.

"I won't do it!"

"You goddamn will!"

"No, I—"

"Shut up," Mars said. He'd seen me coming. Whatever they were arguing about, he didn't want me hearing it.

And angry shade of red stained Stevie's cheeks. The worry lines around his eyes were starting to look like canyons.

The image of the dead apprentice jockey was freshly stamped in my brain, and now I saw desperation in Stevie's eyes. Like Becky Joe, I didn't like it.

2

Staring at the ground, I passed by Mars and Stevie, careful to leave my face expressionless. I could feel the tension between them, but pretended to be oblivious. Instead, since the stable's talented and famous colt resided only four stalls ahead, I looked toward his stall as if my only desire was to catch a glimpse of him.

Ziggy Stardust did not fail me, pushing his dark bay head out over his door as Bionic and I approached. The three-year-old colt rarely disappointed anyone, having won two-thirds of the recent Triple Crown, the two-year-old Breeders' Cup Juvenile race the previous fall, and millions of dollars in purse money for his owners. Of course, Mars had received a fat percentage of the cash as well.

But a thorny question still chafed his fans, the racing hand-icappers, and network talking heads. What had happened to Ziggy Stardust in the Belmont, the third leg of the Triple Crown? Inexplicably, the horse had stopped running after the first half-mile. The battery of after race tests provided no clues. I suspected Mars had given the horse an untraceable drug, turning him into a slug so his trainer could bet every other horse to win. Ziggy Stardust had gone off at nine-to-five odds with the world hoping, that after decades without one, they would finally witness a Triple Crown winner.

I had been at Belmont that day, and the uproar of anger and disappointment from fans had threatened to bring the grandstand roof down on our heads. Mars, who always bet big on his horses and bragged about it, kept his lips zipped that day, hurriedly removing himself from the public's wrath by making a quick dash into the restricted backstretch.

Now, as Bionic and I drew close, Ziggy's luminous eyes studied our progress. He squealed once, then nodded his head up and down, making the large star on his forehead shimmer. Beneath it, little spangles of white cascaded down his face, reminding me of stardust pictures from children's storybooks. The famous dots were Ziggy's trademark. The public loved them.

Mars planned to run the colt back in the Jim Dandy at Saratoga in the coming weeks. If that went well, he would race in the one-and-a-quarter-million-dollar Travers Stakes at the end of August. Both the New York Racing Association and the TRPB wanted to keep a close eye on him and Mars between now and then. It wouldn't do to have bettors believing the top races were rigged.

After we passed Ziggy and circled the end of the barn, Bionic and I ambled past the thirty stalls on the barn's far side that belonged to one of Saratoga's few female trainers, Maggie Bourne. She was standing outside a stall talking to one of the track vets. Her conversation, apparently about the chestnut filly inside, appeared serious, yet Maggie glanced up and smiled at me. I liked that about her. She didn't treat stable help like something that crawled out of the manure pile. Inside the unlighted stall, I glimpsed the back of a man with long dark hair, and a frisson of recognition coursed through me, but I passed by and the moment was gone.

Bionic and I traipsed on until a bantam rooster, flaunting a fine set of glossy, blue-black tail feathers, interrupted our progress. Perched atop the wooden rail that enclosed the shedrow, his yellow feet and sharp toenails clutched the wood. Raising his red comb, he looked at us with disdain, then flapped his wings furiously. I tightened my hold on Bionic's lead shank as the horse shied backwards.

The way the rooster pumped himself up with air as he prepared to crow reminded me of Mars. I glared at the arrogant bird. "Don't you crow, or I'll put you in a stewpot."

Of course, there was no stopping him, and the raucous cry that burst from his open beak warranted earplugs. Bionic ripped the shank from my hands, rocketed down the shedrow, and reaching the far corner, disappeared from sight.

"Loose horse!" I yelled, breaking into a run. I hoped no one got hurt. I hoped Mars wouldn't fire me.

Behind my pounding feet, I heard Maggie Bourne call, "Sorry! We've been trying to catch him . . ."

I assumed she was talking about the rooster and not the horse, but I didn't respond, just kept running as a tight knot formed in my stomach. If Bionic blasted down Mars's side of the barn, he could run down a groom, crash into another horse, or do something crazy like try to jump the rail and kill himself. What would anger Mars the most, though, would be if Bionic upset Ziggy and caused the trainer's star horse to injure himself in his stall.

I streaked around the end of the barn and turning the last corner, almost fainted with relief to see Becky Joe clinging to Bionic's shank, and Stevie grasping the horse's halter. A quick glance down the shedrow showed no sign of Mars. I was lucky.

"Thank you, guys!" I gasped.

"Horse was in a full-tilt boogie, for sure," Becky Joe said, her knuckles white on the shank.

I hadn't heard that expression before, but it seemed appropriate.

"Bet it was that little shit rooster of Maggie's," Becky Joe said.

"That's the one."

"I got plans for that little man."

I didn't ask her what she meant. Might be one of those "the less you know" situations.

Stevie's hand dropped away from the leather halter and his gaze traveled over the horse. "He seems all right."

"Are you?" I asked, curious about his altercation with Mars.

His mouth tightened. "Yeah," he said, staring at a point over my shoulder. "I gotta go."

"Sure." I took the shank from Becky Joe, who gave me a look beneath brows that hadn't seen a tweezer in twenty years.

Without a word, Stevie hurried to where he'd parked his Motobecane bike, mounted it, and wheeled away. Becky Joe walked alongside me as once again I headed down the shedrow with Bionic.

"Stevie's hurting," Becky Joe said with a sidelong glance as if to study my reaction.

"Mars was being pretty hard on him before," I said. "When I asked you what was going on, you said you couldn't say. Would you like to say now?"

"Aren't you the one with the questions? I can't because I don't know. But I can sense something bad. Mars took that boy under his wing a year ago, gave him better horses to ride and at the bigger tracks. Now it's like he's turned on him."

"How do you mean?" I asked.

"Couldn't say."

I rolled my eyes, clucked at Bionic, and moved ahead of Becky Joe. I'd had enough mystery for one day. After a few more turns around the barn, I was finally able to hand Bionic over to his groom.

Unfortunately, my work wasn't finished. One of Pizutti's men had been fired earlier that morning and the job of cleaning his three stalls had fallen to me. Stepping into the first one, I crinkled my nose with disgust.

I'd cleaned enough stalls in my life to know my predecessor had removed a minimal amount of soiled bedding, then covered it over with fresh straw. No wonder the guy had been fired.

With a pitchfork, I lifted pile after pile of filthy straw into a wheelbarrow as heavy lumps of manure increased the weight and charm of the job. Beneath the top layers, I found a web of older, crushed droppings woven into a moldy mat of urine-laden straw. Each time I crammed the barrow full, I trundled the stinking load off to the manure pile outside the barn.

Another hot walker led each of the three horses around the shedrow while I labored in their stalls. The ammonia from the urine burned my nose, and I was relieved when I'd scraped the stalls down to dirt and could sprinkle them with lime to neutralize the acid and cut the stink. With that done, I shook out bales of fresh straw in each stall.

The next job my predecessor left me was washing his horses' dirty stable bandages before hanging them over the wood rail to dry in the sun. I finished my work for the day by dragging a heavy, rubber hose down the shedrow to top off each of the thirty-something water buckets. After turning off the spigot and coiling the hose, I collapsed on an empty, overturned bucket by the barn wall. I desperately needed a shower, but was too tired to move.

Closing my eyes, I lay my head back against the wooden barn wall, enjoying the sun that streamed into the shedrow and warmed my face.

At least while I slaved away with manual labor for Mars, it was comforting to know that the TRPB analysts in our home office in Fair Hill, Maryland, were sorting and filtering through the wagering data for Pizutti's races, looking for the odd spike or other tell in the amounts bet. They scanned for red flags, which suggested the trainer had drugged a horse, causing the animal to run the race of its life. With me working the barn, and analysts working the computers, we hoped to put Pizutti out of business before the end of Saratoga's six-week meet.

Footsteps approached, but I left my eyes closed, waiting for whomever it was to pass.

"Starbucks?" a male voice asked. The rich smell of hot coffee wafted under my nose and I opened my eyes, squinting at the silhouette standing over me. *Calixto Coyune?*

"What are you doing here?" I whispered, sitting up straight. He looked good for someone recovering from a gunshot wound. I wanted to ask him how he was. Questions crammed my mind, but cop instinct won out. "You'll blow my cover!" My last words came out in a rush.

"A most unpleasant cover," he said, waving his free hand before his nose. "You reek. But don't worry, *pequeña leona*, I am also operating under the radar."

I hadn't seen him for months, but the sound of his voice calling me "little lioness" in that Cuban accent sent a thrill right to my gut. "What do you mean?"

"Do you want *me* to drink your coffee, Fia?"

"No," I said, snatching the cup away from him, trying to ignore the snug fit of his leather chaps. I couldn't, and if the container hadn't had a lid, I would have spilled coffee all over myself. I glanced around hurriedly, but didn't see anyone on the shedrow. As the most recent hire, I'd been given the longest, dirtiest job, and everyone else appeared to be long gone. Still, I whispered. "So, what are you doing here?"

"I'm the new assistant trainer for Maggie Bourne."

So it was Calixto I'd seen in Maggie's stall. "How will that work?" I asked, taking a sip of hot coffee. I almost groaned with pleasure as the sweet liquid rushed down my throat and rinsed the ammonia burn still clinging to every membrane.

"Gunny isn't stupid, Fia," he said, referring to our TRPB boss. "He's known Maggie a long time. She's one of the good guys, and she hates Pizutti. She's delighted to play her role in this."

"Seems risky to me, you showing up as an assistant trainer that no one's ever heard of." Had he really had time to heal? "Are you fit enough?"

He made a dismissive noise. "Of course I'm fit enough, and I was a trainer at Gulfstream for several years, Fia. People will believe I just decided to get back in the game."

He'd trained racehorses? There were so many things I didn't know about this man. We'd briefly worked a case together and though I'd trust him with my life, I knew very little about him. Except that he was way too handsome and at the moment was giving me a long, assessing stare.

I tried to peel my gaze from this brown-eyed heartbreaker who'd saved my life. Damn those killer lips and cheekbones. The wide shoulders, long legs, and narrow hips. And, God help me, his—abruptly, I stood up and took a half step away from him.

"What?" he asked, his eyes bright with amusement.

I swallowed two more sips of coffee, grateful for the surge of energy as the caffeine and sugar kicked in. "So what will people think you've been doing since then?"

"I'm the wealthy son of a Cuban coffee mogul. I do what I

like, train when I feel like it. And Saratoga is the place to be in the summer, right?"

I took in the large diamond pinky ring he wore and what appeared to be Lucchese ostrich boots beneath his chaps. He looked like a damn playboy, except his face was too hard and he had those cop eyes that gave away nothing.

"So," I said, "I'm supposed to pretend I don't know you?"

"No. I have a plan, and Gunny approves."

Why hadn't they included me when they put this together? I swallowed more coffee. "What?"

"You're a natural for the role. At least, when you're clean."

"Calixto, I don't want to play guessing games. I'm tired. What role? And for the record, it's not smart for us to engage in a long conversation on Pizutti's shedrow."

"But that *is* the plan. I work for Maggie, we meet, and become, what is the expression you Americans use, oh, yes, we become an *item*."

"Calixto, you *are* American."

He gave me a palms-up shrug. "I'm more Cuban."

"You seem to be whoever you need to be," I said.

My comment caught him by surprise, then brought what might have been a smile to his lips. When I'd first met him, he'd been undercover at Gulfstream Park racetrack near Miami. I'd fallen for the subterfuge, and, convinced he was a bad guy, had done my own due diligence on the man.

He wasn't Cuban. He was Cuban-American. Calixto's father had fled Cuba in 1958, leaving behind a wife and two other children. The father, who'd divorced his Cuban wife within a year, must have arrived in Miami with a lot of money and connections. He'd started a lucrative coffee business and some years later, snagged a top Cuban-American fashion model. The resulting marriage had produced Calixto.

He still had the half smile as he said, "And you, *leona,* have a talent for becoming whoever a man wants you to be."

"Deception's the name of my game." But my joke sounded flat. Truth be told, I suspected I could fall for him in a New York minute and was wary of this pretend game he proposed. I didn't want to lose control of my emotions. I couldn't read him. I'd never know when he was lying to me or when he was telling the truth. Not for sure.

"I've got to clean up before I asphyxiate myself," I said. "Besides, in those six-hundred-dollar boots, no one will buy that you're interested in a grungy hot walker."

"True," he said, his smile now unmistakable, "but there is beauty in my little lioness. Even if it is invisible at the moment. I know how nicely you clean up, Fia."

"It's *Fay.*" I tilted my coffee cup and found it was empty.

"I think I will call you *pequeña leona* to avoid the mistake."

I crushed the coffee cup and searched for a change of subject. "Did you hear about the suicide this morning?"

His smile disappeared. "Yes."

"I was close, Calixto. I heard the shot."

He glanced right, left, and lowered his voice. "What did you see?"

"Nothing, the fog was too heavy, but I was the second one on the scene, and it looked like a straightforward suicide. If there is such a thing."

His eyes drifted away from me. His gaze swept across the green grass next to the barn. I followed his glance through a gap between the two barns next to ours, and onto the Oklahoma Training Track and the path where the jockey had shot himself. The sun shone there now, and a blue canopy arched high above the large, leafy oaks, maples, and tight conifers that grew so profusely on the Saratoga backstretch.

"Gunny is here, Fia. He wants to talk to you."

"Here, as in Saratoga?"

Calixto nodded.

Why hadn't my boss called me himself? Then I remembered turning my phone off to free both hands for stable work. "Do you know what it's about?"

"No. I do not." He hesitated a moment, his eyes searching my face. "Possibly he wants to know how you are feeling now that you are out in the field again?"

"I'm not the one who got shot. I'd think he'd be more concerned about you."

"Easy, *pequeña leona*. He has been checking on my progress. But what happened to you is less straightforward than a gunshot wound, no?"

I couldn't argue with him—not after my hellish experience of being abducted by criminals and injected with mind-altering drugs. Flashbacks, and an inability to perceive what was real and what wasn't, had haunted me for weeks. As a result, Gunny had confined me to desk work at Fair Hill.

"I'm doing okay."

"I can see that, but I believe Gunny has a fatherly attitude toward you, yes? He needs to see for himself."

"*Fine*. When does he want to talk to me?"

Calixto glanced at his watch. "Soon. I have some things to do for him. Call him. He did say there's a question on one of Pizutti's owners."

What a surprise. "Sure," I said. "I'll call him."

A hay dealer's truck rolled up to the shedrow, and two workmen started to climb from the cab. Calixto gave me a curt nod and left. As he walked down Pizutti's aisle, the heels of his ostrich boots left sharp prints in the sandy dirt.

My role at Saratoga was set up. It was running smoothly. Yes, a jockey had committed suicide, but I was an accepted worker in Pizutti's barn and now I had Calixto watching my back.

As I sighed and stared out through the bright sunshine to where the jockey had shot himself, a sense of something dark and hidden touched me like a cold finger.

3

I headed for the room I'd found in a towering, four-story Victorian off Union Avenue, within walking distance of the track. The owner, an older fellow who'd inherited his family's home but not the money to go with it, had cut the house into apartments to take advantage of the lucrative prices he could charge during the summer racing season.

The TRPB had subsidized my rental, but even so, I'd had to take the cheapest unit offered, a tiny room squashed in a corner of the attic. After climbing three long flights of squeaky, wooden stairs, I unlocked my bedroom door, and stepped inside. The cramped room featured a Victorian spool bed, a brightly colored comforter with a merry-go-round print on top, a fine old walnut dresser, and a night table.

I rolled my eyes at the mini refrigerator and chipped microwave wobbling atop a laminated counter bolted onto rusty legs—an adventure in kitchen design that belonged in a Dumpster.

After shedding my foul-smelling clothes, I stepped into the teeny bathroom with the requisite toilet, sink, and shower. The last was big enough to turn around in—if I turned slowly. Still, I almost purred when the shower's hot jets of water hit my back and lavender-scented suds foamed over my skin and hair.

I rinsed and toweled off. Didn't need a dryer, since I kept my hair short. In the past, as a Baltimore city cop, I'd kept it long and more feminine. That vanity had almost cost me my life, most recently during a domestic dispute call in West Baltimore. The meth freak who'd been beating up his girlfriend had grabbed a hunk of my pinned-up hair and slammed my head into the bedroom wall. Fortunately, a backup patrol car had responded, and that officer had zapped the meth-head with a stun gun. He'd cuffed him, while I reeled drunkenly, fighting a black hole of unconsciousness.

One CAT scan and a bottle of ibuprofen later, I'd taken a pair of scissors and whacked off my hair. Nothing to latch on to, nothing to blow-dry. But I have a streak of vanity and I'd kept the super short hair a hot, electric blond, at least until Gunny had told me about the Saratoga assignment. Knowing I'd be visibly back on the racing circuit with a different name, I'd let it grow into a gamine, pixie-like style, and dyed it black, a few shades darker than my natural brunette. To transform my looks further, I adopted a Goth look, wearing black eye makeup and a pair of skull earrings.

After toweling off, I pulled on clean jeans, a T-shirt with a silk-screened death's-head moth, and boots, all black. Truth be told, I favored the color anyway. It never shows dirt, goes with everything, and has a tough quality that appeals to me. And it was the obvious color of choice for my latest adventure in camouflage.

When I'd reached Gunny earlier, he'd told me he'd be waiting for me at Congress Park. A glance at the clock on the walnut dresser told me I still had a half hour before our meeting, so before making the long descent to the front door, I walked to my dormer window and gazed out. Across the slate and shingled rooftops of neighboring houses, I could see Union Avenue and its handsome Victorian, Greek Revival, and Italianate homes. I knew Union Avenue eventually dead-ended at the park where I was meeting Gunny. My rental house was in the opposite direction, closer to the racetrack.

Through the glass, I could see Saratoga's historic grandstand, the main track, and part of the huge expanse of backstretch stables. In the distance, the Adirondack Mountains rose to meet the skyline. As I turned from the window, my cell dinged, and I was surprised to see the caller was my brother Patrick. We'd been estranged for years, but had managed a partial reconciliation when I'd seen him in Florida the previous winter.

"*Patrick?*"

"Fia, I have a great surprise for you. You're in Saratoga for the summer, right?"

"Yes." My foot started to jiggle. This happens when I'm nervous. "Why? Are you coming up here, or something?"

"No, of course not. But you needn't sound so *thrilled* with the idea. Besides, you know how hard it is for me to leave the office. I'm about to close a huge deal. It involves—"

"What's the surprise, Patrick?"

He hesitated a moment, then his words rushed at me like a runaway manure spreader. "I know you two had a falling-out when she left, but she *is* your mother and she's in Saratoga. She's dying to see you, Fia."

I was not dying to see her. Why did Patrick stick up for this bitch?

"I've given her your number," Patrick was saying, "and she'll be calling you. Thought I'd give you a heads-up. You really need to see her, Fia. She's your *family*."

An old, familiar rage swept through me. "For God's sake, Patrick, she's the woman who walked out on us for a wealthier man, the gold digger who cleaned out Dad's bank accounts. She's the reason Dad had to sell the farm, yank me out of private school, and shove me into probably the worst public school in Baltimore. *That* was fun. Of course by then, *you* were at the University of Florida, which *she* paid for, right?"

"Jesus, Fia! I can't change what happened back then. You should move on. She's your *mother*. You should see her."

Trembling with rage, I disconnected the call, raced down three staircases, and burst out the front door, inhaling fresh, cool air. I scrambled into my starlight-blue Mini Cooper, too pissed off to admire its shiny black roof and bonnet-stripes. After firing up its surprisingly powerful four-cylinder engine, I cranked up the volume on Nirvana and McCartney's "Cut Me Some Slack," and laid rubber on the way to the park.

I spotted Gunny's fading red hair behind the *Daily Racing Form*. The newspaper hid his face where he sat on a bench facing a landscaped pond. At its center, a small fountain sprayed cool water into the air, and a duck hen paddled lazily across the pool's ruffled surface. Six ducklings followed in her wake.

Watching their leisurely pace, I took a mental deep breath as the flock swam past an ornate, marble folly that rose from the shallow pool. I was grateful my brain was quiet now, and no longer playing the echo of gunshots or the screams of a man as feral hogs ripped him apart. I'd had a terrible experience in Florida a few months earlier, and for a while these sounds had been so loud, I'd thought they were real. Healing from the emotional trauma had not been easy.

I breathed in the calmness of the park, focusing on the historic beauty of Saratoga. On the far side of the pond, manicured trees and bushes dotted a sweep of green lawn that led my gaze to the 1870s Canfield Casino. In its day, the casino was considered the "Monte Carlo of America," notorious for high-rolling gamblers, entertainment stars, and the occasional mobster. These glory days had stopped abruptly in 1907 when anti-gambling, Bible-toting reformers shut the casino down.

Still walking toward Gunny, I pulled my iPad from my tote bag, and pretending to study the screen, sat a few feet from him, where I caught a familiar whiff of his Old Spice cologne.

He flattened his *Form*, took out a red pen and scribbled on the page listing Belmont's races, as if marking his bets for the day. Not looking at me, he said, "How you doing, Fia?"

"I'm good."

"No more flashbacks?" He did look at me now. A quick search of my face, a careful study of my response. He'd been a cop a long time and was deft at reading people's expressions. Even better than the cops I'd worked with in Baltimore.

"No flashbacks, no hallucinations." I held his gaze a moment, than looked back at my iPad. "I will admit that if a truck suddenly backfires, or I hear any unexpected loud noise, I'll jump. But that's about it."

"Good. I'm glad to hear this." His lips curved in a smile. "How's Pizutti doing?"

"He's a piece of work," I said. "But I've found no illegal activities in his barn. Yet. He's putting some kind of pressure on his stable jockey, Stevie Davis, but I don't know why."

"Keep a watch on that. And an eye on one of Pizutti's owners, a guy named Al Savarine. He seems determined to start up an unusual investment group that could be troublesome."

"That's the guy who owns Ziggy Stardust," I said.

"Right." Gunny twirled his pen before tapping it against the *Form* for emphasis. "Apparently he wants to start a company called Savarine Equine Acquisitions or SEA for short. Possibly a racehorse hedge fund."

"Oh, that'll work," I said.

Gunny caught my sarcasm. "*Exactly*. Bad idea. You and Calixto need to keep your ears open and let me know what you hear."

The ducks had circled and were heading back toward us. I googled SEA on my tablet and nothing came up. Then I put in Savarine. His picture appeared. I didn't like his face. Dark lids hooded his eyes and he'd avoided looking at the camera. He was a Wall Street investment broker.

"Savarine looks like a New Jersey thug," I said. "Who would fall for an equine hedge fund, anyway?"

"Anyone chasing get-rich-quick schemes. Think of the people who got sucked into the tech bubble of 2000 and the mortgage scams of 2008."

We sat on the wooden bench for a few beats without speaking. A sudden strong breeze kicked up the surface of the pond and brought the odor of water, mud, and barnyard fowl. The gust must have disturbed the hen, who quacked noisily and paddled briskly toward us. The ducklings motored hard to keep up with her.

"Maybe Savarine plans to have Wall Street meet the backstretch," I said.

Gunny's only response was a snort of derision.

The duck and her chicks reached the shore, marched up the bank to our bench, and stared at us with beady, expectant eyes. Like everyone else, they were looking for a free ride. I did a mental head shake. Maybe Savarine's idea *would* work.

"You know," I said, "Ziggy Stardust has made so much

money, and Pizutti's runners are doing really well. Maybe the idea isn't that crazy. What would burn me is if people invested because they know Pizutti's crooked."

Apparently it was already burning Gunny, because he pulled a packet of orange-flavored Tums from his pocket and tore it open. At the sound of crinkling plastic, the ducks, who lingered nearby, rushed to his feet.

I reached for the oyster crackers I'd left in my pocket, crumbled some up, and threw them to the birds. The hen quacked, the chicks peeped, and the flock gobbled up the cracker bits as Gunny chewed his Tums.

After swallowing, he said, "Knowing Pizutti's bent would be a strong draw for a number of owners."

"Sometimes, I just want to smack these people."

"Easy, Fia. Procedure may be slow and tedious, but you can't go back to your hotheaded ways." His voice had taken on a sharp edge. "That cost you your last job, remember?"

"Yeah. I remember." The internal affairs division of the Baltimore Police Department had pushed me off the force, accusing me of being an "avenging angel" when I'd shot and killed a man who was trying to strangle a woman to death. The IAD guy had made it clear he didn't want me in the department. I was a liability that could bring lawsuits, and claims of police brutality. I'd been lucky Gunny had taken me into the TRPB.

"So, what do you want me to do?" I asked.

"Same as always. Keep a low profile and your eyes open wide for illegal substances in Pizutti's barn. And keep track of anything you hear or see about Savarine's intended operation."

"Okay," I said. "I can do that."

"And," he continued, "I won't be meeting you again. You funnel your information through Calixto. Okay?"

"Sure. Can I ask you a question?"

"Shoot."

"What do you know about the jockey who committed suicide?"

He paused before answering. "The county police are investigating. The jockey, Jose Fragoso, wasn't being treated for depression. Nor did they find prescription or illegal drugs in his room. There's no indication of foul play, and no reason to think it's anything beyond a straightforward suicide. If I hear anything, I'll tell Calixto. You sit here awhile. I'm heading out."

The ducks scattered when he stood and walked away from the bench. His stride was long and easy as the sun hit the remaining red strands in his fading hair, momentarily turning them the color of molten metal. He must have been a real pistol when he was young.

By now, the breeze had calmed, and the ducks waded into the water and drifted toward the fountain. I thought about Jose Fragoso. I'd seen his body, smelled his blood, and I was sure a darkness the police couldn't see had driven him to his death.

4

Opening day at Saratoga arrived on the third Friday in July. By Wednesday of that week, racing fans had crowded into the town's hotel rooms and the Victorian bed-and-breakfasts on Union Avenue. Cash registers in restaurants and clothing boutiques on Broadway were spitting out purchase receipts like confetti, and the air held a buzz of anticipation I hadn't felt before.

After finishing work on Friday, I walked up Union toward my rental, enjoying the sunshine and blue sky arching overhead. The fans moving with me on the sidewalk held racing tip sheets and some, like me, carried copies of the *Daily Racing Form* for the afternoon's races. At the corner of Union and East Avenue, a red light halted our flow.

Beside me, a heavyset guy with a cigar turned to a man holding a tip sheet.

"Hey, what do you think of Lightning Lily in the fourth today?"

The tip sheet guy stared at his paper through drugstore cheaters. "Not much. Don't like her. She's a sprinter. Why would they put her in for a mile-and-a-sixteenth?"

A woman in jeans and a sweatshirt moved closer to the tip sheet guy, pointing to his paper. "But look at her pedigree. I *know* that dam. She won at a mile-and-a-quarter. Her daughter should go long."

He shook his head. "I'm telling you. She won't. Her sire was a stone-cold sprinter. Never go the distance."

The guy with the cigar frowned. "So, who *do* you like?"

"Daisy Do Right. Look at her last work."

The light turned green, I stepped forward, and their discussion became muffled behind me. Stevie was riding a filly named Wiggly Wabbit for Mars in that race, and I liked her. Though I'd kept my eyes and ears alert, I'd found no trace of drugs in Pizutti's barn, and I thought the filly could win on her own ability. I might lay a bet on the horse, so I wasn't about to voice an opinion to the people behind me. I felt a smile curving my lips. Racing fever had infected me, just like everyone else.

I'd watched Stevie ride in the mornings. He knew his way around a racetrack, had a good timing clock in his head, nice hands, and confidence, but he'd only ridden at second-rate tracks. Mars must have seen something in the kid to bring him in as the stable jockey. Though Stevie's stats were good at smaller tracks, Saratoga was a whole other universe, and I was anxious to see how the kid measured up that afternoon in the fourth. No doubt Stevie was, too. As third choice on the morning line, Wiggly Wabbit and Stevie had a shot to win.

When I got to my rental, I ate a small carton of yogurt and a package of trail mix. After showering, I darkened my eyes with black shadow and liner, then pulled on a T-shirt with a graphic of bleeding red roses on the front. I added ankle chains to my black boots, and was about to head for the track when I saw my *Racing Form* on the floor and leaned over to pick it up.

The paper had opened to a page I hadn't read before and a headline caught my eye: SARATOGA JOCKEY COMMITS SUICIDE.

So the police *had* ruled it a suicide. My eyes raced through the article. Jose Fragoso was from Peru and had been in the U.S. for only two months. I searched for an indication of why he would have taken his own life, but found none. The reporter had used an interpreter to interview a friend of the dead jockey. Named Oscar Mejias, and also Peruvian, he'd said, "Jose was very happy to be in America. It was his dream to ride here."

Some dream. How hard it must be to ride here if you spoke no English. Who could these young Latinos rely on? I read further, but the article provided no clues to Fragoso's state of mind when he shot himself. I folded the paper, tucked it under my arm, and headed for the track.

The third race had gone off by the time I walked through the entrance gates. I hurried, since our filly would be coming into the paddock soon. The huge wooden grandstand, built in 1864, stood to one side of the path I followed, the paddock area on the other. The mile-and-one-eighth track and its stadium seating hid on the far side of the grandstand.

Kiosks selling programs, food, and beer crammed the paddock grounds. Red and white awnings sheltered these crowded concessions. The smell of grilled chicken and french fries teased my nose, while the lines of customers slowed my progress. I didn't mind—people were having fun, and their electricity put a positive charge in the air.

After slipping between a couple eating hot dogs and a family negotiating two baby strollers and a pizza, I finally reached my destination.

When I leaned against the white-painted rails surrounding the paddock, two guys in their twenties stood next to me. They held mostly empty beer cups and wore military-short haircuts. They stared at my Goth tee, skull earrings, and blackened eyes.

With a derisive look, the guy closest to me said, "Funeral parlor's over on North Broadway, lady."

"Why?" I asked, giving him my dead-eyed cop stare. "You need a ride?"

His buddy smothered a laugh, and spilled his beer onto the bed of red begonias beneath the rail.

"Let's move," the first guy said. "This one gives me the creeps."

"Roger that," his beer-spilling buddy said. "But she is kind of hot." His last comment elicited a glare from his friend as they moved away.

Two young women in short dresses immediately filled the space, and the closest one, a bubbly blonde, gave me an appreciative smile. "Love that Goth thing you got going."

"Thanks," I said.

She opened her program. "Who do you like in the fourth?"

I liked her open, friendly face and the fact she'd been nice to me, so I gave her a tip. "That one," I said, pointing to where Becky Joe Benson had just entered the paddock leading Pizutti's horse.

The blonde glanced at the numeral three printed on Becky Joe's vest, then at her program. "Wiggly Wabbit? *Seriously?*"

"Yes. I'd box an exacta with her and Starlight," I said.

She frowned. "Box an exacta?"

"You know, bet them to come in first and second, in either order."

"Oh, okay."

By now, Becky Joe was leading Wiggly Wabbit past me on the other side of the rail. The gray filly looked good and Becky Joe did, too. She'd shined up her cowgirl boots and put on a newer hat. Beneath her numbered vest, she was wearing what she called her "special occasion jacket." The fringed-leather piece appeared to have seen a few too many such occasions, but Becky Joe wore it with pride.

I called to her, "What do you think?"

She grinned and gave me a thumbs-up.

My rail neighbor said, "Oh! Do you own the horse?"

"Nah. I work in the barn."

The two women nudged each other, and knowing they had inside information, rushed off to find the nearest betting window.

About the time they returned with their tickets, Pizutti, wearing a shiny gray suit with a floppy red tie, strutted into the paddock, reminding me of the annoying rooster in Maggie Bourne's barn. He waved at the fans lining the rail who called his name and wished him luck.

To the ones he knew he yelled, "Hey, babe, how ya doin'?"

When Mars thought he was being cool, he liked to call people "babe," be they male or female. Some people cast disparaging looks in his direction and muttered to their companions. Probably, their remarks weren't complimentary. People either loved or hated Pizutti.

He crooked a finger at Becky Joe, then waved her and Wiggly into the number three stall of the saddling enclosure. Built from whitewood panels, it stood beneath one of Saratoga's signature red-and-white-striped awnings. The colorful design was all over the track and provided a county fair atmosphere. I almost expected a barbershop quartet or an old-fashioned beer wagon to materialize at any moment.

But it was time to check out Wiggly Wabbit's competition. As the horses paraded past, I studied each animal, looking for alertness, a shiny coat, good muscle tone, and proper weight. When I'd studied the *Form* at the barn that morning, I'd told Stevie he should worry about the two favorites, Starlight and Daisy Do Right.

"At least," I'd told him, "they look fierce on paper."

It doesn't always happen, but for this race, the horses' appearances agreed with their written form. Starlight's copper coat was on fire with vitality. Her eyes held a determined look. Daisy Do Right, a solid bay, was close to seventeen hands in height and looked like she'd have a stride that would devour the track.

Remembering the discussion about Lightning Lily I'd heard earlier, I gave her a hard look. She had a blaze on her face shaped like a bolt of lightning and was close coupled, with solid muscle and weight, the mark of a sprinter. If she could steal the lead and hold on to the wire, she might have a shot. These three horses were carrying jockeys with high win percentages. Stevie would have his hands full trying to beat them.

The remaining eight horses weren't much to write home about, with the exception of Wiggly Wabbit. Her gray coat blossomed with silver dapples, her muscles were pumped with blood, and the veins stood out on her coat. Sometimes, you can look at an animal and know they intend to win. Our filly had her game face on. I left the rail and went to place my bet.

When I came back, a glance at the tote board told me the bettors liked Wiggly Wabbit's appearance as much as I did. By the time Stevie's valet entered the paddock with the saddle and two girths, our filly was bet down to second favorite.

In the three stall, Becky Joe held the filly's head, stroking her neck, keeping her calm. With the valet's help, Pizutti cinched Wiggly Wabbit's girth tight, before strapping the second, over-girth around the tiny saddle. This standard practice of using two girths could save a rider's life, a rider like Stevie.

The jockeys paraded into the paddock, their silks like the plumage of exotic birds. Stevie stopped near Pizutti. Nerves tightened the lines on his face, and his eyes darted from Pizutti to the horse as if seeking an answer.

The paddock judge called for riders up, Pizutti tossed Stevie into the saddle, and Becky Joe led Wiggly Wabbit toward the track. With Stevie on her back, the filly's head came up, and the muscles in her neck and hindquarters seemed to swell as if injected with an increased supply of blood and oxygen. The bold look in her eyes said, "Bring it on."

Stevie patted her neck as Becky Joe led them past me, but a shadow of anger and uncertainty flitted across his face. He pressed his lips together, and his eyes squeezed shut a moment. They opened, filled with conviction. I didn't know what was going on with him, but he'd just made a decision.

The horses filed from the paddock into the grandstand pass-through and out of sight. I zipped through the building, stepped onto the track apron, and saw Pizutti standing by the rail ahead of me. I placed myself a couple of feet to his side and slightly behind. Using the JumboTron, I watched the horses warm up. Our gray filly looked even better than she had in the paddock. The fans thought so, too. On the tote board, as the horses loaded into the gate, Wiggly Wabbit was the favorite.

The bell rang, the electronic gates crashed open, and the announcer cried, "They're off!"

The horses exploded out. Lightning Lily immediately gained a half-length lead. The number five horse took a left turn out of the gate and crashed into Daisy Do Right, but Daisy held her ground, her long legs getting organized and gathering momentum. Wiggly Wabbit broke evenly, and Stevie had her well positioned in third place. Starlight lay near the back of the pack, as a different chestnut, probably a future "also-ran," charged into second place.

The colorful silks and gleaming Thoroughbred coats flowed through the first turn and onto the backstretch with Lightning Lily still on the lead. Stevie lay in third, with Daisy Do Right breathing down the back of his neck in fourth place.

Starlight used the backstretch straightaway to power forward, picking off stragglers until she drew even with Daisy Do Right, still in fourth. As the horses flew into the far turn, Stevie looked back to see who was coming. Some riders got busy whipping and driving, especially the jockey on the also-ran chestnut. His stick flashed frantically as his filly's stride shortened.

As she faltered, Stevie and Wiggly Wabbit swept past and took aim on Lightning Lily. Daisy Do Right and Starlight began their final moves, leaving the rest of the field struggling behind. It was now a four-horse race.

Excited screaming drew my attention to the right. The two gals in short dresses had followed me and stood only a few feet away. As I turned back, Pizutti made an angry gesture with his fist. What was his problem?

I could hear the horses rocketing down the stretch toward me. Their hooves thundered, making the ground beneath my feet tremble, the sound of their lungs incredibly loud as they pumped massive quantities of air in and out.

Stevie asked Wiggly Wabbit to give him her soul, and she did, digging in and drawing almost even with Lightning Lily, who struggled mightily to hold to the wire. Behind these two, Starlight raced ahead of Daisy Do Right, whose immensely long legs had lost time switching into high gear. Even so, I feared the big filly could grind past *everyone* if they didn't get to the wire soon.

Around me, the crowd was yelling for their picks. The women in short dresses were jumping up and down, screaming for Wiggly Wabbit and Starlight. I hoped they'd win.

Wiggly Wabbit drew even with Lightning Lily, looked her in the eye, and Lily folded. Wiggly Wabbit swept past, and Starlight followed, her nose at Wiggly Wabbit's flank. Daisy Do Right still motored forward.

By now, the two girls were wild, as Wiggly Wabbit held the lead, with Starlight a neck behind and coming. Behind them, Daisy Do Right inched closer in tireless determination.

Stevie put his stick away, hand-riding Wiggly Wabbit with everything he had. It was beautiful to watch; the kid could ride. His filly held on and flashed under the wire, winning by a whisker.

The bubbly blonde ran to me and threw her arms around my neck, shrieking, "We won! We won!"

Her buddy rushed over, and giddy with excitement, we gave each other high fives. With an angry sound, Pizutti threw his program on the ground. He stomped through the gap in the rail to meet Stevie, who would soon pull up near the winner's circle. Becky Joe was on the track waiting for them.

The bubbly blonde and her friend rushed off to cash in their tickets. I would get my money later. Now I wanted to know what angered Pizutti. I stepped through the gap and walked through the heavy sand, stopping close to him and Becky Joe.

Stevie stood in the stirrups, easing his filly down to a jog, then a walk, as they approached us. He sat proudly in the saddle, his eyes lit with joy and triumph. As they pulled up, Becky Joe grabbed the bridle, and led them toward the winner's circle. Pizutti walked close to Stevie, and I followed. The trainer tilted his head up to say something, and I saw his scowl before he angled his face away. It was hideous and a little shocking. Most of the times I'd seen him, his expression was bland, even pleasant.

Stevie had just pulled off the greatest achievement of his career; he'd won at Saratoga, beating three of the top jockeys in the United States. But Pizutti's anger brought the worry lines crashing back to the kid's face, and an edge of fear into his eyes.

I got as close as I dared.

"And if Rico does anything like that," Pizutti was saying, "it will be on you. You *knew* what you were supposed to do."

My heart sank. I'd bet my last buck Pizutti had told him to lose the race. And who the hell was Rico?

5

While everyone filed into the winner's circle for the win picture, I hung back, not wanting to be in the photo.

Pizutti pasted on his happy face for the camera, but Stevie was pale, his unease obvious in the tight lines around his mouth. The filly's proud owners, two guys wearing black turtlenecks, shiny jackets, and soul patches, beamed for the camera. Becky Joe's face remained expressionless, while Wiggly Wabbit blew hard, working to restore her cardiovascular system after the huge effort.

I glanced at the owners again. They looked a wee bit slimy to me. Good thing that they, along with every trainer, jockey, or track worker, had to hold a license from the state racing commission. And *everyone* was fingerprinted. No exceptions. I'd run their names later. If the owners had legal action against them, I'd find it right quick.

Stevie finally managed a strained smile in time for his win photo. After dismounting, he whipped off the filly's tack, rushing with it to the jockey scales as if unable to get away from Pizutti fast enough. I waited on the track for Becky Joe to lead the filly out, and when they stepped onto the sand, I walked alongside them.

After clearing the grandstand pass-through, we clip-clopped along the path I'd walked earlier. We waited for a traffic cop to halt the cars on Union Avenue, then crossed the street, entered the backstretch, and headed for Pizutti's barn.

"So, Becky Joe," I said, "Stevie wasn't supposed to win, was he?"

She gave me a sharp look, then shifted her gaze away.

I kept my eyes on her, pressing her with the weight of my stare until she responded.

"*What?*"

"Did Pizutti tell him to pull the race?"

She made a small sound of annoyance. "Looks that way. You saw how the boy was before the race, all nervous, scared, and shit. Then he rides like a pro, wins the damn thing, and Mars ain't happy about it."

"You know," I said, "I like Stevie. He looked so torn in the paddock, and then it was like he made a decision, and decided to run his race. That took guts."

"He's a good kid. I hate Mars asking him to pull the horse. But now Stevie's put himself on thin ice. Remember, you're just a walker, I'm a groom, and there's not a damn thing we can do about any of it."

"But what kind of trouble is Stevie in?" I asked.

"Wouldn't know."

The woman held information like a bank vault. I tried again. "I heard Pizutti talk about a guy named Rico. Do you know who that is?"

Becky Joe took a bad step, jerking the filly's shank with the stumble. She gave me a quick look, her face suddenly expressionless. "I couldn't say."

The bank of Becky Joe had closed. Still, her reaction told me a lot. Rico could be an associate who'd gambled big money against Wiggly Wabbit. Maybe Pizutti suspected NYRA was looking at him hard for drug violations, and he'd decided to step away from that danger and try fixing races instead.

I'd call Brian, a guy I knew in the TRPB office. Among other things, he worked with the agency's Betting Analysis Platform. He examined wagering data on an almost real-time basis, and fished for suspicious events. Maybe Rico had left a trail.

Late that afternoon, Calixto came around to my side of the barn. He wore a white Western shirt with pearl snaps, black jeans, ostrich boots, and an enticing smile. He carried two bottles of beer. A suitor bearing intoxicating gifts.

I'd been sitting in a folding chair near the tack room waiting to help with the evening feed. I still wore the bleeding-roses T-shirt, and my Goth look was refurbished with freshly blackened eyes.

"*Querida,*" he said handing me a beer that was cold and beaded with moisture, "would you at least consider removing the skull earrings?"

"It's my cover," I said quietly. "I'm a Goth, remember?"

"You make it hard to forget."

I shrugged, and examined the beer's label. The name was unfamiliar to me. "Where did you find this, anyway? Ommegang Adoration?"

"You don't like the name? I'm supposed to adore you, yes?"

I took a sip. Dark and strong. Maybe a little too intense for my taste, but not bad. Not bad at all. In fact, it was growing on me.

"Ommegang's a local brewery," he said, toasting me with his bottle, before squatting in the aisle before me. The muscles in his thighs tightened against the fabric of his jeans as his face dropped to the level of my shoulder.

I could smell him. All male, with a trace of sweat and a hint of expensive cologne. He put a hand on my knee. My stomach contracted, and I sat farther back in my chair.

"*Pequeña leona*, don't draw away. You are supposed to find me irresistible. Your *amiga* Becky Joe is watching us, as are two other grooms. Drink *la cerveza* and smile at me."

I did. I needed the beer. The way he was looking at me, like he wanted to lay me down in the shedrow and have his way with me, made me dizzy. *For God's sake, Fia, he's not interested in you, he's faking it.* The man was a trained liar. Like me.

Becky Joe Benson was eyeing us from where she stood outside the feed room, an open can of beer in her hand, and a knowing expression on her face. She was waiting for the assistant trainer, Carl Albritt, to hand out the buckets he'd loaded with grain and carefully measured doses of supplements. Carl—tall, thin, and bushy-haired—wore geeky glasses, but the eyes behind them were sharp. He worked hard at his seven-day-a-week job and demanded the same from his employees, and as soon as he'd caught on to the shirker groom I was now covering for, he'd fired the guy.

It was almost dinnertime for the horses on Pizutti's shedrow. The feed-room door hung open, Carl was rattling buckets, and every horse was ready for dinner. Thirty of them had their faces over their stall gates. All stared at the feed room. A few of the more anxious pinned their ears, pawed, then backed into their stalls before whirling and charging forward again.

"Calixto, I have to help feed," I said, pouting as if leaving him would be painful. "But I *love* the beer you brought."

He stood, and touched my hand. As I stepped away, his fingers trailed lightly along my skin. I took a steadying breath, and turned to see Becky Joe grinning at us. Javier, the groom, was smiling, too. *This was good, right?*

I almost ran toward the pair, then slowed down before reaching them. I tried to put on a normal expression.

Becky Joe looked from me to Calixto. "Oh, Lord, if I was twenty years younger. That man is *serious* trouble. I'm sure I saw a chastity belt around here somewhere. You want me to get it for you?"

Javier snickered.

I gave them a cocky look. "I can handle him."

Becky Joe snorted. "Honey, you just failed the straight face test. Failed it bad. Even I couldn't have handled *that* one." She tossed her empty can into the trash, before leaning over and grabbing another beer from a cardboard six-pack conveniently close by on a hay bale. She popped the top and took a long drink. A few drops ran down her chin.

Beneath her scraggly brows, she had big eyes, and under her weathered skin, nice cheekbones. I could almost see her as a young, fit jockey. No doubt a head turner. But sun, booze, and a hard life had done irreparable damage to her skin and eyes.

While I was considering Becky Joe's past, Javier set six buckets piled to the brim with grain in the aisle. Becky Joe grabbed three pails and headed left. I took three, headed right, and walked to the far end of the shedrow, where I dumped two of them into the tubs in the last two stalls. The sweet smell of molasses rose to my nostrils, and I almost scooped out a mouthful for myself.

The third stall belonged to Ziggy Stardust. He was fierce about his grain, and snaked his head over his gate before pinning his ears and baring his teeth at me.

"This is not how we win friends, Ziggy," I said, picking up a hay rake and brandishing it at him until he withdrew into his stall.

Once he backed up to where I could feed him without losing my arm, I tossed his grain in as quickly as possible before scooting back. His bold and fiery nature had powered him to the winner's circle many times, but he was no toy in the barn.

Returning to the feed room, I grabbed three more pails and stopped outside Bionic's stall. It had been a couple of days since his work, and he looked good, like he'd gained weight and muscle tone. Nodding his head up and down, he nickered for his dinner. He was a sweet boy, and let me rub his forehead while his mouth worked ambitiously on the grain.

Wiggly Wabbit was a different story. She appeared interested in dinner, but when I poured it in her feed tub, she picked at it, then turned away. Not surprising, seeing the grueling effort she'd just made to win her race.

Once we'd finished serving oats, I topped off the horses' water buckets, while Becky Joe, Javier, and another groom rotated the horses out of their stalls and hand-grazed them in the grass around the barn. The remaining grooms picked at the stalls, providing a lick and a promise until the morning when, with pitchforks and wheelbarrows, they would dig and scrape the stalls clean.

By the time we finished, the sun sat low on the western horizon, and the air had cooled. We exchanged good-byes and everyone headed out except me. I wanted to take a last look at Wabbit. Zipping up my denim jacket against the increasing chill, I walked toward her stall. My dad had ingrained the habit in me during my days with him at Pimlico. Every night we'd checked our horses to see if they'd cleaned up their feed and were settled and happy. I could still hear his voice, *"Happy* horses win races, Fia."

I heard footsteps behind me and stopped. Stevie had come onto the shedrow. I wanted to ask him about Pizutti's angry reaction that afternoon, but resisted. Prying too hard could backfire.

Instead, I said, "Great ride on Wabbit today."

"Thanks. How are she and Bionic doing?"

"Bionic's great," I said, "but the Wabbit's appetite is off."

We walked to their stalls. Bionic had licked his tub clean, but Wiggly Wabbit's remained three-quarters full.

"What's the matter, girl?" I asked, stroking her head. I glanced at Stevie. "I was hoping she'd be deep in her feed after she ran, but you know how they are. They get too tired, they won't eat."

Stevie nodded. "Especially fillies."

"Especially them. They seem to worry more than the boys."

"Worrying's a bad thing," Stevie said.

He'd provided an opening and I didn't resist. "It is bad. You seem like you have something bothering you."

"Why do you say that?"

But as he spoke, his eyes seemed almost pleading, as if he hoped I'd ask again, as if he wanted to talk.

"Stevie—" The sound of an approaching vehicle stopped me. We both turned. Pizutti drove his dark-blue Mercedes SUV up to the barn and stopped. An older man sat in the passenger seat.

Stevie's face blanched. His head turned left and right as if seeking a place to escape, before he took a breath and grew still. As if unable to keep the thought silent, he said, "He'd only find me somewhere else."

"Who? What is it?"

"*Nothing*, Fay. Forget it. You're done feeding, right?" he asked.

"Yeah, but—"

"Then *leave*. Mars'll be pissed if you act curious about him, or that guy."

"Who is he?"

"Just *go*." He gave me a little push, then walked toward the two men who'd climbed from the SUV. Pizutti had parked near the end of the barn that housed Ziggy's stall.

I sauntered a short ways down the shedrow, then took a quick glance over my shoulder. None of the three guys were looking my way, so I dropped to my hands and knees and scooted into Wiggly Wabbit's stall. Once hidden, I called Calixto, hoping he was still on the barn's opposite side.

He answered on the first ring, his voice sounding amused. "I believe we are the new hot topic around the barn. I *heard* Becky Joe warning you off, and now, Maggie Bourne tells me to watch myself. She says you will drain my blood and put me in a coffin. *Pequeña leona*, I—"

"*Not now,* Calixto. Something's going on over here. Pizutti just showed up with some old guy and Stevie looks terrified."

"What does this older man look like?" he asked, his voice all business.

I peeked from Wabbit's stall, drank in the man's appearance, and withdrew. "Seventy-something. Still has thick hair. Salt-and-pepper, brushed straight back." *The guy used a lot of pomade, too.* "Uh, nice clothes, black glasses . . ."

"You just described a third of the male racing fans up here."

"So sneak over here and look for yourself."

Calixto could be so irritating. It wasn't like the old man had a pointed head or a forked tongue. Using my camera phone, I zoomed in on the guy and shot some pictures. Even with the magnification, it was hard to see his eyes behind the thick glasses.

But he *did* have a large nose, and a disapproving, down-turned mouth. The frown looked carved in place. *Fun guy.*

"I'll check it out," Calixto said as Wiggly Wabbit swung her long gray neck over my head and sniffed at my hair.

Gently, I pushed her head away, then I peered down the shedrow. Mars was leaning into Stevie, jabbing his index finger at the kid. He had the same ugly scowl on his face I'd seen earlier. I couldn't hear what he was saying, but his low tone sounded angry and urgent. The older man remained silent as he stood behind Mars, but his fixed expression of disapproval grew tighter.

Calixto appeared around the corner of the barn, and as he walked past the three men, the older guy jerked his thumb in my direction and said something. The three of them moved close to where I hid, apparently not wanting to be overheard by Calixto, who continued on as if he had someplace to go.

I was sure the three men hadn't seen me, and was glad Calixto had flushed my quarry to me. They stopped outside Wabbit's stall, where I crouched in the dim front corner, partially hidden by the wall.

Wiggly Wabbit swung her head toward me, knocking my arm. I dropped the phone and watched in dismay as the filly moved forward and crushed the phone under her metal-shod hoof. *Damn it.* I pushed on her leg until she moved off the phone. Snatching it up, I found it was dead, the camera and recording options obliterated, with no sound and no signal.

"Listen, Stevie," Mars said, his voice soft, as if trying to reassure. "It's kinda like you do for me, and I'll do for you. You know? 'Course I want you to ride your races and all. But I've given you a big chance here, and you let me down today. You understand?"

"I'm *not* pulling races for you, Mars." Stevie's voice, angry and defiant.

"Shut up, you little shit!" The older man's voice. It was gruff and carried an Italian accent. "You need to understand what happens when you don't do as you're told. Your boss here's nicer than me."

"Jesus, Rico," Pizutti whined. "Don't go breaking the kid's knees. He won't be able to ride, for Christ's sake."

So *this* was Rico. And I couldn't even record this conversation. *Damn it.*

"Nobody's breaking anybody's knees," Rico said. "But, kid. I got sumthin' to show you."

Wiggly Wabbit had retreated to the back of her stall, and thankfully was ignoring me. On my hands and knees, my face almost at ground level, I stole a glance at Rico. He was pulling what looked like a four-by-six photo from his jacket. I eased back, listening.

"*No!*" The word almost a whisper. Stevie grew louder. "How did you find her? Leave her *alone*. She's got *nothing* to do with this."

"She does now," Rico said.

Mars stared at the photo. "Wait a minute. You didn't say nothin' 'bout Lila."

Rico's words came out harsh. "Marzio, your father would be so disappointed in you. You talk like a fucking sissy. You listen to me, Stevie, it's your choice what happens to her. You want one of the boys to work on her?"

"No!" Stevie wailed. "*Don't.* Just tell me what you want me to do next. I'll do it, I promise."

I could hear the sob in Stevie's voice, and it made me sick. I wanted to come out with guns blazing, but sucked in the emotion and swallowed it. I could help him best by knowing what was going on, not intervening right now.

"Come here," Rico said.

I heard their footsteps receding and risked another look.

Rico walked to the trash barrel, near Ziggy Stardust's stall. I wished the colt would snake his head over the gate and bite the son of a bitch.

Rico held the photograph over the trash can. His grin was sick as he watched Stevie's face. Slowly, he ripped the picture into little pieces. "You want this to happen to her?" He laughed as the scraps of paper fluttered into the trash.

Stevie reeled away from Rico and vomited in the sand of the shedrow.

6

It seemed I hid in the stall on my hands and knees for an eternity, waiting for Pizutti and Rico to leave. The intensity of Stevie's fear, emotion so strong it had made him sick, stayed with me as I remembered how Rico had laughed, and told Pizutti to make the kid clean it up.

Finally, I heard the two men drive away, but waited until the sound of the Mercedes's engine faded before ducking under the stall gate. Stevie had disappeared, which didn't surprise me. What did was the ashen face of Becky Joe, staring at me from where she stood near Ziggy Stardust's stall.

I walked toward her. "Did you hear that? What are they doing to Stevie?"

Her eyes were almost hidden beneath the brim of her Western hat, and she refused to look up at me. "I didn't hear anything. I gotta go." She turned away quickly, and scurried out of sight past the corner of the barn.

Damn the woman. I needed to call Calixto, but my phone was broken. I was relieved when I saw him emerge from a door in the barn across the way. Waving him to hurry over, I sped to the litter barrel and dumped its contents. Track maintenance had picked up the trash earlier, so it was easy to spot the fragments of the photo among the small amount of debris. I started to grab the pieces, then stopped, thinking I should use gloves.

"Go ahead," Calixto said as he drew close. "You can touch them. We do not need his fingerprints. I know who he is—Rico Pizutti, Marzio Pizutti's uncle."

He knelt beside me, and we grabbed as many pieces of the photo as we could find, quickly arranging them like a puzzle, until a face appeared.

"Oh," I said. "She's so young." Why couldn't Rico's target be someone older, someone less vulnerable? "God, she looks like *Stevie.*"

"Poor *bambina.* Could be his little sister."

"That bastard," I said. "Using this girl to make Stevie fix races."

"The guy is a thug. He was convicted of extortion in New York. I had not realized he was up here."

"He's with the mob?"

"Was. My contacts at the FBI will know more about his status. I will make some calls. You are aware of our connection with the FBI, yes?"

"I know the TRPB has a past association and you've worked with them before. And I read our first director, Spencer Drayton, was J. Edgar Hoover's assistant. Drayton modeled the TRPB after the bureau, right?"

"Yes, five gold stars for my *pequeña leona.*"

I ignored the comment. At least he didn't pat my head and hand me a toy mouse.

"Rico's connection to the mob may be more serious than you think," I said. "He told Stevie that maybe 'one of the boys' would hurt the girl. Sounds like he's still mobbed up. Maybe he never left the business."

"It is possible. I will let you know what I find out."

"But what can we do for Stevie *now*?" I asked, righting the barrel and replacing the few food wrappers and coffee cups that had been mixed in with the photo scraps.

"*We* cannot do anything. We need our cover, but another agent can step in and talk to Stevie. Offer to protect the girl if Stevie will inform on Rico and Pizutti."

I stared at Calixto. "But that's so dangerous for him. He's just a kid."

"Come on, Fia, you are not new to this game. You know how it works. And put those big, pleading blue eyes away. They are *not* working." But he put a hand on my arm and his expression softened. "Gunny told you there is something else brewing here besides Pizutti and Rico, yes?"

I nodded. "Ziggy Stardust's owner is starting up some sort of hedge fund, using Ziggy as the bait." My fingers were sticky from the wet coffee cups, and I wiped them on my jeans before glancing at Ziggy's stall.

The big colt had thrust his head over the stall gate and was staring at us. In the dimming light, his white blaze and bright spots made a fairly convincing star-spangled banner. People often invest with their hearts, not their brains. Ziggy would be an easy sell.

An hour later, I'd bought a new phone, and was in my room in the Victorian on Union Avenue staring inside the tiny freezer compartment of my refrigerator. Frozen lasagna and a box of chicken potpie stared back. Neither of them lit my fire.

My laptop sat next to me on the tiny kitchen table. I'd searched the internet but found very little on Rico other than his prior convictions. But there *had* to be more, because I could still hear the sob in Stevie's voice. I wanted to tear this Rico jerk into little pieces.

I glanced back into the freezer. Why had this stuff looked good in the grocery store? My phone chirped and I grabbed it off my bed, hoping it would be Calixto with information he'd obtained from the FBI field office in Albany. It was.

"Your friend, Rico, owns a restaurant here in town," he said as soon as I answered.

I leaned forward and shut the doors on the freezer and refrigerator. "I told you he was a mobster. He probably sits in there eating Italian food and ordering hits on people."

"I can tell when you're stressed, Fia. You make jokes."

"Yeah, what else is new?"

"Gunny is bringing in an agent from Maryland to talk to Stevie Davis."

My fingers curled tightly around the phone. "Tell me Pizutti and Rico won't know about this."

"Of course not. I know this agent. He is good."

I sighed. "Okay."

"Have you had dinner?"

I perked right up. "No. What are you thinking?"

"I want to take you to Zutti's Café, a *very* nice Italian restaurant."

"Not *Rico*'s place?"

"Why not? Rico has never seen either of us. Besides, the place is expensive, everyone knows I have plenty of money, and what better way to impress the woman I am pursuing?"

"Um, even so, I'll go disguised as a normal person." I'd find something to use in my bag of tricks.

"Does this mean you will not wear skull earrings?"

"I don't think mobsters are into Goth."

"I am relieved to hear this. Perhaps you could dress like our friend Kate?" he asked.

I thought I'd heard a hopeful note in his voice. So, he'd liked my Kate persona from several months earlier in Florida. As Kate, I'd worn short skirts, low-cut blouses, and high heels. Probably just the right look for a mobbed-up New York restaurant.

"You might get lucky," I said.

One blond wig, tasteful makeup, and short skirt later, I walked with Calixto under a green awning and into Zutti's Café. The aroma of tomato sauce, garlic, and grilled shrimp laced the air as a dark-haired man in black tie greeted us in the foyer. He led us by a refrigerated case. I almost didn't make it past the display of pies, fruit tarts, cakes, cheesecakes, and an assortment of chocolate and whipped cream delights.

A cappuccino machine busily frothed milk into a cup on a marble-topped bar covering one wall. Behind the polished-stone counter, mirrors, and shelves of single malt scotch, vodka, gin, bourbon, brandy, ports, and sherries glowed in the warm light from hanging lamps.

Glossy wood floors, white tablecloths, and fresh-cut flowers added to the ambiance. The maître d' led us to a table fronting a long banquette upholstered in gold-and-green-striped fabric. He pulled the table away from the wall, and as I sat on the banquette, my short skirt slid farther up my thighs. I fluffed up the long blond hair of my wig, removed my blazer, and smiled at Calixto. He ignored the chair on the opposite side of the table and slipped in next to me, causing the maître d' to grin.

"This is cozy," I said.

Calixto's eyes glittered as they swept over the low V in my

blouse. After a rapid discussion with the maître d' about wine, he ordered a bottle. From our host's pleased expression, I suspected the money for the wine would keep me in chicken potpies for a year.

Glancing toward the back of the restaurant, I started slightly. A latticed screen partially hid two tables, and Rico sat at one with an old guy in a striped suit. Behind them a set of swinging doors led into the kitchen.

The two men puffed away on big cigars and had glasses of what looked like brandy. Rico's salt-and-pepper eyebrows bristled over tired, dark eyes. Beneath them, heavy bags sagged onto his jowly face. He had a round belly, probably from too much fried squid and cannelloni. The other guy had a lined, seamed face and a nose slightly pushed to one side. Someone had done a job on him in the past.

"There's your man, Rico," I said, tearing off a piece of warm, crusty bread and dipping it into a bowl of olive oil.

Calixto glanced toward the kitchen. "So it is, and the gentleman he's sitting with is Alberto Rizelli."

"And he would be . . ."

"Another retired mobster from New York. His mother was from the Gambino family."

"What makes you think he's retired?" I asked.

"He is still on parole after twenty years in federal prison. If he is caught doing *anything*, he'll be back in for life."

"Yeah, unless he has a good lawyer." *Fia McKee, cynic.*

Calixto shrugged. Our waiter arrived with a bottle of red wine, opened it, and allowed Calixto a sample taste. When it was poured, an earthy, rich scent drifted to my nose. The ruby liquid gurgled and splashed into my glass. I drank some. Don't know anything about wine, but this stuff tasted wonderful. I drank more.

"So what was Rizelli in for?" I asked, as Calixto's gold double-C cuff links gleamed at me from the starched white cotton that covered his wrists. The man had strong hands, and long, tapered fingers. And they were so close to my hand. Two sips of wine and I was already imagining those fingers—

"Rizelli ran prostitutes and loan-sharking back in the seventies and eighties," Calixto said. "My guy at the FBI mentioned him today. He said Rizelli was tied in with Rico, and committed— they suspected but could never prove—multiple murders."

"But they got him for prostitution and loan-sharking?"

"Yes, for that."

"Nice guy," I said, before swallowing another sip of wine.

The waiter returned, and we ordered mussels and shrimp with linguine. I was glad, that like me, Calixto was not bound by the white wine with seafood rule. I had more wine, a bite of bread, more wine, and a forkful of crisp green salad when it arrived. Then I had more wine.

By now, Calixto was looking pretty good. His mouth was so . . . I pushed my wineglass away. Maybe I should wait for my dinner.

"But," Calixto said, "my guy at the FBI was only half joking when he referred to the 'Saratoga mob.'"

"Saratoga mob?" I started to reach for my wine, but stopped.

"Yes, *querida*, and you should keep your claws sheathed around these men."

"I will, if they leave Stevie alone. But who else is in this gang?"

"Apparently there are five or six of these old mobsters up here. After being indicted—"

Our waiter arrived with steaming plates of shellfish, the rich scent of garlic butter almost as intoxicating as the wine. I pried a mussel from its shell and popped it into my mouth. *Nirvana.*

Calixto dug into his meal for a while before continuing. "So, after being indicted and serving their time, these *viejo mafiosos* could not obtain licenses for any of their previous businesses—concrete, waste management. They were finished in the Big Apple and New Jersey."

I forked up a bite of linguine dripping with garlic butter. Calixto leaned forward and wiped a drip of butter from my lower lip before licking it off his finger. My physical reaction was quick and intense. *Damn him.*

"But," he continued, after a long sip of wine, "though many mobsters retire to Florida, these individuals dislike the Miami scene. They are hard-core New Yorkers, true racing fans, and have decided to settle in Saratoga."

Calixto was into his wine now, his eyes bright with amusement. "They pulled Rico in for questioning last year, and he told them, 'I'm retired from all that now. I got my little restaurant to keep me well fed in my old age.'"

I leaned forward. "Yeah, right. But he can't help himself, can he? Now he's got to play the ponies illegally. How convenient for him that his nephew trains at Saratoga."

Calixto emptied his wineglass, then refilled both of ours. He took a long pull. "You think the *nephew* is convenient? Listen to this. Rizelli owned a horse farm in New Jersey with a racetrack on the property. There's an Irish vet that used to work for him who swears Rizelli had a backhoe on the property and—"

"Buried bodies in the infield! He did, didn't he?" I burst out laughing and reached for my wine, then stopped, realizing I shouldn't be laughing. "But this isn't funny, is it? These are *horrible* people."

"Would you rather cry, *pequeña leona*?" He took my hand and rubbed his thumb lightly against my palm. "I don't want to see you cry."

I drew back. "We should think about getting our check. We have to get up early."

"Of course," he said. "This is good. They will think we rushed out because we cannot keep our hands off each other."

"Yes," I said. "They will think that and that you have more than one woman." My phone vibrated in my purse, and I dug it out to make sure it wasn't Brian. Maybe Pizutti had left a trail of transactions showing us he'd been betting on races that he'd fixed. Only I didn't recognize the number, and let it go to voice mail.

We left the restaurant and walked down Broadway to stretch our legs. The temperature had dropped as it does at night in Upstate New York, and I buttoned my blazer over my blouse. We walked past shops, boutiques, more restaurants, and a Starbucks, when I saw the most amazing building and stopped. "What is this place?"

"The Adelphi Hotel."

"Wow. It's like a fantasy. Was it modeled after an Italian villa?"

"Exactly," Calixto said.

I stared up at the lit façade of the four-story hotel. An ornate porch, maybe ninety-feet long, stretched across the second level. From there, slender three-story columns rose, finally joining intricately carved arches that formed the roofline.

"A famous Saratoga landmark," Calixto said. "Perhaps we should stay here some time,"

"*What?*"

"Only as part of our romance cover, of course."

I couldn't think of a comeback and was grateful when my phone buzzed to remind me a message was waiting. I pushed Play.

Around me, everything receded. A voice I hadn't heard in

seventeen years sparked the anger that still smoldered in my gut. A sense of betrayal rushed forward from the past as I listened to the voice of Joan McKee Gorman.

Calixto stared at me. "*What?* Who has called you?

I could feel the anger contorting my lips. I stared into the dark beyond him. "My mother."

7

Early the next morning, I found Becky Joe passed out in a chair inside the tack room with an empty bottle of gin by her feet. When I leaned over to make sure she was just sleeping it off and not seriously ill, I caught the sour smell of intoxication. I liked her and didn't want her fired, so I placed the bottle in the trash barrel before Pizutti could arrive and find it.

I remembered how the blood had drained from her face after she'd witnessed Rico's cruel behavior to Stevie. Rather than admit what she'd seen, or talk about it, she'd gotten drunk. Had she been here all night?

At 4:15 A.M., it was still dark outside, with only a trace of gray to the east. I hoped I could rouse her before anyone else arrived. They'd be showing up soon.

Using the water spigot by the shedrow, I filled the coffeepot, poured it into the coffeemaker, and spooned a strong portion of java in the filter to brew. When the rich scent of coffee filled the air, I made us both a cup and quickly swallowed a few mouthfuls.

Gently, I shook Becky Joe's shoulder. She didn't wake up, so I shook harder, and when her eyes opened, I held the second cup out to her. She grimaced and pushed my hand away, spilling hot coffee on her knee.

"Ow! Crap . . . I'm gonna be sick."

She rushed out of the tack room with her hand covering her mouth, sped off the shedrow, and barfed in the grass. *Lovely.*

"You drink the whole bottle last night?"

She walked away, jerking an angry, backward wave in my general direction before she lurched along the path leading to East Avenue. This was not good. She was Ziggy Stardust's groom, and Pizutti had scheduled the colt to work that morning. The colt's weekly speed drills were critical, and this was a terrible time for his groom to be missing.

The replacement worker for the one Pizutti had fired should arrive momentarily, but with Becky Joe absent, we'd still be one groom short. It would be a long morning, and I regretted not going to bed earlier the night before. Wished I'd had less wine, too. Couldn't fix that, so I drank more coffee.

Once I'd started working for him, I'd soon realized the trainer liked to use his assistant, Carl, as a hatchet man. Despite his soft spot for his help, if anyone screwed up, Pizutti would see to it Carl gave the offending groom the axe. I was afraid his blade was about to fall on Becky Joe.

A few minutes later, two yawning grooms appeared, and Carl drove up in his truck, leaving it parked near the barn. A couple more grooms shuffled in, and moments later, I heard the sound of Pizutti's diesel approaching. I finished my last sip of coffee, and watched as he climbed from the Mercedes and headed toward me.

Mars had a reputation for loving the fast lane—gambling, flashy women, booze, and drugs. Did these vices ever spiral out of control? His most likely downfall would be gambling debts, unless he had an equally expensive cocaine habit. But he seemed too on top of his game for heavy cocaine use.

From the doorway to the feed room, Carl called out to him. "Becky Joe's AWOL."

"She's not effing here?" When Carl nodded, Pizutti said, "Man, can you believe that woman?" The whining note in his voice intensified. "Carl, I want you to—"

"She's *sick*," I said. "Saw her last night. She had a bug or something."

Pizutti looked doubtful. "Nah. Broad probably hit the bottle."

"No, really," I said. "Last time I saw her, she was throwing up."

"Huh. Maybe you're right, 'cause she usually comes to work no matter how messed up she is. And she *does* know how to get messed up." He nodded to himself, then his gaze came to rest on me. "So, can you rub Ziggy this morning?"

Carl frowned. "Fay may be a bit new to be working on Ziggy. Besides she's a hot walker. What about Javier?"

"Nah, I've watched this one. She knows what she's doing. She'll be fine."

Pizutti's compliment worried me. Was my cover as a hot walker that transparent? My years at Pimlico as a groom and exercise rider for my dad might have seasoned me too much to fool a horseman like Pizutti. Or maybe living a double life just made me paranoid. I shook it off.

"I'd love to groom him!" No need to fake my eagerness; putting my hands on the sleek coat and muscles of a great racehorse like Ziggy Stardust would be a treat.

Pizutti turned to Carl. "Get his breakfast ready." He pointed an index finger at me. "You feed it to him, and as soon as he's finished, get to work on him. He's going out after the eight o'clock break."

When Carl handed me the feed bucket, I grabbed the rake so I could encourage Ziggy to stand back. Happily, I was able to serve the grain without having his teeth embedded in my arm. With that accomplished, I watched him devour his oats while banging his feed tub against the wall. The way he darted fierce glances at me, you'd think he hadn't been fed in weeks.

As soon as he licked up the last oat, I grabbed a brush box and carefully entered his stall, telling myself that if Becky Joe could groom the horse, I could, too. Luckily, he tolerated my presence, but eyed me suspiciously as I squatted beneath him and removed his stable bandages. But when I massaged his neck with the rubber curry comb, he nodded his head up and down with enthusiasm, apparently in equine ecstasy.

"Oh, you're just a big old pussycat," I said, and rubbed harder. Next, I used a comb on his mane, tail, and forelock, a stiff brush on his legs, and a hoof pick on his feet before going over his entire coat with a soft brush. My finishing touch was to polish his coat with a soft, clean cloth until he gleamed.

The energy that flowed from his body into my hands was almost magical, definitely electrical, and totally awesome. I'd always believed the best racehorses possessed a magnetic quality. Some said I had an overactive imagination. Personally, I think those people are obtuse, and don't belong near a good horse.

By now, I'd broken a sweat, had horse dust all over me, but was happy as a sunbeam, at least until I thought about the previous evening. The cloud of indecision about my mother, which I'd ignored all morning, had gathered strength. Now it loomed large, darkening my horizon. Couldn't I just *not* call her?

I'd avoided the bitch for seventeen years, and wanted nothing to do with her. Suddenly, she wanted to see me? *Now?* Did she feel guilty about leaving me behind all those years ago? I hated her for it, and doubted I could ever forgive her. I wiped the sweat off my face with Ziggy's towel, and after easing out of his stall, I stood in the aisle staring at nothing. I didn't want this uncertainty hanging over me.

Find out what she wants, Fia. Get it over with. I decided I would as soon as I got back to my room.

When the track reopened after the eight o'clock break, I was surprised to see Carl give Stevie a leg up on Ziggy Stardust for the speed work. I'd assumed Ziggy's regular jockey, the legendary Cornelio Valentinas, would work the horse. Valentinas must have been unavailable, because I knew Stevie would never be named to ride Ziggy when the horse ran in the Jim Dandy, whether he'd worked the horse or not. The owners would only accept a top jockey like Valentinas for their horse. They'd never want a rider as inexperienced as Stevie.

Once Carl had tossed Stevie onto Ziggy's back, he led the horse and rider for a few turns around the shedrow. This was done in the sometimes vain hope the walk would settle the horse and avoid a sudden explosions of pent-up energy on the way to the track. The trio had just disappeared around the far corner of the barn without mishap, when Calixto, leading another horse and jockey, came around the near corner.

He threw me a meaningful look before glancing up at his rider, and saying, "Oscar Mejias, this is Fay Mason."

Damn. The guy I'd read about in the *Form,* the friend of Fragoso, the jockey who'd shot himself. This one looked to be in his early twenties, his face thin and honed from constant dieting.

"*Hola,* Oscar," I said.

He smiled and said, *"Cómo estás?"* revealing seriously crooked teeth with a gap where one canine was missing.

Was it a coincidence Calixto had hooked up with Oscar Mejias? I doubted it. More likely, Gunny and the Saratoga County Sheriff's Office wanted Calixto to investigate deeper into Fragoso's suicide, and if Mejias was riding for Maggie Bourne, it gave Calixto the opportunity he needed.

Fragoso's death still haunted me at night, the memory of his bloody head crawling into my dreams. I shook the ugly vision off, watching Calixto lead the horse and rider down the aisle instead. The way his leather chaps accentuated his long, lean legs brought a sudden flush of heat.

I almost berated myself, but my desire to live had always burned hottest alongside my fear of death. Nothing wrong with that. It's the way it should be.

Later, I stood on the edge of the Oklahoma Training Track with Pizutti and Carl, staring through binoculars, holding my breath as Ziggy Stardust broke from the gate. He was working five furlongs with two other horses, and Mars had told Stevie to let him rip.

"Wanna see him go really good," he'd said. "Just show him your whip. Don't be hittin' him with it, okay?"

Through the lenses I watched Stevie sit chilly on Ziggy's back, not asking, just seeing what the horse wanted to do. Fast and straight as a falcon dive, Ziggy shot down the backstretch, opening up on the other two horses, leaving them behind.

I'd only seen the horse run live that one time at Belmont, the day he'd stopped running. Now, he took my breath away. He gained more momentum, rocketing around the turn and exploding down the stretch with dizzying speed. When he hit the wire, Stevie stood up in the irons, and Mars clicked his stopwatch.

"Fifty-nine flat! And all within hisself. Man, he went good."

Mars slapped palms with Carl, and through the binoculars, Stevie's face was flushed with happiness. I felt it, too.

Exhilarated, I bounced back to the barn and finished the morning chores, before hurrying up Union Avenue to the rental, where I zipped up the three staircases and entered my room. After showering, I scrolled through my messages for my mother's number.

I stared at it for a moment, my buoyant mood shriveling. I gritted my teeth and hit Send.

When she answered, I reverted back to my childhood.

"*Fia* . . . darling! So delighted you called me back. I really, *really* want to see you." She spoke in the breathless, dramatic, and manipulative voice I remembered from childhood. "When can we make that happen?"

I exhaled a breath, "How are you, Mother?"

"Oh, darling, call me Joan. Patrick always does. I *so* prefer it."

"Fine," I said. "I don't really think of you as my mother, anyway."

"Now, sweetie, don't be like that. I want to see you. I *need* to see you. I've felt so bad about what happened with your father."

I ground my teeth. What was she talking about? "You mean when you took his money and walked out?"

An edge of steel sharpened her voice. "I told you, don't be like that, Fia. Your father forced me to leave. Surely you realize that?"

"First I've heard of it."

She paused, came back with a softened tone. "Fia, please. I want to talk this through. We've been estranged for so long. It's been very *painful* for me."

For you?

"I talked to Patrick," she continued. "He told me you two

have made up, and I was *thrilled* to hear it. But he said you lost your position with the police force? That you're working at some barn up here now?"

The disapproval I remembered so well. Her words oozed with it. I closed my eyes and took another breath. "Yes, *Joan.*" I almost spit the name out. "That's correct."

I heard her sigh, the one that said I was such a trial for her. "Fia, I want to help you. Get you back on your feet."

"Really? Why?"

"Because you're my *daughter.* I want our family to reknit." She paused a beat, then played what she must have considered her ace in the hole. "Patrick says Jilly is *crazy* about you, and I thought I would invite her up. To Saratoga . . . so she can see you."

I adored my niece who I'd only come to know recently. She was cute, tough, and like me, at age fifteen, a handful.

"Do not," I said, "use your granddaughter as a bribe. Don't suck her into your games. Leave her out of it!"

Joan seemed speechless. But I should have known she'd only paused to regroup. "Oh . . . Fia. I am so sorry. I've *hurt* you." Her voice broke with tears. "Please, sweetie, let me see you. *Please.*"

I wanted to scream at her. Tell her she hadn't hurt me, couldn't hurt me, because I cared so little about her, she'd never even come close. But talking to her for the first time in seventeen years had torn the scab right off my wound. I saw the denial I'd clung to for so long was a big fat lie. When this woman had walked out on me, she'd broken my heart, shredded my soul.

But she wasn't giving up. "Fia, you should know I was in that plane crash last month at LAX. If you saw the news, you know sixteen people died! I was one of the lucky ones. And it's made me—"

"You were on that American Airlines flight?" It had been

all over the media. Why hadn't Patrick mentioned this? *Because he knows you hate her.*

"What I'm trying to say," she continued, "is coming that close to death has made me reconsider many things in my life. I want a second chance."

I'd been marching about the room, clutching the cell to my ear, and had wound up standing before the window. I stared at the Adirondack Mountains in the distance. They looked so desolate and cold. Was it possible she wanted to reconnect? If she did, should I let that happen?

A sudden avalanche of emotion buried me and I heard myself saying, "All right . . . I'll see you."

Damn her. Why had I weakened like that? Sounding like a sixteen-year-old. Young and vulnerable. Just pathetic.

"Oh, Fia, *darling.* I'm thrilled to hear it! You won't regret this."

8

I turned my phone off and crawled under the comforter, trying to ignore the large merry-go-round print that covered its surface. I was afraid if I stared at it, the carousel would begin spinning in time to the images that whirled in my head—Stevie's frightened face, the day I'd realized my mother had abandoned us, and the terrible pain she'd left in my father's eyes.

Eventually, the previous evening's events with Rico, followed by too much wine, too little sleep, and the draining reconnect with my mother did their work, and I slid under for almost two hours. I awakened with renewed energy and a text message from Calixto.

"See me at pm feed?" he'd asked.

I made coffee, added a dollop of cream, and drank from my landlord's china mug picturing a pink and green unicorn. Sitting on his merry-go-round comforter, I realized the man had a penchant for fantasy horses. Maybe I'd introduce him to Ziggy Stardust.

A short time later, when I arrived at the barn, Becky Joe was back in action.

"I hear you covered for me, Fay. I appreciate it."

She looked a little gray around the edges.

"No problem," I said, and followed her to the feed room where Carl was setting out buckets of grain.

Unfazed by his sensational work, Ziggy was his usual dev- ilish self, and I had to wave the rake at him before I could dump grain into his tub. Wiggly Wabbit dove into her feed, the fatigue from the previous day's race replaced by a bloom of energy. An- other good sign.

I worked through my chores, finished topping off everyone's water buckets, and wiped my hands with a clean towel, before beating it to the ladies' room to wash my face. After adding more mascara and black eye shadow, I fluffed my hair, and headed to see Calixto.

I found him sitting in a squeaky desk chair in Maggie Bourne's office where the smell of molasses, grain, and liniment seeped in from the shedrow. Calixto was studying a condition book from Monmouth Park racetrack.

"Maggie running a horse in New Jersey?" I asked.

"She wants me to see what is available down there, yes." He closed the book, stood, and came around the desk. Lowering his voice, he said. "Regarding Fragoso. I—"

"You're looking into his suicide through his friend Oscar Mejias, aren't you?"

"No *cucarachas* on you, *querida*."

His grin was so damn cute, I had to resist an urge to touch him. "So what have you found out?"

His cautious glance around the office told me he worried the walls might have ears. "We will graze Secret Wish, yes?"

I nodded and followed him onto Bourne's shedrow, where he grabbed a lead shank, haltered a chestnut filly, then led her from her stall out to the grass to graze. We walked to where no one could hear us. Still, Calixto kept his voice so low that I had to stay close. Close enough to smell his light spice cologne and feel his body heat in the cooling air.

"Jose Fragoso was living in a rental house with three other young Peruvian jockeys. The oldest of the three is only eighteen."

"And Mejias is one of them, right?" I asked.

"Yes. All up-and-coming jockeys who rode at the Hipódromo de Monterrico in Lima, and not one of them speaks a word of English."

I asked the obvious question. "Who sponsored them to come into the U.S.?"

"A Peruvian named Marco Tolentino. He became a citizen five years ago, and brought the boys to New York recently. He travels between here and Lima several times a year."

Secret Wish had found a small clump of clover. She tore the tender stems from the ground, chewing them up and swallowing them before spotting another cluster. She dragged Calixto to it.

"When you females want something, there is no stopping you," he said.

Careful what you wish for, Calixto.

I breathed in the filly's horsey scent and the wet smell of crushed vegetation as her teeth ground the clover to juice. I thought about the four jockeys, foreigners who didn't speak English, living in a house together in Upstate New York. These riders had come to the U.S. with dreams, hoping to follow in the footsteps of successful Peruvian jockeys like Edgar Prado, Jorge Chavez, and Rafael Bejarano. But Tolentino would have ways to control them, to force them to follow orders. Legal or otherwise.

"Does this Tolentino guy have a record?"

"Not yet, *leona*. Right now, we are more concerned with checking the status of jockeys' families."

"But not to see if they have records, right? You're thinking Tolentino will threaten their relatives in Peru, and these boys will do exactly what they're told. That's what you're afraid of, isn't it?"

"Yes." He held my gaze a moment.

I was surprised by the depth of pain in his eyes and had to look away. He really cared about these people. My glance swept to the path by the racetrack where I'd found Fragoso's body. Had someone threatened him so horribly he'd killed himself? The thought spread like gasoline onto the anger that flickered inside me.

"*Damn* it, Calixto. This is what Rico is doing to Stevie. Threatening his little sister."

"Fia, I wish we had something solid that would allow us to bring charges against Rico. But we don't."

"Or this guy, Tolentino." My anger intensified. It always did when I wanted to protect an innocent and couldn't. "Calixto, there must be something we can do for Oscar and the other two!"

"Gunny is meeting with two NYRA officials and an FBI agent tomorrow. I believe they will strongly suggest to Tolentino that he send the boys back to Peru. Gunny indicated it will be suggested to him in a manner he will not refuse."

"But that's all we can do? Send them home?"

Calixto put a hand on the neck of Secret Wish as she nipped and tore at the blades of grass near her feet. "There may be channels to notify officials in Lima. I am not familiar with Peru, or the level of corruption that might exist within its police department. At least these three can ride in Peru, and be at home with their families."

I didn't like this, didn't like that the fate of these Peruvians was out of my hands. But Stevie was American. If I could help him, I would.

"I have to go back to my barn," I said.

Calixto's look was questioning, but he simply nodded as Secret Wish pulled him away from me, tugging him toward another clump of grass.

I hurried around the corner to Pizutti's shedrow. The sun was lower in the western horizon, and the backstretch had quieted. Pizutti hadn't shown up that afternoon, and most of the help had already left. Carl was still in the office, and I waited until he came out before slipping inside and rifling through the office notebook with its contact information on vets, feed companies, hired help, and so forth.

I found Stevie Davis's phone number, and more important, his address. I memorized both and left the backstretch.

Stevie's address took me to a brick ranch on a side street off Lake Avenue. I parked the Mini and walked to the front door. When I rang the bell, a bent old man, who'd probably been over six feet in his youth, opened the door. Our attempts to speak were drowned out by two Jack Russell terriers that barked incessantly while rocketing up and down like fur-bearing firecrackers.

I leaned over and let the dogs sniff my hand. Once that was accomplished, they clearly expected me to pet them, so I did.

When I could finally explain why I'd come, the old man said, "Oh, you're looking for young Stevie. He's renting the little apartment over the garage back there." He waved an arthritic hand toward the back of his house. "He should be there now. Just walk down the drive. You'll find it."

After I thanked him and stepped outside, one of the terriers bolted through the door and tore after me with great enthusiasm.

"Take him with you!" the man shouted, and shut the door.

With the brown and white dog bouncing alongside, I followed the drive to the garage, where Stevie's yellow Motobecane leaned against the wood frame wall. I climbed a staircase, and was about to rap on the door, when it was opened by a slender girl with long hair. It was unmistakably the girl in the torn photo, her hair the same light brown as Stevie's. The dog raced past me into the apartment, catapulted through the air, and landed on a battered couch. A little king on his throne.

My gaze returned to the girl. The words "tiny ballerina" came to mind. She looked about twelve, had lovely dark eyes, and like Stevie's, they were bright with intelligence.

"Hi," I said. "My name is Fay. You must be Lila?"

She nodded, and I heard footsteps from the back of the apartment.

"Lila! I've told you not to open that door. Who is it?" Stevie's voice sounded worried. He jogged past the kitchen and into the living room with only a towel wrapped around skinny hips. His hair was wet and tension shadowed his eyes.

"I'm sorry, Stevie, it's just me. I guess I should have called first." Except, as an agent, when I needed to talk to someone, I didn't call. I just showed up.

The terrier flew off the couch and jumped on Stevie, his front paws hooking the towel as if determined to tear it off.

Lila giggled, apparently delighted by her brother's predicament.

"Raymond, stop it!" Stevie's glare switched from the dog to

me. "Fay, why are you here?" He took a breath, then said, "I mean . . . come in. You can sit while I put some clothes on."

He escaped into a bedroom and shut the door. As soon as I sat on the couch that faced a TV, Raymond sprang through the air and crashed onto my lap. Lila, who'd seated herself cross-legged on the floor, giggled again.

"He's a silly dog, isn't he?" I asked.

A sweet smile curved her lips as she nodded.

Raymond squirmed in my lap and shoved his head under my hand, leaving me no choice but to pet him. *Demanding little bugger.*

"Are you Stevie's friend?" Lila asked.

"Yes. I work with him at the track. I like him."

Her eyes widened. "Are you his girlfriend?"

"No. Just a friend."

I glanced around the tiny apartment. It smelled fresh. The kitchen was tidy and the red-and-white-checked cloth spread over the metal table was clean and smooth. Something tasty was cooking in the oven.

"Are you baking something, Lila?"

"Yes, we're having chicken with stuffing!"

"Did you make it?" I asked.

"Stevie helped."

These kids were taking care of themselves, which was great, but I had to ask. "Lila, do your parents live here, too?"

Her face clouded, and her gaze drifted to the floor. "No."

She'd clasped her hands so tightly together, I decided to leave it alone, and a strained silence grew between us. I was relieved when Stevie, minus the towel, plus clothes, came back into the room.

Lila stood up. "May I take Raymond outside to play?"

"Of course," Stevie said. "But stay close, okay?"

She nodded and hurried out the front door with the little dog.

Stevie stared at me and remained standing. "So, what do you need, Fay?"

"It's more about what you need, Stevie. And your little sister."

His lips pressed together. "I don't know what you mean."

"Come on. Something's going on with you and Pizutti and that creep Rico. I think you need help."

"You don't know what you're talking about!" His words lashed at me like a whip. Then, he took a breath, and spoke more softly. "How could you possibly help me?"

How indeed? Again, I berated myself for letting Wiggly Wabbit break my phone. I would have had all the evidence I needed. I couldn't tell Stevie I worked for the TRPB, and I couldn't turn Pizutti or Rico in with only hearsay evidence.

"I know they've threatened you. I heard them last night. You could go to the stewards and tell them." As I said it, I knew how stupid it sounded.

"Are you crazy?" Stevie asked. "They wouldn't believe me! All that would happen is I'd lose my job, and Rico might . . ." He stared at a spot on the floor. "I need my salary to take care of Lila. You've seen her. She's just a little girl!"

He hadn't been able to say that Rico might hurt his sister. Hell, I couldn't bear to think about it.

"Where are your parents, Stevie?"

His eyes turned cagey. "They're around."

"Where? It looks to me like you two are living alone. You wouldn't want Child Protective Services to get involved, would you?"

He threw me the hard look of an angry man. There was nothing youthful in it. "You'd better butt out of this!"

I raised my hands, palms out. "I'm not calling them. I'm

just afraid they might catch on to this. Are your parents really 'around'?"

Stevie's shoulders sagged. He walked to the couch and sank down next to me.

"Listen," he said. "We ran away, okay? My dad drinks, our mom's a junkie, all right? She'll let him do anything as long as he brings her the next fix."

"Jesus, Stevie. I'm sorry. Did he hurt you?"

He waved it away like it was nothing. "Yeah, he beat me, but then he started looking at Lila in a way that made me want to kill him."

I closed my eyes. "I'm sorry."

"Stop saying that. We're *fine!*" He gazed at the ceiling a moment, then exhaled. "See, what happened is, I met Pizutti up at Finger Lakes. Rode a few races for him. He saw what was going on with my parents and gave me this job. But he didn't know anything about Lila. I thought he didn't even know she existed. Anyways, as soon as he offered me work, Lila and I were like outta there. I owe Pizutti a lot. I wouldn't turn him in. He fronted the rent for this place."

"But he let Rico threaten Lila."

Stevie dropped his head in his hands. "I know, I know." His voice sank to a whisper. "If I have to pull a race, I'll pull a race."

I didn't need to tell him he could go to jail for that. I sighed. The kid didn't even have a car, only a bicycle. "If you two have to run again, I'll drive you anywhere you need to go, okay? In the meantime, maybe just sort of play it by ear?"

I didn't know what else to say. I couldn't tell him the TRPB was watching him, hoping he'd provide a conviction for Pizutti. And if Stevie did pull a race, he might be the only one who got nailed. Pizutti could simply say he had nothing to do with it.

Stevie pulled away from me and stood up. "I'm glad you came to see me. I'll do what you said. Take it a day at a time." His smile was weak. "Maybe things will work out."

"I'll do whatever I can to help you."

"Thanks," he said. "I should get Lila in for dinner." He moved toward the door. "See you tomorrow, okay?" He'd ended our meeting.

I nodded, and when I stepped outside, the air had chilled, leaving the sky cold and empty. I followed Stevie down the stairs and watched him walk to Lila. She was holding on to a piece of rope, playing tug-of-war with Raymond.

Pizutti confused and angered me. He'd taken this kid under his wing, brought him into Saratoga, and now, just like Becky Joe had said, he'd turned on him. At times, Pizutti had exhibited a kind heart. But he was weak-willed and a coward. He'd pushed Stevie into a situation I suspected was terribly similar to that of the jockey who'd shot himself.

Damn it. I had to get him out of this.

9

Al Savarine showed up at the barn a few mornings later, during the eight o'clock break. Ziggy Stardust's owner struck me much as his photo had. He looked like a thug. His suit and Italian shoes were expensive, but excessive. He had an overbite, thick lips, and a narrow depraved-looking face, as if he'd turned away from what was right in life years ago.

When he removed his designer sunglasses during Pizutti's introduction, his eyes were shifty, his expression arrogant. Yet I sensed insecurity in the man—always a dangerous combination.

Never one to hesitate, and since Pizutti had neglected to mention I was only a lowly hot walker, I jumped right in. "Mr. Savarine, I've been hearing about your plans for a hedge fund. It sounds really cool. I'm impressed!"

Savarine puffed with importance. "Yeah, it's looking really good. It'll be something nobody's ever done before. New, like, cutting edge in finance. Our clients will be able to buy a piece of everything, get in on *all* the action."

"That's awesome," I said.

"Hey, did you hear we plan to build an equine clinic? Gonna be state of the art."

I hadn't. "Really? And your clients will get a cut of that, the purse money, and breeding stock?"

"Absolutely."

This went against everything I knew about breeding and racing. Profits at the track were impossible to time or predict, if they came at all. Every year owners put something like $2 billion into a game that returned only $1 billion in purses. I couldn't imagine Savarine's idea having legs. Would people believe he could produce regular profits, month after month, year after year?

"So," I said, "I guess people will have to fork out a lot of money to fund all this, huh? What would happen if you had a really bad year? Wouldn't they be kind of upset?"

Savarine's expression darkened. He glanced at Pizutti before sliding his dark glasses back on.

"Don't pay any attention to her," Pizutti said quickly. "She doesn't know what she's talking about. She's a hot walker."

"Oh," Savarine said, his mouth forming an unattractive grin. "With all that fancy eye makeup, I thought she was . . . I don't know, something."

"Forget her," Pizutti said. "Let's go look at your horses."

They turned away from me and walked toward Ziggy's stall. What *did* the man plan to do if the fund became a reality and horses inevitably lost tens of thousands of investor's money? Something Gunny wanted to know, too. I imagined the SEC and the United States Postal Inspection Service might also be lurking in the wings, scrutinizing Savarine's plan.

I turned when I heard footsteps behind me. Becky Joe

emerged from a stall carrying a grooming box. Although she had an amused smile on her mouth, her eyes held a hint of worry.

"Man, you sure stuck it to that larcenous loon. You trying to get yourself fired?"

I shrugged. "Just asking a question."

"Better lay off it, Fay. Smarter to leave stuff alone."

"I can't help it," I said. "It's my nature." Aside from that, I was more than a little agitated since I had agreed to see my mother that afternoon.

Muttering something about hotheads, Becky Joe disappeared into the stall, and a little later, Stevie showed up to gallop Bionic. We exchanged glances but no words. We hadn't spoken about my visit to his apartment, and so far it seemed he was holding up. At least, the shadows around his eyes had lightened a little.

Since I wanted to watch Stevie gallop Bionic, I volunteered to lead the horse and rider onto the track. After I released Bionic, Stevie jogged him the wrong way for a mile, then turned, and set the horse into an open gallop. I stood on the rail watching the colt who looked strong and smooth. I felt a little thrill as I realized he was stretching into a faster clip while Stevie sat chilly on his back, asking for nothing. I'd never spent this much time around a top barn, and wasn't used to seeing so many nice horses. I told myself not to get used to it, as my next assignment could be far different.

"Hey," Stevie gasped when he pulled Bionic up and was walking beside me again, "you see that? He was moving! He's not the same horse I worked last time."

"You got that race coming up, too," I said. "He should be good in there."

Stevie grinned, his hand stroking Bionic's damp neck, "That's what I'm thinking."

"How's Lila?" I asked.

"Oh, she's great. Mars says we can get her enrolled in school down in Hallandale Beach when we go to Gulfstream for the winter."

"Sounds good." Was Pizutti in la-la land? Or had he worked things with Rico so Lila wasn't at risk anymore? I didn't ask, just walked alongside Bionic, hoping things would be okay, but not believing it.

Using the Mini's navigation system, I drove toward my mother's house, to the north of the city, near Skidmore College. After following a narrow lane through a wooded area and passing heavily landscaped homes that were barely visible from the road, I found Spring Street. It led me across a stone bridge with an ornate iron railing into a tony development of five- to ten-acre lots. Money, lots of money, which had always been my mother's goal.

All I knew about her husband, the stepfather I'd never met, was that he had racehorses, no doubt how my mother had met him in the first place. And I knew Richard Gorman had made a fortune creating, building, and finally selling a technology company called Horizons Unlimited. My brother Patrick had mentioned their primary residence was still in California, but Gorman had built a summer home in Saratoga so they could "enjoy" the season each year.

The address led me to a large wooded lot at the end of a cul-de-sac. A single-story stone mansion with large chimneys at either end rose from the middle of the property. Tall, elegant windows were laid in granite walls beneath a slate roof. The builder had left several massive conifers and deciduous trees flanking the house. Red roses and carefully trimmed evergreen bushes partially surrounded a circular drive that was paved in flagstone.

I parked next to a large black Mercedes, but when I climbed

out of my Mini, it was the red Maserati convertible that seemed to scream, "I'm your mother's car!" Yes, sirree, she had made quite a life for herself.

I walked over the stone pavers to a heavy wooden door and rang the bell. I expected a butler, or at least a maid, to respond and was caught off guard when Joan opened the door. I barely saw a flash of polished skin around beautifully made-up eyes before she threw her arms around me.

"Oh, sweetie! It's been so long." She put her hands on my shoulders and stepped back. "Fia, don't stiffen like that. Let me look at you."

I felt like a child again, like she was making sure I'd washed my face and tied my shoes correctly. Thank God I'd removed the Goth makeup and earrings, and was wearing a simple pair of jeans and a plain sweatshirt.

I hadn't forgotten the acid comments I'd received from her as a child.

She was still gorgeous, and somehow, I felt obligated to comment. My mother had that effect on people.

"Mother—I mean, Joan. You look great."

She responded with a quick smile and a slight shrug that seemed to say, "Of course I look great." Tall, with midlength brown hair gleaming with blond highlights, she was toned and thin. She'd obviously received good cosmetic surgery, and didn't appear a day over forty. But I knew she was fifty-six.

Her eyes slid up and down my body, assessing me like a dress on a hanger at Saks Fifth Avenue. I struggled not to squirm.

"Didn't I say you'd turn into a lovely woman?" Her sudden frown was almost imperceptible on her Botoxed forehead. "But why do you wear your hair so short like that?"

"I like it this way." She should have seen it before I let it grow three inches.

"You need a better sense of style, Fia." She sighed. "I suppose that's my fault. . . ." Then she brushed the thought away. "But you were always such a tomboy. Never interested in clothes, or pretty things. Always wanting to go the track and those *horses*."

She'd spit out the word "horses" like it was dirtying her mouth.

"I still love them."

"But you're working at some stable here in Saratoga?"

"Yes, I *told* you that."

"Well, don't get all defensive. Come in. Let me show you the house." She led me through her home, her silk tunic flowing like a river of blue over black leggings and jeweled flats.

Twelve-foot ceilings soared overhead, and the six-foot windows emitted long shafts of yellow light. Richly hued silk and wool carpets dotted polished stone floors. The living room boasted a massive granite fireplace and at the other end of the house, I later discovered, its twin dominated the master suite. The kitchen should have been in *Architectural Digest*. Richard Gorman had made a lot of money with his tech company. I was curious to meet this guy.

"Let's sit here, in the living room," Joan said, waving at one of two beige couches. "Rich and I so enjoy the view."

I glanced out the tall windows to where a large stone-paved patio met the lawn that swept gently down to a stone wall fronted by cypress trees, dogwoods, and more roses. A gardener was busy with clippers.

"Very nice," I said, as I sat and brushed my fingers against the rich, velvety texture of the upholstery. "You've done well for yourself, Joan."

She made a small sound of irritation. "I *did* want Rich to put in tennis courts." Her mouth turned down, showing her disappointment with Rich's apparent failure to do so. "But I'm working on that."

I remembered that tone. She'd always been working on some-thing.

She rose from the couch and walked to a long antique cre-denza and opened the bottle of wine sitting on top. At one end of the credenza stood a magnificent bronze statue of a rearing horse, at the other end, a huge silver vase of red roses perfumed the living-room air. Joan poured the white wine into two crys-tal glasses and brought them to the couch.

She handed me a glass. "Oh, Fia, you should relax. Let's enjoy our afternoon together."

And then we can cook a pot roast and sing camp songs by the fireplace.

"Sure," I said, taking a good dose of wine. I needed it.

"I want you to meet Rich," she said, kicking off her flats and folding her long legs onto the couch. "We're having some people over for cocktails Saturday evening. I want you to come."

"Don't know if I can."

"Nonsense. You work at a *barn*. Of course you can come." She took a sip of wine. "You people and your horses. I wish I could get Rich away from those damn things." Again the down-turned mouth.

You married him.

"Anyway," she continued, "you certainly have time for a party. Do you have anything to wear?"

"Not really."

"God," she said, her lips curling with annoyance, "you're just like your father."

I boiled over. "I can't believe you would—"

Her eyes got the cold edge I remembered as she cut me off. "Let's forget about that, Fia." She gave me a brilliant smile, gleam-ing with capped teeth. "I'm sure we're the same size. I'll lend you something of mine."

"No. Don't. I'll find something."

She shrugged. "If you must." Her gaze dropped to my boots. "I see you still wiggle your foot. You can't learn to control that?" She made an effort and smiled. "So, tell me about your work as a policewoman."

Was she really interested in my life or just making conversation? I was pretty sure it was the latter, but she was about to regret bringing it up.

"After Dad was murdered . . ." I felt my jaw slacken with the disbelief I'd felt eight years earlier when I'd found his body. "I still can't believe you didn't come to his funeral."

She looked away, spoke to her wineglass. "I was in California. Richard's business was totally consuming my time . . ."

"Of course," I said, and took a breath. "So, with both you and Dad gone, I was at loose ends, and angry at the world. Can't imagine why I was angry." By now, I was afraid my foot jiggle was wearing a hole in Joan's Oriental. "Anyway, I went back to school and got a degree in criminal justice."

"You have a college degree?" She sounded thrilled. Probably because I'd changed the subject.

"So I became a Baltimore city cop, but had to leave after I killed a man."

"*What*? You *killed* someone?" She clutched her wineglass and, for once, was speechless. But she recovered, her eyes narrowing, becoming calculating. "But that happens sometimes in the police force. I mean, sometimes it's necessary, isn't it?"

"Yes, but my supervisors didn't like it. They worried about bad press and lawsuits."

"Oh, for heaven's sake," she said, waving the problem away. "Everyone worries about bad press and lawsuits. Rich was always concerned about that before he sold Horizons Unlimited." She studied me closely, her eyes shrewd. "Tell me, why did you kill a man?"

I gave her an abbreviated version, telling her about the woman who was almost dead from strangulation before I'd shot the guy. I didn't tell her about the repercussions or my weird connection to the perpetrator.

Joan gave me a curious look. "Was it hard? Killing a man, I mean."

"No, it wasn't. Not under the circumstances."

"Interesting," she said, and seemed to stare at something inside I couldn't see.

"So," I finished, "I gave up being a cop and went back to what I love most." I wasn't about to tell her I worked for the TRPB. I'd trust the Saratoga mob with a secret before I'd trust her.

Her mouth pinched with disapproval. "The damn racetrack. Fia, you could do so many other things! Rich has excellent connections—"

"Leave it, okay? Just don't."

She shrugged and sipped her wine. Her long manicured fingers slowly twisted the crystal stem. "I'd just hate to see you turn out like your father."

"Screw you," I shouted. All these years and I'd I never said a word to her. Inside a dam was breaking. "I loved Dad. I'd be proud to be half the person he was. And you treated him like shit!" I felt the sting of tears in my eyes.

"Fia, I'm sorry. I shouldn't have said that."

"No, you shouldn't." The smell of her roses had become cloying. I felt like I couldn't breathe, and stood up.

"I said I was sorry, Fia. Please don't leave."

"I've got to go to work."

She stood quickly, stepping back into her jeweled flats. "Let me walk you out."

"Whatever."

"I want to make all this up to you, Fia," she said, hurrying to keep up as I rushed toward the front door. "Please come to the party this Saturday. *Please?*"

"I wouldn't miss it," I said. "I really want to meet this guy. See what he's got that made you walk out on us." I stopped, glanced around her entry foyer, where I stood on what was probably a shockingly expensive Oriental rug. I waved at the paintings on the wall, the long, ornate mahogany chest. "But it's obvious, isn't it?"

I beat it to the front door, rushed outside, and slammed the heavy wooden door behind me.

10

The next morning, about the time most of our chores were done, I stood with Becky Joe on Pizutti's shedrow, watching an eighteen-wheeled commercial van roll up to our barn. The air brakes hissed and the smell of diesel filled the air as the carrier ground to a halt.

Moments later, Javier led a horse off the van and into a stall we'd made ready for the new arrival. Named Glow West, the chestnut colt had previously been stabled at Belmont Park with another of Pizutti's assistant trainers.

Becky Joe handed me the *Daily Racing Form* she'd been studying, and as I examined Glow West's past performances, an alarm bell rang in my head.

The *Form* had posted two brilliant works for the four-year-old colt, who was coming back from a layoff after suffering a foot abscess. He was entered to run that very afternoon, and Pizutti had named Stevie on the horse.

"This colt is going to go off favorite," I said to Becky Joe, keeping my voice soft. "Did you see these works, and the races he won last year?"

"Yeah, I saw."

The name of another entry in the race caught my eye, raising a red flag that waved in time to my mental alarm bell.

"Becky Joe, look at this! Pizutti's got Dodger running in the same race."

"Saw that, too. I think Mars is up to his dirty tricks."

I was surprised she admitted that much to me. Then again, I'd covered for her when she'd had that sick hangover. Maybe I'd earned her trust. My attention shifted back to the *Form*. Dodger belonged to Savarine, and though the colt's stats showed slow works, rumor around the barn had it that he was way faster than he appeared on paper. Was he already earmarked for Savarine's hedge fund?

"Pizutti's not going to let Stevie win on Glow West, is he?" I said.

"That's how I see it," Becky Joe said. "Nice setup for old Mars and Savarine to bet the wallet on Dodger and walk away with the bank. Gonna leave poor Stevie to pretend he's riding Glow West to the wire, and if the stewards catch on, it won't be pretty."

I hoped we were wrong, but the pieces were in place on the board, just waiting to be moved by Pizutti. The "slow" Dodger would go off at long odds, then surprise the fans by running second or third, possibly even winning. Having studied the *Form* and knowing what I knew about Dodger, I'd bet Glow West was his only serious competition.

Stevie had already told me, if Pizutti ordered him to, he'd keep the horse from winning. I thought about the girl that reminded me of a tiny ballerina and her innocent eyes. I couldn't really blame Stevie.

"You're not on Facebook, are you?" Becky Joe asked.

"What? Facebook? No way." I could see it now, *Fia Mckee, undercover agent for the Thoroughbred Racing Protective Bureau.* With pictures of me in various disguises.

"How come?" she asked.

"Not my thing."

"Maybe you should try it," she said. "I've got, like, a thousand friends who are racing fans and you should hear the things they say about Pizutti. They *hate* him."

"Then NYRA should read their comments."

Becky Joe went on about the wonders of Facebook until I told her I had to make a call. As soon as I was able to move out of her hearing range, I rang Calixto.

"How is New York's most beautiful Goth this morning?" he asked.

"Troubled. Look at the fifth race this afternoon. Savarine has a ringer in there named Dodger. Stevie's going to be on the favorite, Glow West, and I think he's going to pull the horse." I'd already told Calixto about my visit to Stevie's apartment and how I'd met Lila.

"Hold on while I look." A moment later, he said, "I see what you mean. Are you finished over there?"

"Yes."

"Good, I'm bringing you a gift," he said, and disconnected.

A gift? This could work for me, this bearing of presents every time he saw me on Pizutti's shedrow.

A few minutes later, he strode down the aisle wearing lizard boots, black jeans, and a Western shirt. He held a small box in his hand. When he passed Pizutti's office, the trainer stepped out and stared after him.

"Hey, Coyune, nice boots, babe. Why you always gotta look like you walked off the cover of *GQ*?"

"I like to keep the fans happy."

Pizutti grinned. "Yeah, well don't go stealing my help, okay? We like Fay right where she is."

"I'm not here to steal her," Calixto said, stopping next to me, "I'm here to win her love."

I knew his words were bullshit, but they still jolted my heart.

Pizutti gave an eloquent shrug. "Yeah, whatever. Just let her do her job, okay?"

"No *problema*." Calixto turned his back on Pizutti and handed me the box.

"You want me to open it now?"

"Yes, *querida*."

"Aw, jeez," Pizutti said, and went back into his office.

The box was wrapped in shiny black paper with a dark red ribbon. "You're catching on to my Goth look," I said, untying the bow.

"Wait until you see what is inside."

"What you got there?" Becky Joe asked, heading down the aisle toward us. She stopped about two feet away from me and watched as I tore the paper off and opened the box.

A necklace lay in sheets of black crepe paper. Black titanium bat wings were attached to a center medallion. The wings hung from a dark chain. A dazzling black stone was set into the medallion. I couldn't quite grasp what I was looking at.

"Is that a *diamond*?" Becky Joe asked.

"No, of course not," I said, "it's—it's a . . ."

Calixto leaned forward and withdrew the necklace from the box. "A black diamond, two carats."

"Holy shit!" Becky Joe said.

If Becky Joe hadn't been there, and if Pizutti hadn't just materialized from his office again when he heard her exclamation, I would have said, "I can't keep this!" Instead I said, "Wow."

The piece was attractive in a kind of dreadful way. And the little gleam I saw in Calixto's eye told me he was amused that my Goth act had resulted in me receiving an expensive piece of frightful jewelry.

I could wear this to Joan's party . . .

"What are you thinking, *leona*? You have an evil look in your eye."

"You don't want to know."

He shrugged. "Then would you be so kind as to turn around?"

After a brief hesitation, I did, and Calixto fastened the clasp made of two titanium skeleton hands. When his warm fingers touched the lock of hair on the nape of my neck and brushed against my skin, my body responded. *Traitor.* I stepped away quickly.

"Fay, babe," Pizutti called from his office doorway, "sell the fucking diamond."

Calixto glanced at the trainer, his face expressionless. "Mars, can you not display a little class?"

"Not as easily as you do that smarmy act. Man, you're something." He waved an annoyed hand at Calixto and disappeared into his office again.

"I'd sell that diamond in a New York minute," Becky Joe said.

"I *love* it. I'm keeping it. Calixto, thank you."

"Thank me later," he said, and Becky Joe snorted.

"I need to talk to you about something," I said to him.

Becky Joe made a rude noise. "I bet you do."

I'd had enough of the comments and glared at her. "Could you *excuse* us for a minute?"

I grabbed Calixto's arm and pulled him off the shedrow onto the grass. "This romance thing is getting out of hand," I said.

His penetrating stare ruffled my composure. Then he leaned

forward and touched the diamond where it rested in the hollow of my throat. "I find it to be the best part of the job."

Was he *serious?* "Whatever," I said, taking a half step back. "Can we please return to the matter at hand? Did the agent talk to Stevie? Because I'm thinking Stevie could wear a wire. We could catch Pizutti telling him to pull Glow West."

"The boy will not cooperate. Our agent, Turner, got nowhere. Stevie insisted he didn't know what Turner was talking about, and Turner told me he didn't want to push any harder. He was afraid he'd tip the boy off that someone close to him is watching."

"If he didn't already. If only we could get Stevie to work with us. The way he's going, he's headed for jail." *What would happen to Lila?*

As we quietly discussed the problem, Pizutti's vet arrived in his white pickup truck. Short, fair-haired, with a boyish face, I figured Doctor Paxton for about thirty-five. He hopped from the driver's side and threw Calixto and me a smile.

With his cute dimples and blue eyes, his face was the soul of innocence, which immediately made me suspect him. I'd found cynicism to be an unfortunate by-product of law enforcement.

Paxton opened one of the boxes built into the sides of his truck and started setting a few vials of medicine onto a tray. He added some needled syringes and began drawing liquid from the vials.

"Prerace time," I said, figuring the vet would be injecting Glow West and Dodger with vitamins, permitted painkillers, and the diuretic Lasix, which was still legal in New York. These additives would give the two runners an edge, the same edge that every other horse in the race was probably receiving.

Unless, of course, Pizutti had one of those magic, as yet untraceable drugs, like Dermorphin had been when it first appeared, delivering a painkiller up to a hundred times stronger than morphine. U.S. racetrack labs worked hard to stay on top of this stuff. It was especially difficult since the rules kept changing, not only from state to state, but from year to year. Fortunately, the labs, for the most part, were successful.

"I think I'll go see if Dr. Paxton needs any help," I said, as the vet stepped into Pizutti's office.

Calixto nodded, and I stuffed my empty gift box into a pocket and strolled past Paxton's pickup. Glancing into the compartment Paxton had left open, I saw more rubber-topped bottles, vials, and jars of pills than you could shake a stick at.

Hearing Paxton and Pizutti talking inside the office, I slowed to read some of the labels. Lasix. Corticosteroids, like the muscle-building synthetic testosterones stanozolol and boldenone. The anabolic steroids were there, too, like the anti-inflammatories prednisone and hydrocortisone. As long as these steroids were administered no closer than thirty days before a race, it was okay, but Pizutti's horses had tested positive on race days before.

If my suspicions were correct, and Savarine expected Dodger to provide his shareholders with a big paycheck, then Pizutti would be doubly anxious for the horse to score. Would he rely on Dodger's hidden speed to secure a win? Or something else?

I'd asked Brian at TRPB to check on Paxton a week earlier, and he'd found no dirt. But Paxton was working for Pizutti, and Pizutti had committed more infractions and received more suspensions than any other New York trainer. Remembering what Becky Joe had said about the angry fans on Facebook, I did a mental head shake. Why had it taken the New York Racing Association so long to call in the TRPB?

Paxton emerged from Pizutti's office and went inside Dodger's stall. I followed, stopping outside, where I snuck a peek at Dodger and Paxton.

Javier held Dodger's shank as Dr. Paxton inserted the needle of a syringe into the large vein that ran down the side of the horse's neck. He pushed the plunger, then flicked a glance at me. "Fay, isn't it?" he asked.

"Yeah. You need any help today, Dr. Paxton?"

He flashed his dimples. "We're good."

"He getting Lasix?" I asked, making conversation while I stared at the other syringes poking from the top of Paxton's breast pocket.

"You bet." He whipped another shot from his pocket and shoved it into the neck muscles that lay just to the front of Dodger's withers.

I hung around until he was finished with Dodger. No way to prove what the injections were without grabbing the empty syringes and having them tested by a lab, but Paxton's relaxed attitude made me doubt he was administering illegal drugs. I almost wished he'd loaded Dodger with some kind of jet fuel. Without it, the win hung on Stevie's ability to stop Glow West.

Without getting caught.

11

When Pizutti called me to his office later that morning, I found the calico stable cat sprawled across the top of the desk. She'd settled herself on a copy of the *Daily Racing Form* and was purring mightily as the trainer stroked her fur.

Despite my cop experience, a part of me still wanted to believe that animal lovers aren't bad people. But even angels can fall for the lure of easy money, and Pizutti was no angel.

He stopped petting the cat. "Listen, Fay, I want you to run Glow West this afternoon. Okay? You can do that, right?"

"Run" was track parlance for taking the horse to the paddock and keeping him under control until the jockey mounted and rode him onto the track. Nodding, I said, "Sure."

If you've never done it, it's hard to imagine the difficulty of leading a fired-up, thousand-pound Thoroughbred past a crowd of excited racing fans. Your legs struggle through the pull of deep, heavy sand on the track or in the paddock. Inevitably, the horse seems hell-bent on dragging you into the next county.

As soon as I left Pizutti, I walked to the other side to confer with Calixto. His plan for the race was to hang near the betting windows in the section reserved for box holders. Pizutti would be there, too, sitting with the horses' owners. The TRPB agent, Turner, planned to float. While Glow West was racing, I'd be stuck on the rail with the other grooms holding halters and lead shanks.

After the race, I'd take the colt back to the barn, unless he won, in which case I'd lead him into the winner's circle, making sure to turn my face away from the photographer. I didn't need my picture on the internet.

But late that afternoon, when the jockeys entered the paddock, I knew the winner's circle was not in Glow West's immediate future. Stevie's face was flat, his eyes staring into the distance at something no one else could see. He kept lifting his hand to his mouth, worrying a hangnail on his thumb.

He stopped next to me, where I held Glow West, who was being saddled by Carl and Stevie's valet. Stevie avoided my eyes as he licked a drop of blood from his thumb.

Moments later Carl tossed him in the saddle, and Pizutti, who was two stalls down, lifted another jockey onto Dodger.

"Good luck, Stevie," I said, but the boy didn't seem to hear me.

The field paraded onto the track, the horses with bowed necks, the jockeys a rainbow of colored silk. The board showed Glow West a solid favorite. But Dodger's odds were twenty-to-one, a dream for bettors who were in the know.

I glanced around the apron, through the crowd of people holding beer cups and hot dogs. Rico and his mobster buddy,

Alberto Rizelli, stood near the rail. Though the day was warm with high clouds and bright sunshine, the two old men wore nylon vests with big zippered pockets over their shirts.

As the horses jogged past the crowd at the rail, the two men drifted apart. A number of mostly young people materialized from different directions and eased toward the two mobsters. These ordinary-looking and easily forgettable newcomers took turns standing close to Rico or Alberto. Each time one conferred with a mobster, he'd hold out his or her program, like they were handicapping the race or trading tips. The old guys would dip into a pocket and slide a small envelope into the person's program.

No doubt the envelopes were stuffed with cash, and these folks were running bets on Dodger for Rico and Alberto. The bets would be low enough their payoffs wouldn't exceed the $9,000 limit that raises a red flag for the IRS.

Running bets was still one of the best ways for crooks to remain anonymous. Though online betting is widespread, it's hard to hide when you have to list your Social Security number to open an account. Sure people could and did supply false information, but running unidentified cash bets at the track worked better.

Pretending I had a phone call, I shot dozens of pictures of the young runners and the arthritic mobsters' hands dropping cash into racing programs.

Watching the young people's movements, and glancing at the time on the tote board, I realized they were waiting to place their money until the last possible moment. They played a fine line. While they risked the windows shutting down before they placed their bets, they couldn't alert the crowd that the "smart" money had jumped on Dodger. At least not until it was too late for anyone else to bet on the horse.

No doubt these old mobsters had people running bets in New York City at Aqueduct, spreading cash in New Jersey at Monmouth or the Meadowlands, and retired mafia cousins spending money at Gulfstream Park and Tampa Bay Downs in Florida.

When I had enough pictures, I put my cell phone away, but continued to watch Rico and Alberto. They had the pumped-up, sly look of criminals about to make a score. I sent a text to Calixto telling him what I'd seen.

He texted back, "Some of Rico's boys are up here, too. Watch the odds."

I heard a low rumble of voices around me, and glancing at the tote board saw Dodger's long odds had shrunk from twenty-to-one to ten-to-one.

Seconds later, the field loaded into the gate, the starter sprang them loose, and the betting shut down. If Dodger won, the mobsters would make a killing.

Out on the track, a dark bay long shot rushed to the lead. Dodger and the bright chestnut, Glow West, followed close behind.

After a quarter of a mile, the jockey on the dark bay eased his horse into a more sensible pace, trying to save him for the finish, maybe trying to steal the race after gaining the early lead. Though Dodger's rider sat chilly, the ten-to-one long shot moved up, thrusting his head level with the dark bay's flank.

Glow West sailed a length behind Dodger. The remaining six horses rolled along in the wake of the three front-runners until the last turn, when everyone got busy making their moves.

Stevie and Glow West weren't supposed to finish in the top three, a tall order since the colt looked like he was blasting along with a ton of firepower left in the barrel.

Holding my breath, I watched the field come out of the turn into the stretch. Dodger shot past the dark bay and took the lead.

Glow West tried to go with him, but Stevie hit his horse hard, two times, left-handed, making the chestnut lug into the path of the horses coming up from behind. Two of these had to check sharply to avoid clipping Glow West's heels. I could imagine the obscenities their jockeys were screaming at Stevie for his erratic move.

Even though Stevie had smacked Glow West halfway over to the parking lot, the game chestnut spurted forward and gained ground on Dodger and the dark bay. If Stevie was only pretending to ride, he did a darn good job of flashing his whip and gyrating his body to mimic a hard finish to the end. *Maybe it didn't matter where he finished.*

The three front-runners flashed under the wire with Dodger a clear winner, the dark bay hanging on for second place, and Glow West rushing up so fast, he would have beat them both had his sideways movement not lost so much ground. A moment later, the board flashed with an objection raised against Glow West for interference. Somewhere in the grandstand the stewards were reviewing tapes of the race, and I prayed they'd take Glow West down.

As Stevie galloped his horse back to me, I saw him glance anxiously at the board. Suddenly, I realized the kid had *planned* on a disqualification. Glow West's number was lit up in the three spot, but flashing with the objection. Bettors held their tickets, stared at the board, and grumbled. I held my breath.

With cheers from some patrons, and groans of anguish from others, Glow West's number came down and was placed last. I let out a long breath, and as Stevie approached me on Glow West, relief flooded his face.

Pizutti walked past with Dodger and Carl, on their way to the winner's circle. He glanced at Stevie, and said, "You did good, kid." He kept going, not waiting for the boy's reply.

On the apron, near the winner's circle, Rico and Alberto held plastic cups with ice floating in amber liquid. Their lips clamped on smoldering cigars, and they both wore crooked smiles. Rico said something, and Alberto chuckled and slapped the other man on the shoulder. He even did a little dance and didn't seem to mind when part of his drink sloshed onto the pavement.

Assholes.

The afternoon heat had risen and the sun was radiating off the track surface beneath my feet. Slogging through the heavy sand and dirt had built up my appetite. The aroma of fried food drifting across the track from the burger, fry, and hot dog stands made my mouth water.

Next to me, Stevie slid off Glow West, removed the saddle, and hurried off to weigh-in at the scales. I slid the halter over the horse's bridle and led him back to the barn. Because he'd been disqualified, he wasn't required to go to the test barn for blood and urine samples. Waiting for my horse to pee in a jar is not how I wanted to spend the afternoon.

When I got back to our shedrow, Javier took Glow West and gave him a bath. As rivulets of sweat and dirt sluiced from the horse's coat and pooled at his feet, the scent of damp earth and salt filled the air. When Javier shut the water off, I led the colt around the shedrow until he was cool and dry. "You should have won," I whispered, rubbing my palm against his face.

My phone chimed with a text from Calixto. "Call me."

Thinking I'd give Glow West another turn around the barn while we spoke, I hit Calixto's speed dial, and he answered.

"How much black is on my favorite Goth's face today?"

"Enough," I said. "What's up?"

"I talked to Fair Hill. The betting analysis tech says dozens of bets were placed up and down the East Coast, all cash. No accounts were used. There were some placed with offshore book-makers, but through third parties."

"Can *any* of this be traced back to our mobsters?"

"Not easily. Did you get pictures, Fia?"

"Yes. But the money was hidden in packets," I said.

He sighed. "In my photos as well, and first reports indicate the packets were opened out of sight of the track video cameras. By the time it got to the betting windows, the money was transferred to wallets."

"Well, they *are* connected to the mob . . ."

"This is what I like," he said, "a painted woman with annoy-ing observations."

"Listen, Stevie's here. Can I talk to you later?"

When he agreed, I ended the call. Stevie stepped onto the shedrow, and I studied his face as he walked toward me and Glow West. I could still see relief, but his frame seemed to sag with exhaustion, as if the emotional load he'd been saddled with was breaking him down.

"Hey, how's he doing?" he asked as he reached us and slid a hand down Glow West's neck.

"Good," I said. "He's ready for his stall. Help me put him in." I led Glow West into his stall and removed his halter.

"What about Bionic?" Stevie asked. "I think Mars is gonna enter him soon."

"He's good, too." But would Pizutti let the kid ride Bionic to win? "How about you?" I asked as we left Glow West in his stall.

Stevie glanced around and lowered his voice. "Better than I was. There's two trainers up here might want me to ride for them. They liked my win on Wiggly Wabbit and that bullet work on Bionic."

"Do you have a written contract with Mars?"

"Nah. I didn't sign anything."

"Good. It would be terrific if you could get out from under him and Rico."

But there was his sister, and she was more binding than any contract. I kept the thought to myself, and said a silent prayer for both of them.

"You know Lila liked you," he said. "She's still doing okay, and maybe after today, those guys will, you know, leave us alone. Anyways, I appreciated your offer about driving us somewhere, but I think we'll be okay."

"Hope so," I said, watching a cloud bank that had formed on the western horizon drift toward us. It would bring rain; I could smell the moisture in the air.

A car I didn't recognize drove up to the shedrow in a hurry. It stopped abruptly, and a guy I'd never seen before got out and strode quickly toward Stevie. The man was maybe forty, had a hard face, and a radio clipped to his belt. When he got close enough, I could read his badge. FITZGERALD, NYRA INVESTIGATIONS.

"Stevie Davis?" he asked.

Stevie's eyes widened. "Yes, sir?"

The man held a clipboard. He pulled a form off and handed it to Stevie. "Mr. Davis, this is a summons. You need to appear before the racing stewards tomorrow morning at ten A.M."

Stevie's thumb slid to his mouth and his teeth went to work on the ragged hangnail. "Is this because of my horse lugged out?"

"Don't know. I'm just delivering the summons."

Fitzgerald was being a prick. Of *course* he knew.

"Mr. Fitzgerald," I said, "it would be nice if Mr. Davis was told what this is about so he can prepare for it, don't you think?"

The man gave me a cold look, then shrugged. "You can call the stewards' office and ask."

"We'll do that," I said, watching the sky darken.

A cool breeze hit my face, and the rain began to fall. The investigator left, hurrying through the drops to his car, and when I turned back to Stevie, his lip was smeared with blood.

I called the track operator and asked for the stewards' office. Their secretary, who was pleasant enough, told me since I wasn't the kid's attorney, she had to speak with Stevie. I put him on the phone. As he nodded his head and said, "Yes, ma'am," his jaw looked tight enough to crack a bullet.

The secretary spoke some more, then Stevie said, "Yes, ma'am, I'll be there. Thank you."

He handed the phone back, his eyes anxious, his shoulders hunched with tension. "They *know* I stopped the horse."

"They don't know that," I said, dismayed to realize I was helping Stevie find a way out. "You hit the horse left-handed by *mistake*. As soon as you realized he was veering into the path of those behind, you stopped, right?"

"But it was too late. I'm, like, *totally* screwed."

"Listen to me, Stevie. You tried to straighten him out, right? And you rode him to the finish with everything you had, didn't you?"

He shook his head miserably and didn't answer.

"I watched the race, it *looked* like you rode the hell out him. Right to the wire."

"It did?"

"Yes, it did. And that's what you tell them, okay?"

"I'll have to. I can't give Mars up. He'd kill me!"

His last words shook me. "You don't mean that?"

"No, it was just a . . . figure of speech is all."

But he was right, he didn't dare give Mars up, not with Rico threatening Lila. I didn't know how, but I had to fix this. *Damn Rico, anyway.*

"Okay," I said, "I understand. But speaking of Mars, you

should talk to him about your summons. He can give you some pointers. He's had plenty of practice."

Was I really helping Mars and Rico keep their dirty money? By now, the rain was beating down in windswept torrents, and even under the shedrow roof, we were getting wet. And cold.

"Let's go see Bionic," I said.

We hurried down the shedrow, opened Bionic's stall door and went inside. The plain-looking blood bay crowded against us, spreading his warmth. He wanted us to rub our hands on him, and we were happy to oblige.

"He don't look like much," Stevie said, "but he's got pedigree up his eyeballs. Got that Curlin line in his blood."

"Oh, he can move," I said. "He showed that in his last work."

"I can't wait for him to run!"

A sudden silence hung between us. But we were both thinking, *If he's allowed to run.* The rain beat down in sheets outside the shedrow, but on the western horizon the sky had lightened. The storm wouldn't last.

"It might be okay," Stevie said. "Mars was talking about the race and he seemed excited about Bionic's chances. It's a stake race, too."

If the kid won a stake, more trainers would try to pick him up, and this was exactly what Stevie needed.

"I'll be rooting for you."

"Thanks. You're pretty cool, Fay." He blushed slightly.

Outside, the rain eased to a drizzle. Stevie gave Bionic a gentle slap on the shoulder. "Dude, we can't rub on you all night." Glancing at me, he said, "I can ride my bike now. I better get home."

"Time for me to leave, too," I said.

We left the shelter of Bionic's stall. Stevie grabbed a small barn towel, and we walked to the bicycle he'd left leaning against a tree. He wiped off the wet seat, and handed me the rag.

As his skinny body pedaled the bike away, the drops of water on its yellow frame glistened like a thousand tiny stars.

12

I sat with Calixto outside a small café on Broadway. A cold front had ridden in with the earlier rain, and brought an evening so chilly I'd slipped a down vest over my long-sleeved tee.

A brown Stetson hooded Calixto's eyes, and he wore a suede vest lined with sheepskin over a white shirt, with jeans. Two fresh cups of hot coffee sent spirals of steam into the air next to our almost emptied plates. We'd been devouring Angus chopped steak, mashed potatoes, and green beans. Sometimes there's no substitute for comfort food.

"So," I said, "what's Gunny going to do about the fixed race and illegal betting?"

"He has contacted the FBI. They will send a couple of agents up from Albany to sweat Pizutti and Rico. It is a shame there is not enough evidence to warrant their incarceration. But the FBI will, no doubt, flex their bad cop muscles. Effective to a degree, since it does inject fear and make them more cautious."

It wasn't enough. "But we can't nail them?"

"No, Fia, we cannot."

I took a sip of coffee and set the mug down hard enough my silverware rattled. "This is just peachy."

Calixto stared at me, his eyes unreadable. Then, they softened. "You are quite captivating when you are angry, *querida*."

In the cool air, I felt a blush rise to my cheeks. It was hard to ignore the effect this man had on me. But I sidestepped it and forged ahead.

"I'd like to captivate Rico right into a jail cell. I'm worried what this clown will do after Pizutti enters Bionic in the upcoming stake. He'll probably threaten Lila again."

We were both silent a few beats. Calixto's long, tapered fingers held his coffee cup, his eyes never left mine.

Nervous, I scooped up the last of my mashed potatoes, swallowed a bite, and took a sip of coffee. An older man came down the sidewalk on Broadway with a leashed dog, reminding me of the old man who rented his garage to Stevie. As the dog padded past us, I could almost hear Lila's delighted shrieks when she'd played tug-of-war with the terrier Raymond.

"Calixto, did anyone find out why that jockey killed himself?

He looked away from me for a moment. "You mean Jose Fragoso?"

"Who else would I be talking about?"

"Fia, Fragoso's sister was murdered in Peru. We think he killed himself because he still had two younger brothers at home and didn't want them hurt. Or worse."

"That's horrible!" It was what I'd been afraid of, and made me doubly fearful for Stevie's little sister. "Can Gunny find a safe house for Lila? Maybe through the FBI?"

"Possibly."

At times like this, following my mantra is hard. I didn't want to sit chilly and wait for an opening. I wanted to force one, blast on through, and rescue Stevie and Lila. My knuckles hurt where they gripped the handle of my coffee mug.

"Don't look so impatient, *querida*. We'll find a way to make this work. But following procedure is the safest route, is it not?"

I sighed. "That's what they tell me." My phone chirped with a text message. Glancing at the screen I saw it was from my mother. Short and not too sweet.

"Don't forget party tomorrow night! Wear something nice. Be there by seven!"

"What?" Calixto asked. "You look like you swallowed *una cucaracha*."

I squeezed my eyes shut, then said, "My mother."

"Please, tell me about *tu madre*. Is she really so horrible?"

I glanced at him, meeting his eyes. They held no sign of amusement, only compassion. For the moment, I decided to believe it was genuine.

I took a shallow breath and exhaled. "She walked out on Patrick, Dad, and me when I was fifteen. Left us for a wealthy man, and wiped out Dad's bank account when she left. Do you remember the last time she left a phone message?"

"When we had dinner at Rico's café?" Calixto asked.

"Yes. It was the first time I'd heard from her in seventeen years."

"Then for you, *pequeña leona*, her calls are more like swallowing a scorpion, are they not?"

"Yes, and they burn and sting all the way down."

Calixto leaned forward and placed his hand on mine. "What does she want?"

His touch was comforting, his presence reassuring. "She says she wants to make up for what she did, for the lost years."

"And you do not believe her?"

"I don't know what to believe. She's having a party Saturday night and insists I come."

"You will go?"

"Yes, I'm curious about my stepfather." The warmth of his hand on mine radiated energy. And courage. "Will you come with me? I could use your support."

"Yes, *querida*, I would be honored. Besides, I am eager to meet your scorpion."

Suddenly, I was looking forward to going to Joan's soiree. "Thank you," I said, meeting his gaze. A thrill shot through my gut and I forced myself to look away from his brown eyes, his beautifully formed eyebrows. Those damn lips.

"I am sorry you lost your father, Fia. So often we lose the good and are left with the bad." His sympathy felt genuine.

"What about you?" I asked. "Your father lives on Fisher Island? Your mother was a fashion model?"

A breeze kicked up, scuttling debris down the sidewalk past our feet beneath the wrought-iron table. A shadow crossed Calixto's face as if brought by the cold current.

"She was beautiful and sweet. I loved her very much."

"*Was?*"

"Cancer. Pancreatic. She was only forty, still working on fashion shoots. She was dazzling."

"I'm so sorry."

We sat in silence a moment, the loss of things loved filling the air between us.

Finally, he spoke. "When she died, my father took it very hard. He never leaves Fisher Island anymore. He has become a recluse."

"What about his coffee business?"

"Others manage Coyune Coffee for him."

I knew I was prying and possibly treading on dangerous ground, but I was curious. "And his first wife and your half siblings?"

His eyes widened slightly. "You did perform your due diligence. You know then that they are in Cuba."

"But have you met them? Aren't you curious about—"

"Not half so curious as you." His mouth had hardened. The planes of his chiseled face became more pronounced. "Let us leave them in Cuba, *pequeña leona*."

"Okay . . . sure." But the cat in me was dying of curiosity. Had he met them? Did they hate him because their father had abandoned them and married a younger woman who had produced a new heir? Did they see Calixto as interloper and thief?

"Whatever you are thinking, Fia, stop it. I meant what I said. Leave them in Cuba. Forget about them."

Damn the man. He could read my face like a billboard. And I could see a wound in him at the mention of the Cuban family. But this was not the time to pry. Maybe there never would be. "So, um, you've been to Saratoga a lot, right?"

His responding nod was so wary, I was glad my next question was innocuous. "Is there a dress shop around here with clothes the scorpion would approve of?"

As much as I wanted to annoy Joan by Goth-bombing her party, the satisfaction would not be worth her acute displeasure. Besides, I was thirty-two, not thirteen.

"If my mother were still alive and as young as you," Calixto said, "she would probably go to Violet's. It's here on Broadway."

By keeping my curiosity hidden behind a façade of mundane conversation for the remainder of the evening, I avoided the icy slap of Calixto's cop eyes.

———

In the morning, after work, I went in search of Violet's. As Calixto had indicated, the posh boutique was on Broadway near Lake Avenue. A deep purple awning crowned the display window, and I spotted a rack of pretty dresses before I got four feet inside the door. Their price tags were alarming.

A saleswoman saw my face and, not unkindly, said, "We have a sales rack in the back."

I started in that direction, when behind me a little bell rang as someone entered the shop. I turned to look. A woman, probably a little younger than I, glided into the store like a queen. Her coffee-and-cream skin was radiant under her long, curly black hair. Her almond eyes tilted up at the corners, her nose was long and slender, her mouth full, and her body a schoolboy's dream.

She stopped at the first rack of dresses, and another saleswoman rushed to greet her. I kept going toward the clearance rack, and my salesgal whispered, "That girl was Miss Jamaica two years ago!"

"She's beautiful," I whispered back.

Leaving Miss Jamaica behind, I passed mannequins displaying elegant pieces of jewelry, richly hued silk tops, scarves, and skirts. Small tables held high-heeled leather boots, shoes, and expensive-looking belts. It occurred to me these "things" were part of why Joan had abandoned her family.

I shook the thought off, found the rack of discounted spring clothing, and spotted a simple black sleeveless dress. My salesgirl, who'd remained hot on my heels, moved to stand beside me, then leaned forward and briefly studied my face. Though her eyes slid down my body with Joan-like scrutiny, there was no criticism in her eyes.

"You're a size four, right?"

"Yes," I said.

"And you need a dress for an evening function?"

I nodded, and she whipped a vibrant blue dress off the rack that had laser-cut detail along the V-neckline and hem.

"This will bring out the blue in your eyes," she said.

Miss Jamaica swept toward us with her saleswoman staggering under a load of clothing on hangers. They disappeared into a changing room.

I reached a hand to grasp the price tag on the blue dress. Reduced twice. From $255 to $95.

The woman had been watching my face as I saw the price. "It's been here waiting for you. Try it on."

I did and the dress fit like it was custom-made for me. It made my eyes look an intense blue. It showed a lot of leg, but not too much.

"I'll take it," I said.

The salesgal grinned. "How could you not?"

13

I stood outside the Victorian wearing my new dress, strappy black heels, and a choker made of lapis and black onyx. I clutched the obligatory little black bag that contained my cell phone and a few essentials.

Probably, I should have added a small flask of vodka for courage, since I was way too giddy about taking Calixto to meet my mother.

Though I'd kept it understated, I'd gone all out with my makeup, applying four different hair products, three subtle shades of eye shadow, two types of mascara, one rose-colored lipstick. *And a partridge in a pear tree?* I tried but failed to shake "The Twelve Days of Christmas" that began earworming my head. No doubt, the impending introduction was driving me over the edge.

Glancing up the street, I was relieved to see Calixto's red, 550-horsepower Jaguar XK cruising toward me. Hopefully, its impressive sound system would overpower the annoying tune in my head. Sleek and shining, the car cruised closer. Being a busy-body, I'd looked the Jag up. Its base price started at $132,000. Since he was playing the role of Cuban-American playboy, this was a good car to do it in.

The muscular engine purred to a stop at the curb beside me. Calixto climbed out wearing a black silk suit. His tie and pocket square held brilliant blue accents that matched my dress.

"Did you follow me to Violet's?" I asked as he approached.

"Of course not." His eyes narrowed as he took in my appearance. "I wanted to wear something that would match your lovely eyes. I see you did, too."

Who could believe this man? But damn he looked good. A childish thought hit me. *Wait 'til Joan meets this guy and sees his car. . . .* Of course, her Maserati started at $132,000, so maybe she wouldn't be impressed. At least, not with the car.

Calixto held the door for me before he climbed into the driver's seat. After I sank into the interior's smooth white leather, he hit the gas, and we sailed up the street, heading north to Joan's. When we arrived, at least twenty cars crowded the cul-de-sac and front driveway.

The uniformed maid I'd expected on my first visit met us at the door and indicated we should go to the patio out back. As we walked through the house, Calixto took in the fine carpets and paintings on the wall.

"*Very* nice. It appears your scorpion stung her prey and sucked him dry."

"She knows how to do it," I said.

Outside, the patio was strung with party lights and dotted with unlit torches. Farther along, a large tent had been erected. The evening was clear and warm, but as the eastern horizon grew darker, I could sense the cooler air of night creeping in.

Several long tables were laden with food in silver serving dishes, and bars were set up on either side of the tent. A jazz quartet was playing a Miles Davis tune and everyone was dressed to the nines. Diamonds sparkled, and tanned women with long, toned legs crowded the stone pavers. Men in expensive suits and Rolex watches sipped liquor and wine while layering the air with the scent of booze and cigars. The lilt of conversation, laughter, and the rattle of ice in crystal glasses filled my ears.

Next to me, a cynical smile passed so quickly over Calixto's face, I wasn't certain I'd seen it.

"Why do I feel like I'm on a movie set?" I asked him.

"Perhaps you are. We should find our host and hostess, *pequeña leona*."

I scanned the crowd and spotted Joan in a long, close-fitting coral dress, slit partway up her left thigh. A photographer with a camera lens the length of Secretariat took her picture as she draped her arm around a man in a white linen suit. Was he my stepfather? I probably should have googled for pictures earlier, but devoting any time to Joan and her affairs wasn't on my list of priorities.

"That's the scorpion," I said, nodding in the direction of the coral dress. "Let's do this."

As we approached, Joan's gaze swept past us, then darted back, coming to rest on Calixto. Her eyes widened ever so slightly when she recognized me. A confused expression flitted across her face, then disappeared.

Had she expected me to arrive in manure-laden boots with a groom holding a pitchfork?

She stepped away from the linen suit, and approached us with a brilliant smile. "Fia, sweetheart, you look fantastic! Who is this *delicious* man?"

"Joan, this is Calixto Coyune."

He stepped forward, took her hand, and said, "It is a pleasure to meet you, Mrs. Gorman."

"Call me Joan," she said, holding his hand longer than necessary.

"Where did you *find* him?" she asked me.

"At the racetrack."

"Well . . . how nice."

While she recovered from meeting arguably the sexiest man in New York, I looked around for the linen suit. He'd disappeared.

"I really want to meet Rich," I said. "Is he here somewhere?"

"Of course. Over at the bar."

She waved to a stout man with a florid complexion, who headed toward us. He was a big, beefy guy, whose well-cut beige suit, I suspected, hid a lot of flesh. He had a pleasant smile and a face dominated by crudely formed, heavy bones. His eyes held humor and the crafty look of a man capable of creating a major company.

"Fia," he said, stretching his hand to take mine, "I've heard so much about you."

When I clasped his hand, he pinned my fingers between a gold signet band and a large diamond pinky ring. His smile revealed slightly bucked teeth.

"It's nice to meet you, Mr. Gorman."

Still grasping my fingers, he said, "Call me Rich."

Turning to Calixto, Rich released my hand. I rubbed my fingers and mentally shook my head as he greeted Calixto. My dad had been athletic and trim from working with the horses and riding the track pony every day. That Joan would leave him for a toad, no matter how much money the toad had, astounded me. But then I'd never understood my mother.

Joan zeroed in on my date. "Rich, don't these two make a *gorgeous* couple?"

Rich showed his bucked teeth, and Joan continued. "What do you do, Calixto?"

"Mostly, I manage the family money and dabble in horses."

Joan's eyes gleamed. I'd bet my life savings she was dying to know how much money.

"Yes," she purred, "watching over the money. It's a full-time job isn't it, darling?" she asked Rich, sliding her arm around her husband's waist and giving him an affectionate squeeze that seemed genuine. Rich responded with more teeth.

"Georgina," Joan cooed in the direction of a fiftysomething blonde in a black dress. "Come meet my daughter."

Tonight, she was proud to be my mother. I looked good, and was on the arm of a handsome, sharp-dressed man with money. *What more could a mother want?*

Georgina arrived, her black taffeta swishing, her hair a helmet of blond. Her hand was cold, her handshake limp. "Joan, you didn't tell me she was so lovely! Oh my, the two of them are absolutely the couple of the evening! Just *fabulous*, both of them!"

I could imagine her reaction if I'd come as a Goth with Becky Joe as my date.

Calixto leaned into me and whispered, "I see the evil look in your eye, *querida*. Be careful."

Rich was talking to Georgina, and Joan was staring at Calixto like he was a box of chocolate truffles.

Calixto turned back to my stepfather. "Are you from Kentucky, Rich?"

"As a matter of fact, I am. You have a good ear, son."

I'd spent time in Kentucky with Dad when he ran horses at Keeneland in Lexington, and like Calixto, I could hear the accent. Except my stepfather's voice lacked the refined quality of a landed Kentucky horse breeder. He sounded more like his family had come from the mountains. Regardless, his being from

Kentucky might explain why he'd been involved with horses, which had probably led him to Joan. For all I knew, Dad had introduced them.

When another man joined us, Calixto excused himself and headed for the bar. When the two remaining men started talking about horse racing, Joan rolled her eyes and launched into a conversation with Georgina about some scandal at the local country club.

Rich was telling his new companion about a top racehorse he'd owned, named Behold the King. "Stop in at the house," he said. "See the statue of him I commissioned from Pierre Lemarque."

Rich's companion made impressed noises. "Lemarque, you say? Must have cost you a damn fortune."

"It's an investment," Rich said. "Take a look at it. It's on a credenza in the living room. You'll enjoy seeing it."

I remembered the statue from my first visit to the Gormans' home. It *was* a fine piece. Probably cost more to insure than I earned in six months.

"I'm starving," I said to no one in particular, and left the group. I made a beeline for the bar and asked for a vodka tonic. Armed with a stiff drink, I hit the buffet table and nibbled on salmon mousse and fresh strawberries. Beyond the table's end, among a small group of people, I spotted Al Savarine. I hadn't realized he knew Rich, but then it was hardly surprising as the lives of wealthy racehorse owners had a tendency to intersect.

At the other end of the table, a man from Joan's catering service was carving a steamship round of beef. The tasty aroma wafting off the roast drew me toward him. I was reaching for a roll to put some beef on when the catering man stopped slicing abruptly.

I followed his gaze. A rough-looking, dark-skinned man with Rastafarian dreadlocks was approaching the meat carver.

"Excuse me," the carver asked, "are you supposed to . . . are you a guest of the Gormans?"

The Rastafarian's mouth split in a wide grin that revealed yellow teeth. "Ya, mon. Dis be true. Mi wit Mr. O."

The carver's brow creased in momentary uncertainty. "You mean Mr. Onandi?"

"Ya, mon. Mi wit him."

I tried not to stare at the guy's shaggy dreads and brightly striped knit hat that puffed up high on his head like a popover.

The carver threw me a quick apologetic smile, then turned back to the Rastafarian. "That's fine, dude. Maybe you should find Mr. Onandi?"

The Rastafarian, glanced at the four-piece band and stretched his arms wide. "I like jazz, mon. But mi go to house, find Mr. O. Make you happy." He smiled again, but the warmth never reached his eyes, and I wondered if his long colorful dashiki might hide a weapon.

Stop thinking the worst of people, Fia.

The Rastafarian disappeared into the house, and I sampled some grapes and Stilton cheese. The man from the caterers sliced me some beef which, after I placed it on a roll spread with butter, melted in my mouth and almost made me whimper. Heading back to Calixto, I stopped at the sight of the former Miss Jamaica walking toward the dance floor in a long emerald caftan.

She wore gladiator sandals with four-inch heels, making her at least six feet tall. Through the slit in her skirt, I glimpsed leather laces snaking up her calves—a fashion statement that brought the word "bondage" to mind. Did she know Joan? She was far too lovely and refined to be connected to the Rastafarian.

When I reached Calixto, Georgina and Rich had gone elsewhere. Joan stood closer to Calixto than necessary.

"Oh, you're back," she said. "This man is *terrific,* Fia. I'm so glad you two are seeing each other."

She'd have us married in a minute. Then she'd be after *his* money.

"Fia is special," Calixto said, leveling his intense gaze on Joan. "And I see now where her beauty comes from."

Joan fluttered and blushed. I had never seen my mother flutter. She reminded me of a baby bird hoping to receive a worm. It was embarrassing. *Did I act like that?*

As if hearing my thoughts, Joan slid a mask of composure over her face and threw Calixto a dazzling smile. "You are very kind. I'd love to stay and chat with you both, but I should mingle with our guests. You two enjoy yourselves and, Fia, before you leave, I'd like a word, dear."

Now what? "Sure," I said. She swept away from us, a column of coral, her tan perfect, her hair luminous.

Calixto's gaze followed her departing figure. "Damn good-looking woman."

"Yes," I said, "if you can survive the venom."

Movement on the dance floor caught my attention. The four jazz band members were returning from a break. They gathered their instruments and slid into a smooth rendition of "Misty."

"Dance with me," Calixto said.

Although it's the women who love to dance—you see them all the time rocking it out by themselves on the dance floor—I'm convinced it's the men who dreamed up this slow dance scheme. After all, how else can a male walk up to a strange female and take her in his arms and press himself against her?

Which is exactly what Calixto did, brushing his starched white shirt against the bodice of my blue dress. Pressing his hand

into the small of my back and clasping me into him, he caught
me so off guard, I had an instinctive fight-or-flight reaction. At
least until his heat reached my core and my thighs melted into
his. *Get a grip, Fia.*

"*Querida*," he murmured.

His lips grazed my cheek near the corner of my mouth. His
light cologne mingled with his male scent intoxicated me. He
was a good dancer, light on his feet, rhythmic. His body radiated a sense of controlled power that unleashed would be . . .

Mental head shake. I shouldn't have had that vodka. Or
maybe I should have another and take what we both wanted.

His mouth curved in a wicked, knowing smile. Could I keep
nothing from this man? I used my irritation to douse the sexual
desire he ignited in me. I felt my face harden with forced composure. *Like my mother.*

"What is it, *leona?*"

"Nothing."

Mercifully, the song ended, and he released me. The band
picked up a fast tune and Miss Jamaica, without a partner, walked
onto the floor. Her body swayed as she danced like a wild and exotic animal. The men stared at her. Calixto was not immune,
either, his eyes narrowing, his nostrils flaring slightly. Between her
supple, lush body and beautiful face, she was a testosterone igniter.

"She won't be alone for long," Calixto said, as two guys in
their thirties or early forties zeroed in on her. "If she came with
a date, I hope he is not the jealous type."

"Yeah, me, too," I said, "since she's staring at *you*."

"It pleases me to think you are jealous, *leona,* but it is hardly
my fault that she is a discerning woman."

"Maybe you should go over there and *discern* with her," I
said. "I'm going in search of the ladies' room." I gave him a little
finger wave and headed for the house.

Inside, someone had already occupied the powder room off the entry hall, so I headed for Rich's study. Joan had shown it to me during my previous visit and I remembered it had its own private bath.

My stepfather's office was a masculine retreat with mahogany bookshelves, a deep brown-red Oriental carpet, and a tufted leather couch in the same rich shade. Clearly, Joan had gone all-out to decorate for him. The bathroom door was opposite the room's main feature, Rich's elaborate, paw-footed desk.

I was startled to see the Rastafarian there, his sandaled feet lounging on the desktop as he smoked a cigar-sized blunt. The smoke drifted to me, its pungent, fruity scent unmistakably marijuana. Who had invited this guy, anyway?

He smiled happily, and held the joint out to me. "Hey sista, ya want a hit a dis?"

"No, thanks." I ducked into the bathroom, closed and locked the door.

My mother certainly had some odd people at her party. Did she even know this weird Rasta dude?

After using the bathroom's facilities, I grasped the doorknob, but held my breath before leaving. Getting high on the Rasta's smoke while exiting through the study seemed like a bad idea. But a second voice in the room outside stopped me.

14

"Where is she?" a man's angry voice demanded. "I told you to watch her!"

"Di empress be fine. She like de dance."

"She's dancing? And you're in here smoking weed? We are not in Jamaica, you idiot."

The new man's accent could have been Jamaican, but was so slight, I wasn't sure.

"Put that out!" the new voice said. "You want me to tell Kamozey you screwed up? Find her. Bring her to the limo!"

I barely heard the Rastafarian's next words, his voice was so low and quavery. His don't-worry-be-happy mood was apparently shattered.

"Ease up, mon. Mi go."

Was it the name "Kamozey" that had shaken him? I wished there was a peephole in the door to see the newcomer's face, but as much as I wanted to see him, instinct told me it was better he didn't know I was there and had heard him.

I wasn't worried about the Rastafarian. He was so stoned, he'd probably forgotten I was in the bathroom. But the second man's voice raised hairs on the back of my neck. By now, my ear was pressed hard against the door, straining to hear their words.

"Mi mon, someone is coming. What yuh tink—"

"Shut up," the second man's voice hissed in warning.

"Oops, sorry," a third male voice said. "Somebody said there's a bathroom in here?"

"Sure, buddy," the second man replied. "We were just leaving."

"Hey," the third man said, "aren't you—"

"Like I said, buddy, we were just leaving."

I heard footsteps leaving the room and assumed it was the Rastafarian and his angry companion. My breath caught in alarm when the doorknob turned. The lock held, and a discreet knock followed.

"Just a minute," I said. I took a deep breath, fluffed my hair, and opened the door.

The man in the white linen suit stood outside. He had an appealing face, or would have, if it weren't drawn so tight with worry lines. His eyes were wide as if something had spooked him.

"It's all yours," I said, waving a hand at the bathroom.

"Um, thanks." He sniffed at the lingering smoke, compressed his lips, and shook his head.

"It's enough to get high on, isn't it?" I asked.

He looked at me, focusing for the first time. He paused a beat, then his face lit with recognition and he smiled.

"Aren't you Joan's daughter?" he asked.

When I nodded, he said, "I'm Rich's racing partner, Matt Percy."

We shook hands, and though he had a confident grip, sweat dampened his palm.

"I don't know my stepfather that well," I said. "Actually, I've just met him for the first time, but Joan tells me he loves the ponies. So, you two own horses together?"

Before he could answer, his phone chimed. He stared at the screen. "Excuse me, I have to take this."

I nodded, and edged around him, intending to see if Calixto had been seduced by Miss Jamaica. Or would it be the other way around?

"Thanks for calling me back," Percy said to his caller, as I started to leave the room. "Come to your *office*? I can't be seen talking with the FBI."

He sounded so alarmed, I stopped, and pretended to adjust the ankle strap on one shoe.

"No, I just wanted to alert you guys. I'm not *alone* right now. Okay, okay, I'll come in. But tomorrow's *Sunday*!" His sighed was filled with exasperation. "Look, I'm just trying to do the right thing here. All right, all right, I'll be there."

He ended his call. I stopped fiddling with my shoe and stood up. I was curious about the conversation, but Percy was so rattled, I didn't want to spook him by asking questions.

"Nice meeting you," he said, before walking into the bathroom and closing the door.

When I stepped into the hall, the sweet smell of marijuana seemed to emanate from the Gormans' bedroom. Wasn't the Rastafarian supposed be looking for the angry man's woman?

Curious, I followed the scent until low, agitated voices reached me. I slowed, trying not to let my heels clack on the stone floor, then stretched one leg forward and took a large step to reach the Oriental runner that lay outside the bedroom. I crept on until I was almost at the bedroom door, then leaned forward to peek inside.

Rich stood with his profile to me, as did the man opposite him, a man I had not seen before. But I knew his voice. The angry man from Rich's study. He was tall and thin, with a large hooked nose. The Rastafarian was nowhere in sight, yet I could smell his smoke.

I drew back before they saw me, and listened to the heated words of Rich's companion.

"You fool! How could you let this happen?"

"It's not my fault," Rich said.

"Isn't it?"

"What difference does it make now, Darren? Listen, it's not safe to talk about this. Not here in the house. Can't I meet you at the Adelphi later?"

"All right, but you better have a plan to fix this, Rich. *Damn it.*" There was a momentary silence before he continued. "You should return to your guests and your wife before the situation worsens."

The man's words were sharp enough to draw blood. I waited for Rich's reply, but only heard their footsteps coming toward me.

I scooted backwards on the thick runner, then continued in that direction, tiptoeing back several feet on the stone floor. Then I clacked forward purposefully.

"Hey," I said as they came through the bedroom door, "bathrooms are at a real premium today."

Rich's face wore a pleasant mask. I would never have known he was upset. "The one in here is available, Fia." He gestured into the bedroom behind him.

Smiling, I stole a glance at Darren. He had small piercing eyes and narrow lips. Curly hair and light khaki skin suggested he might have some island blood in his veins.

I paused and put my hand out. "Hi, I'm Fia McKee."

His thin lips pressed into a smile. "Yes, it's nice to meet you." He kept going right past me.

I gave Rich a questioning look, hoping he'd introduce his friend. But, whatever Darren's last name was, I wasn't going to get it from these two.

Continuing my act, I strode into the bedroom and headed for the bathroom. Pausing to listen, I heard the men's footsteps fading down the hall. Joan's impressive granite fireplace took up much of one wall and faced a lavishly upholstered king-size bed. The bed had a heavy silk coverlet the same river-blue as the tunic she'd worn on my first visit. Must be her favorite color.

Why did I still smell weed? As if answering my question, the bathroom door opened and the Rastafarian poked his head out and stared at me. His red-yellow-and-green-striped hat drooped to one side.

"Hey, sista, they be gone?"

"If you're asking about the two men? Yes, they left. You're not still smoking that stuff in there, are you?"

He revealed the yellow teeth with his wide smile. "No, mon. Mi put it in de toilet."

"Okay," I said, wondering if he'd smoked the blunt down to where it would flush without jamming Joan's pipes. Of course, it wasn't like she couldn't afford a plumber. I gave him a nod and said, "I gotta get back to the party."

"Be well, sista."

I followed the hall past a guest bedroom and a library, crossed the entrance hall, and entered the large living room that smelled of roses. Through the tall windows I could see the crowd outside, and to my right, beyond the dining room, I could see Joan in her *Architectural Digest* kitchen talking to a caterer in a white uniform.

After stepping outside, I walked across the patio and carefully mown lawn into the tent, where I saw Miss Jamaica sitting at a table with Calixto. *Big surprise.*

As Calixto lounged back in his chair, Miss Jamaica leaned toward him. She had a beautiful profile. As I watched, the side of her mouth curved into a smile as her hand touched Calixto's arm. Whatever she said made him laugh, and I did not like the way this made me feel.

This was exactly why I did not want to get involved with him. He was a babe magnet and I didn't want to deal with it.

But you're already involved, an inner voice whispered.

No, I'm not!

Deny all you want. It won't change anything.

Calixto glanced at me. "Come join us, Fia. Can I get you a drink? You look like you need one."

I could wear a bag over my head and the man would still read my thoughts like they were lit with neon. "Vodka tonic, please," I said as I sat in a chair next to Miss Jamaica.

"Hello," she said softly, extending a manicured hand. "I'm Julissa Jolivet. You were at Violet's today, weren't you?" Her smile was hard to resist.

"Yes." I was surprised she'd noticed me in the shop.

"I almost bought that dress last month. You look beautiful in it."

"Thanks," I said, and told her my name. I felt bad for previously dismissing her as self-centered and empty-headed. So much for my detection skills. Glancing after Calixto, I saw he was caught in a line at the bar. I turned back to Julissa.

"You were Miss Jamaica two years ago?"

"Yes, I was." Her tone seemed wistful.

"Are you up here on a promotion tour?"

"Oh, no," she said. "I don't do that anymore. I am traveling with my—my gentleman friend."

My interest kicked up, and when I saw the Rastafarian heading toward our table with his eyes on Julissa, I knew. "You're with Darren?"

She started slightly. "Yes. Darren Onandi. How did you know?"

Before I could reply to her question, she saw the Rastafarian and stood abruptly. "I'm afraid I have to go. It was very nice meeting you, Fia."

I didn't like the tension radiating from her. "Is everything okay, Julissa?"

After a brief sigh, she said, "Yes, everything is fine."

The Rastafarian jerked his head toward the house, grasped Julissa's arm, and led her away. I stopped myself from following them. I didn't like seeing her manhandled, but she hadn't asked for help, and it was none of my business. I left it alone.

Again, I glanced at Calixto, still stuck in the bar line. He caught my eye, and raised his palms in a what-can-I-do shrug.

The problem could be fixed by raiding Joan's living-room bar, but thinking about her had been a mistake, like thinking about the devil. She came through the patio door, scanned the crowd, and spotted me, making a beeline in my direction. She passed the Rastafarian and Julissa who kept going until they disappeared into the house.

As Joan drew closer, I stood quickly. Her face was white, her eyes wide with something like shock. I grabbed my purse and rushed toward her. We met halfway to the house, where a woman in a pink dress with her husband in matching pink-and-green-plaid pants crowded between us.

"Joan," the woman gushed, "what a magnificent event. Everything is just—"

"Not now, Charlotte!" Joan steadied herself, then plastered on a smile. "I'm having a crisis in the kitchen. If you'll excuse us?"

Not waiting for Charlotte's response, Joan clutched my hand, her grip clawlike.

"What is it?" I asked.

"You have to come. Something terrible has happened!"

I rushed with her into the house. Behind us I heard Charlotte say to her husband, "Well, I've never been treated so shabbily. You would think . . ."

Her voice faded as Joan and I reached the patio doors and dashed inside. I expected to find an explosion in the kitchen, possibly an injured caterer, but Joan hurried past the kitchen, across the main hall and sped toward Rich's study.

Outside the room, her stride faltered. She stopped and turned to me, her face so pale I was afraid she would faint.

"I *can't* go back in there," she said. "Please, Fia, you were a cop. You know how to handle these things." She became silent, rooted to the floor. She gestured toward the study. "*Please.*"

I stepped into Rich's office to the middle of the plush Oriental and stopped, my senses on high alert. The room was empty. No sound, no rustle, no one breathing. Careful not to touch anything, I stared at the leather couch, Rich's paw-footed desk, and the bookshelves behind. The room appeared undisturbed, the heavy curtains still drawn.

But a heavy metallic odor overpowered the residual scent of the Rastafarian's marijuana. The smell came from the bathroom, and I dreaded what I would find there.

15

I walked cautiously across the carpet toward Rich's bathroom, careful not to touch anything, wishing I had my Walther. But who brings a handgun to a garden party? Outside the door, I stopped and stared inside.

It took a moment to recognize him. He lay in the bathtub, covered with blood. His throat was so severely slit, his head was barely attached. I fought against the nausea that rose in my throat. *You're a cop, Fia. Get a grip.*

Once I drew a tight enough rein on my emotions, I recognized the suit. It was, or had been, white linen. *Matt Percy.* The fabric was soaked with his blood, the coppery smell so strong it was almost unbearable. No murder weapon was visible. I backed out of the doorway, pulled my cell from my purse, and called 911.

When the male dispatcher answered, I quickly relayed who, what, when, and where. The "why" I couldn't tell him, but

I suspected it had something to do with the phone call that had left Percy so agitated.

Glancing around the study, I did not see a single drop of blood. There had been no bloody footprints in the bath. The killer must have worn plastic coverings over his clothes and shoes. *Premeditated.* Who could carry plastic sheeting into a garden party without being noticed? The caterers. Members of the band. Any woman with a large purse and, of course, the owners of the house.

"I'm securing the scene the best I can," I told the dispatcher who was still on the line.

"Yes, ma'am, and please stay with me until the patrol officers get there."

"Of course."

Spinning with an overload of adrenaline and nothing to use it on, I exited the room, and pulled the door closed behind me. I stood with my back against it, facing Joan. "I have to stay here until the police come."

"The *police?* Oh, Fia, no!"

Good old Joan, asking for my help with a murder, yet thinking I wouldn't call the police? I put a shushing finger to my lips, then spoke into the phone.

"Sir, how far away is the nearest patrol car?" Joan needed to understand the dispatcher was listening.

"Five minutes."

"Thank you."

Always quick to regroup, Joan said, "This is so terrible, Fia. I'm not thinking straight. I need to find Rich."

"Do that," I said. "Tell him what's happened and tell him to keep anyone from leaving."

"But we can't keep people here if they want to leave!"

"You have to, Joan. Don't you understand the police will need to talk to *everyone*?"

"This is so awful . . . in our *home*. My God"—her voice rose in panic—"whoever did this could still be in the house!"

Leaving the line to the dispatcher open, I tapped out a quick text to Calixto about Percy, finishing with, "Get in here, *please*. Bring Rich. Joan's losing it."

As I sent the message, the police dispatcher said, "Ma'am, a Saratoga PD cruiser's arriving at your location."

Fast-moving footsteps turned my head. Calixto rushed toward us, his cold cop eyes assessing Joan. Behind him, Rich struggled to keep up. He was breathing hard and the skin stretched over the rough bones of his face was wet with perspiration. As he panted to a halt, I studied his eyes and body language, and found no tell. If he was going to commit murder he wouldn't do it in his own home, would he? Would Joan?

"Calixto," I said, "there's a cruiser outside. I'm going to meet it." He nodded, then glanced at the closed door to the study, his brows raised with the obvious question.

"In the bathroom," I said. He nodded, and I sped down the hall, through Joan's entry foyer, and out the front door.

A police car, with flashing red and blue lights, had parked in front of the house. Two officers climbed out and headed toward me.

Two more vehicles rolled into the drive and continued on to the house. The first was a long black limousine, the second another police cruiser that seemed to be herding the limo to the house. I remembered Darren Onandi telling the Rastafarian to "bring her to the limo." Good for the cops, making the limo turn around and come back. I hoped no one else in the house had managed to leave since Percy was killed.

When the two officers were close enough, I said, "I'm the one who placed the 911 call."

Before the inevitable barrage of questions started, I mentally ticked off who I'd seen in the house before Percy died. Joan in the kitchen. Rich arguing with Onandi in the master bedroom. The Rastafarian in the master bath. The caterers, who had access everywhere. The one or more people who'd used the powder room, or stood in the library, or hidden in the guest bedroom. With a crowd this big, who knew?

The limo had parked with the second patrol car right behind it. The Rastafarian had climbed from the passenger seat where he'd been sitting next to Onandi's chauffeur. Now, he was confronting a tall muscular police officer.

"Hey, mon, why yuh want to be like dat? Nobody done noting. We afta go!"

The tall cop's voice was audible and firm, "Sir, nobody's going anywhere. Now, I need the rest of the people in your limo to get out and go back into the house."

As I, and the two cops near me, paused to watch the confrontation, a female cop climbed from the other cruiser, hurried toward the limo, and joined the tall cop. Onandi emerged from the car and Julissa climbed out slowly behind him. Something was wrong with her movements. She kept her face turned away from us.

The female cop asked, "Ma'am, are you all right?"

"Of course, she's all right," Onandi said. "This is preposterous! Do you know who I am?"

I doubted the cops gave a crap who he was, but I kept the thought to myself. Julissa finally turned toward us, and my breath sucked in. A vicious red bruise marked one swollen cheek, and finger-sized welts marked her arms.

I started toward her, but the officer closest to me put a stay-

ing hand on my arm. "Ma'am, I think it's time we go inside."
His eyes were not unkind, just insistent. "Why don't you show
us what you found?"

"I will, but you need to call in someone from homicide."

"We'll make that decision. Ma'am, you need to take us inside."

I did, and the officers pulled on rubber gloves, stepped boldly
into the bathroom, and visibly deflated when they stared at Percy's partially detached head. I retreated from the bathroom as
the nausea I'd felt earlier reeled through my stomach again. By
now the blood stench was as bad as the sight, and I had to turn
my face away and breathe slowly through my mouth.

The two officers backed out of the bloody scene, careful
not to touch anything in the study while they stepped gingerly
through the room and closed the door. As soon as they'd secured
the scene, one of them keyed the radio strapped to his shoulder
and called homicide.

Within minutes, the house was crawling with cops. Two
homicide guys arrived and stationed police at the front door, the
back garden wall, and the side gate to keep guests from leaving the
grounds. The entire house, except for the living room and powder
room, was cordoned off. The master bedroom, the guest room,
and the library were considered the "second crime" scene, and
only Joan, Rich, police officers, the head caterers, and I, were allowed in. Probably because we'd be questioned first.

The two homicide detectives disappeared into Rich's study,
followed by the medical examiner and crime scene investigators
who lugged in bags of equipment. The rest of us waited.

The party mood died a quick death as people realized a man
had been murdered, and they were not allowed to leave. Joan's
friend Georgina sat beneath her helmet of blond hair casting
dark, suspicious looks at the other guests. Her taffeta dress seemed

to have wilted. People's angry complaints and distrustful stares at one another created an ugly atmosphere. The scent of perfume, cologne, and freshly washed bodies was soon replaced by the smell of sweat and fear.

Fortunately, the bar remained open, and people eventually settled down with exasperated sighs and a drink. A woman in pink silk said, "That fellow seemed like a nice man, I can't believe someone found it necessary to kill him."

Next to her, her gentleman companion said, "Quiet, Lucille. Let's not talk about it."

A woman near them in a rumpled green suit said, "Why shouldn't she talk about it? It's on all our minds, for God's sake!"

Before a fight broke out, the two homicide detectives reappeared. They introduced themselves to the crowd in the living room as Clark and Ferguson. Clark was tall, lean, and chocolate-skinned with a strong jaw and large hands. Ferguson, who did the talking, was short, with a New York City accent, maybe from Brooklyn. He wore glasses with small, round frames that made him appear studious. The shrewd eyes behind the lenses said otherwise.

Ferguson asked the crowd for their understanding and thanked them for their patience.

Lucille ignored her companion's attempt to shush her and said, "We certainly understand the severity of the matter, but do not assume we are patient!"

Her companion rolled his eyes and shifted his body as far away from her as his seat would allow.

When Ferguson finished his speech, Calixto and I managed to buttonhole Detective Clark. We told him we worked for the TRPB. He studied us a moment, then told us to rejoin the cattle herd. He must have made a call to confirm our identities, because a short time later he led us into the library.

"Okay, your stories check out." He zeroed in on me. "You're Mrs. Gorman's daughter."

"Yes, sir."

"And you were formerly an officer with the Baltimore PD?"

"Yes."

He turned his attention to Calixto. "And I'm told, Mr. Coyune, you've worked with the FBI?"

Calixto nodded. "Agents from the Albany field office are already involved in the case we are working on here in Saratoga."

I barely kept from blurting, "They *are*?"

"So," Calixto continued, "it would be most appreciated if you would keep our identities concealed. If our work is successful, it will benefit your city."

"Not a problem," Clark said. "In fact, you two might be useful to us on this homicide." He swung his cop gaze back to me. "But I still have questions for you both and want to start with Ms. McKee."

Calixto left us in the library, and Clark asked me his questions. He recorded my responses on a small video camera he set up on the library desk. I told him everything I'd seen, heard, or knew about the demise of Percy. He looked dubious when I told him I'd only recently reconnected with my mother and that I hadn't seen or spoken to her for seventeen years. Eventually his well of questions dried up and he excused me.

When I left the room, he called in a beat cop who'd been stationed outside.

"Could you bring in Mrs. Gorman?" Clark asked him.

Love to be a fly on the wall for that one.

If I'd wanted to, I could have called a cab and left, but chose to wait for Calixto and the bitter end of the questioning. I liked to watch people's expressions as they were led into the library or guest bedroom to be grilled by Ferguson and Clark, and their faces as they came back out. First, I wanted to find Julissa.

She wasn't in the living room, so I went out the patio doors. I saw the Rastafarian, Onandi, and the chauffeur sitting at a table inside the party tent, but no sign of Julissa. I walked through the darkened grounds as a caterer lit torchlights and finally spotted her sitting on a stone bench near the back garden wall.

"Hey," I said, settling next to her. Even in the gloom I could see the raised profile of swelling on her cheek. "Does it hurt much?"

"I took some painkiller. It's no worse than usual."

"Than *usual?* Onandi has hit you before?"

"Yes, if he gets jealous. I should have been more careful."

She was accountable for his brutality? Typical response of an abused woman. Nearby, a caterer lit a torch and its flames reflected on her face. My perception of her and her life tilted as I studied her, wondering what I could say. She must know people who could help her. Did she have no money left from her run as Miss Jamaica?

"Can't you leave him?" I asked.

"The techs from his bank hacked into my accounts. They removed my money."

"*His* bank?"

She slowly shook her head. "It's a long story."

"Well, that sucks. Can't you just walk away?"

Her laugh was bitter. "We came here on his private jet. He has my passport, my papers. I have no cash!"

"Then how were you shopping at Violet's earlier today?"

If she was angry that I doubted her, she didn't show it. "Darren opens accounts for me at shops like that. Sometimes I take the clothes to consignment stores and trade them for cash. It's never enough."

Anger sparked inside me. Who was this Onandi, anyway? "Can't you go to the Jamaican consulate?"

"Sista, please, I understand you would like to help me, and I am grateful to you. But you have no idea how powerful Onandi is. The people at the consulate? If I was able to get there, they would turn me over to him. Then he would beat me." Her voice had broken, and I could feel her trembling in the dark next to me.

She didn't need me pushing her like this. How nice it would be if Onandi was wanted for some crime, something that had the FBI on his tail. But when I'd asked Calixto about Onandi earlier, he'd known nothing about the man.

"If he had a connection to the Saratoga mob," he'd said, "I would have heard about him."

Next to me, the torch flames flickered on Julissa's bruised skin. There was nothing to support taking her into protective custody. Like the Peruvian jockeys, she was not a U.S. citizen, and I had no control over her fate.

"Julissa," I said, "if I can find a way to help you, I will."

"Thank you, sista, but I don't want any more trouble. Please, forget about me." She looked defeated as she stood up stiffly and walked away. She headed through the dark, back to the tent where Onandi drank liquor and smoked a cigar. The Rastafarian's mouth split into a wide grin as he watched her approach.

16

At 2:00 A.M., I sat on Joan's velvet couch with Calixto. Rich and Joan had collapsed onto a damask-covered love seat, Joan sipping a brandy, while Rich chain-smoked cigarettes.

Earlier, two additional detectives had arrived to assist Clark and Ferguson with the questioning of the Gormans' guests. After the crime scene technicians gathered their initial evidence, Joan and Rich had undergone a second round of questioning, apparently about the people they'd invited to the party.

Now, everyone, from smartly dressed guests straight off the pages of *Town and Country* to the saxophone player and bartenders, had been interviewed and dismissed. Their buzzing cloud of suspicion, fear, and anger had departed with them.

Tiredly, Joan waved away Rich's cigarette smoke. "I asked you once to put that out. You know better than to smoke those things in the house." Like before, he ignored her request.

Still, their physical closeness while surrounded by adversity suggested their relationship might be a good one. Rich, who'd seemed calmer earlier, had grown more agitated, repeatedly rubbing his free hand over his face or tugging the pants' fabric near his knees. Apparently, the murder of Matt Percy was sinking in.

Across from me, Joan took a large swallow of brandy, and gazed at Rich. "You don't really think Sam or Jim could be involved in this, do you?"

He rubbed his forehead with weary fingers. "I don't know what to think. This whole thing is . . . immense."

I didn't know who Sam or Jim were, but Calixto and I exchanged a look. We would find out. Calixto had been using his phone to contact the TRPB office in Maryland. He'd already run a number of guest names through the agency's server and come up empty.

Now we waited for Clark and Ferguson to release the Gormans. The detectives had informed them their home, now a crime scene, would be off-limits for at least twenty-four hours. Rich had made arrangements for them to spend what was left of the night at the Adelphi. As Joan polished off the last of her brandy and Rich sucked on his umpteenth cigarette, I leaned close to Calixto.

"Correct me if I'm wrong, but it seems the one thing we haven't found tonight is a connection to the Saratoga mob."

"Not so far, *leona*. I don't believe a link exists between Percy's death and Mars or Rico Pizutti. But there is one odd thing."

"What?"

"Ferguson told me that the limo Onandi arrived in is bulletproof."

"That *is* interesting." I sighed and sank back into the couch cushions. A moment later, Ferguson entered the room and told us we could leave.

————————

In the morning, bleary-eyed from only two hours of sleep, I roboted my way through stable chores, glad news of the murder hadn't reached the track grapevine yet. Though the papers carried the story, people on the backstretch were unaware of my connection to the Gormans, and the two horses owned by Percy and Rich were in a barn on the other side of the backstretch. Still, I was careful to Goth myself up with plenty of black eye eyeshadow, white makeup base, and a T-shirt featuring a coffin on the front and a skeleton on the back.

When I finally staggered back up the long staircases to my room, I sank into a short but deep sleep. When I awakened, I thought of how best to find information on the racing partnership between the murder victim and my stepfather. Knowing the Saratoga racing office would have a record, I called Brian at the TRPB.

Before I could get a word out, he said, "I heard about the murder up there at your mom's house. That's totally bizarre."

"Very," I said.

"Any news from the local police yet?"

"No. Calixto may have something. I'll talk to him later, but I want to ask you about something else that might be related." I told him about the partnership.

"Let me call the racing office. They can fax me a copy of what Gorman and Percy wrote about the partnership when he renewed their ownership licenses."

While waiting for Brian, I pulled a small carton of coconut yogurt from the refrigerator and spooned into it. A half hour later, Brian called me back.

"The arrangement," he said, "seems very straightforward. No other partners are listed and there's no indication of a silent partner. I checked out the two horses and found no issues there, either. Your stepfather is listed as sole breeder and sold a forty-nine percent interest in both horses to Percy."

This wasn't unusual, as a lot of owners liked to keep a controlling percentage when they sold shares of a horse.

"Who's the trainer?" I asked.

"Feinberg."

"That's a dead end." Feinberg was a competent trainer who had no issues with either the NYRA or the TRPB. As I tossed my empty yogurt carton into the trash, I remembered I'd seen Al Savarine at the party.

"I need one more thing."

"You always do, Fia."

"Can I help it if I'm an amazing agent?"

"No comment," he said.

Will you look to see if there's a link between my stepfather, Percy, and Ziggy Stardust's owner, Al Savarine?"

"Savarine? He the guy with the hedge fund?"

"He may be starting one," I said.

"Where have you been, Fia? It's a done deal. The fund was opened two days ago."

"You got a file on it I can read? Is he calling it SEA?"

"No and yes. I should have something to send you tomorrow. It's really taking off. Folks are pledging away their life savings."

All the more reason to find out if Percy was involved with Savarine. Ditto my stepfather.

"Okay, Fia. I'll get back to you."

After disconnecting, I booted up my laptop and googled Savarine Equine Acquisitions. This time, I found a Web site for SEA with the familiar thuglike photo of Savarine. In addition, the page displayed a company banner, a picture of Ziggy Stardust winning the Derby, and a boatload of reasons why anyone with a grain of sense would be eager to invest in SEA.

Understandably, the fund was collecting management fees. But what were the *performance* fees they were taking? The Web site stated Mars Pizutti would pick out all future stock. Pizutti wasn't *that* good. Who would fall for this?

I thought of Gunny's words that day at Congress Park and how he'd reminded me of the thousands who'd eagerly stampeded into the tech bubble and mortgage banking scams. Fools have always fallen for get-rich-quick schemes and it seemed they always would.

When I arrived at Pizutti's barn late that afternoon, Stevie was standing outside Bionic's stall. When he saw me, his face broke into a grin.

"Fay, I got good news. I met with the stewards and they're giving me three days, and—"

"How is not riding races for three days good news?" I asked.

"You didn't let me finish. Mars is gonna enter Bionic in a fifty-thousand-dollar race tomorrow and name me as the jockey! My suspension doesn't start for five days, and the race is in three!"

"You got lucky there," I said. "I hope you win!"

"We got a shot," he said, stroking Bionic's reddish brown face before turning back to me. "You're gonna watch us, right?"

"Absolutely." As I spoke, Bionic raised his head, grabbed Stevie's ball cap with his teeth, and jerked if off the boy's head. Still grasping the hat, the horse nodded his head up and down. With his upper lip curled up and his teeth showing, Bionic appeared to be laughing.

"Give that back!" But Stevie was grinning as he tugged at the cap and snatched it from the horse's teeth.

A moment later, Stevie told me he had to get back and fix dinner for Lila. I watched as powered by youthful exuberance, Stevie scooted across the grass, mounted his bike, and swiftly pedaled away. When he was gone, Becky Joe and Carl showed up, and we began the evening feed.

As Becky Joe and I lugged buckets down the aisle, she paused and stared at me. "I hope that kid gets a fair deal on this race."

"I was under the impression Pizutti wants to win this one," I said.

"Maybe."

"Did you hear something? And don't tell me you 'can't say.'" I'd be ready to smack her if she did.

"Didn't hear anything. It's just that boy is so happy, I hope nothing goes wrong."

She stopped at Wiggly Wabbit's stall and busied herself dumping feed into the filly's tub. I kept going, hoping Becky Joe was only exhibiting the glass half-empty side of her nature. But even if Pizutti wanted the horse to win, like my dad always said, "There's only one way to win a race, and a hundred ways to lose it."

A minute later, Calixto came around the corner of the barn, but stopped when he saw me brandishing a rake at Ziggy Stardust. He understood the importance of focus when I was around a colt as fierce as this one. When I had the horse's feed in his tub, and had stepped away without sustaining teeth marks, Calixto continued toward me, making a wide arc around Ziggy. The colt pinned his ears and snapped his teeth at Calixto.

"I think this horse won the Derby through intimidation," he said.

"No doubt." I glanced around and lowered my voice. "Any news on Percy's death?"

"You know it is too soon, but I admire your eagerness."

His eyes drifted from my head to my toes, admiring more than eagerness. I felt myself flush.

"However," he continued, "I did place a call to Detective Ferguson, which he has not yet returned. Brian tells me you have already asked him about a Percy-Gorman connection."

"Anything new there?" I asked.

"No. There is not."

I shrugged, picked up Bionic's feed pail, and headed toward his stall. The scent of molasses rose from the grain, enticing and sweet. I glanced back at Calixto. "There's something I forgot to tell you last night. I saw Al Savarine at the party. Did you?"

Calixto's nostrils flared slightly. "No. But that is interesting, yes?"

"Very. And Brian told me that Savarine's fund is off and running. Did you know that?"

"Gunny told me earlier. It is one of the reasons I came to talk to you. You need to spend more time with your mother, Fia. Find out why Savarine was at her party."

Spend time with Joan?

He held up a hand. "I know you don't want to, but Joan is a window to questions that need answering. You have access to her, and no one else does."

Terrific. I dumped Bionic's feed into his tub, banging my rubber pail sharply against the wire stall gate. "I'll do what I can, but this is tricky. It was one thing to go to her party as her well-dressed daughter, but if people see me with her at the track or downtown in Saratoga, they might realize I'm also the Goth they've seen on the backstretch. I can't risk that."

Calixto folded his arms across his chest and leaned back against the barn wall, his eyes never leaving my face. "That goes without saying, *pequeña leona*. But you are far too clever to allow that to happen, are you not?"

I hoped so.

17

I spent a frustrating evening on my laptop researching the names Matt Percy, Richard Gorman, Al Savarine, and Darren Onandi. Brian was already working on this and had access to far more information through the TRPB servers than I'd be able to find, but I couldn't leave it alone.

The only relationship I saw was what I already knew—the partnership between Rich and Percy. Though I unearthed no other affiliation between these men, I'd bet my paycheck something hid below the surface. When I saw Brian's name pop up on a secure e-mail a moment later, my fingers flew to click it open.

"Sorry, Fia. So far no ties between these four men."

Damn. "There must be something?" I typed back.

"Nope. Will keep digging."

I thanked him, then stretched out on the merry-go-round comforter and stared aimlessly at the ceiling. As so often happens when I'm not focused on anything in particular an idea presents itself. *Patrick.* He might know something about Rich. I grabbed my cell and called my brother.

"Fia?" he asked, sounding surprised. "Are you going to hang up on me again?"

I couldn't blame him for the cheap shot. "Sorry, Patrick. When you called about Joan, it caught me off guard. Some of the things she did in the past left me pretty angry. I took it out on you. I shouldn't have."

He was silent a moment, then, "Apology accepted. How are you?"

"Worried. Did you know a man was murdered at Joan's house last night?"

"*What?*"

I told him about the homicide, standing up and pacing around the room as I related the gruesome events.

"My God, Fia, is Joan all right?"

Wasn't she always? "Physically, she's fine. But she and Rich are pretty upset. They've had to leave their house until the Saratoga PD finishes working the crime scene. They're at the Adelphi."

"Jesus! I'm going to call her right now."

"Patrick, wait." My pacing had taken me to the window. I looked down at the streetlights. A stiff breeze stirred the treetops below me, causing eerie shadows to scurry across the ground.

"I want to call Joan, Fia."

I drew back from the window. "Let me ask you something first. What do you know about Rich?"

"Rich?"

"Yeah, you know, our stepfather?"

"He's a great guy. Why?"

"Have you met many of his friends? Some interesting people were at the party, and I was wondering if you knew anything about a man named Matt Percy, or Darren Onandi, or Al Savarine."

"I met Matt. He was very personable and a good friend to Rich. I don't recognize those other two names. But don't worry about Rich, he's a good guy. He's been wonderful to Joan. Still, I know you, Fia. You shouldn't be snooping into Rich's business."

"A man was *murdered* in his home last night!"

"I get that, but shouldn't you leave it to the Saratoga PD? You're not with the police department anymore, remember? Aren't you still working at the track?"

Thunder rumbled in the distance. Our conversation was going nowhere and arguing with Patrick was pointless. "Yes, you're right. How is Jilly?"

"She's great. Since we gave her that filly, her grades are up, and she's staying out of trouble."

I was happy to hear this, especially since family history had repeated itself for my niece. Her mother had walked out, too. But Patrick owned a prosperous real estate company and unlike Joan, Patrick's wife hadn't cleaned out his bank accounts when she left town.

"Give Jilly my love," I said.

After we disconnected, I reviewed the events of the previous evening. I thought about the Rastafarian, and the conversations I'd heard between Onandi and Rich, hoping a clue might reveal itself. No such luck. I was glad Patrick thought Rich was okay. Though we didn't get along that well, Patrick had pretty good instincts about people, probably one of the reasons his business was doing well.

Remembering Gunny's request that I stay close to Joan, I called her cell, hoping she'd finished talking to Patrick. She answered on the second ring.

"How are you?" I asked.

"I'm . . . managing."

Her voice sounded shaky, the usual confidence gone. Having a murder in your home could do that.

"I'd like to come see you," I said. "Will you be back in your house tomorrow afternoon?"

"I don't know."

I heard a noise in the background and Joan drew in a quick breath as if startled.

"I'm worried about you," I said. "That was pretty awful what happened last night."

"Yes. Well, thank you for calling," she said and abruptly disconnected.

What was that about? It had almost had sounded like she was afraid to talk to me. I called her back, but was sent to voicemail. I called Patrick again with the same result.

I left him a message. "Did you talk to Joan? She sounded weird when I called her, like she was afraid or something. Let me know how she seemed to you. Thanks." I tossed the phone on the bed, wandered back to the window, and stared out.

On the far horizon, a jagged bolt of lightning lit the outline of the Adirondack Mountains, and the trees below began to whip back and forth. A strong gust rattled the old windowpanes, and I drew the curtains against the coming storm.

When I awoke in the morning, I checked for messages. Patrick had not returned my call, and there was no word from Joan. I didn't like the way she'd hung up on me. A person or unexpected incident had alarmed her the night before and I was curious to know what. But as soon as I opened the bedroom curtains, another event captured my attention.

A huge oak had crashed on the lawn below. I'd never heard

it fall. The thunder and wind had been so loud the previous night, it must have obliterated the sound. One gigantic limb had narrowly missed crushing my Mini.

After dressing, I hurried outside to check the car for dents or cracked glass. I'd been lucky, the Mini was fine. After cleaning leaves and twigs from the windshield, my drive to the backstretch took longer than usual. So many trees had come down during the storm, I had to abandon my normal route more than once in a search for passable streets.

On the backstretch, men with chain saws were cutting limbs and the trunks of trees that had fallen in the high winds. It looked like a small twister had ripped through. The damage was widespread, and the noise of wood chippers was deafening. Track management was lucky it was a "dark day" with no live racing.

Stevie was just disappearing into Pizutti's office when I arrived at the barn, and Becky Joe was walking Glow West, whose heaving sides told me he'd just finished galloping on the track. Pizutti's door closed sharply behind Stevie, and Becky Joe glanced at Pizutti's office with a down-turned mouth.

"What's up?" I asked.

Before she could answer, Javier poked his head out of Dodger's stall. "Fay. You're *late*. I already pulled the tack off Dodger. You need to walk him!"

"Sorry," I said, and hurried to the stall.

Once I got the horse walking on the shedrow, I urged him into a faster pace to close the distance between us and Becky Joe. By the time I caught up with her, we'd reached the short end of the rectangular barn. The walls here were solid—no stall openings, no people.

"Becky Joe," I called, "what's up with Stevie and Mars?"

"I'm thinking that sumabitch Mars is squeezing the kid, again."

"Bionic's race?"

Becky Joe glanced back. "Could be *Rico*'s decided the horse shouldn't win."

"He controls Mars?" I already knew the answer to that.

"Money and influence, Fay. Man's got connections."

I closed my eyes in frustration. Gunny had asked for a court order to bug Marzio Pizutti's office, but hadn't been able to get a judge to sign off on it. Not enough probable cause. Opening my eyes, I looked down at the bits of hay and straw passing beneath my boots. As far as helping Stevie went, I felt as useful as the dirt beneath my feet.

Stevie's face, when I saw him, would tell me if he was being pressured. The kid was easy to read, and if he was upset, maybe I could get him talking. Since Agent Turner had already approached him about giving evidence, perhaps I could push the kid in Turner's direction by suggesting it was past time for Stevie to get help. And that wouldn't blow my cover.

When Dodger and I finished our first turn around the barn, we passed Pizutti's office. The door was still closed. I slowed and listened, but heard nothing from inside. On our next turn, Stevie had emerged and was walking away from me down the shedrow.

"Hey, Stevie," I called, forcing my lips into a smile.

When he turned, the tight, pale skin on his face spoke volumes. "I gotta get Wiggly Wabbit out," was all he said before hurrying into the horse's stall.

I walked toward him, stopping Dodger outside outside Wabbit's stall. "Everything okay?"

"I can't talk to you, Fay. I don't have time." He had his back to me and wouldn't turn around. "Don't you got work to do? You should keep that horse moving."

He'd never spoken to me so sharply. In my peripheral vision I could see one of Maggie Bourne's grooms behind me leading another horse, so I had to hustle forward.

When I finished with Dodger, Stevie was already off Wabbit. Javier handed me the hot horse, and I had to keep moving. When I got Wabbit cooled out and settled in her stall, I glanced around for Stevie but didn't see him. His yellow bicycle was leaning against a tree, so he must still be around.

The sound of chain saws and wood chippers accompanied me as I finished my chores. The sweet-and-sour smell of sawn wood permeated the air, along with the tang of raw pine, liniment, and sweet feed. When I was finished topping off the water buckets, I saw Stevie walking toward me, eating an apple. He spotted me and stopped abruptly.

"Hey," I said, hurrying toward him before he could scamper off. "How are you today?"

His eyes slid left and right as if looking for a way out. Then he looked at his feet.

"I'm fine. I don't have time to talk, Fay."

He spurted forward and tried to sidestep me, but I grabbed his arm and saw fear in his eyes. His hands were shaky.

"Stevie, wait. What's wrong?"

"Nothing! Now leave me alone before you make it worse."

"Make what worse? Is it *Lila*?"

"Fay, I'm asking you nicely. Leave me alone." He jerked his arm from my grasp, ran to his bike, and wheeled quickly away.

If he threw Bionic's race, this time the stewards would fine him severely. He might not be able to ride the rest of the meet, not to mention he'd get a bad rep that would follow him throughout his career. *If* he still had one.

I decided to pay a visit to Stevie's apartment later, but first I wanted to talk to Calixto.

I found him lounging in Maggie Bourne's office chair behind her desk. He wore jeans and a black sleeveless T-shirt. Seeing his trim, muscular arms, so pumped with blood that the veins stood out, sent a little thrill to my gut. *Steady, Fia.*

"You're looking unusually casual this morning," I said, before noticing the bits of sawdust clinging to his cotton T-shirt. "Been using a chain saw?"

"You are very observant. Have you thought about becoming a detective?"

"Too dangerous," I said.

"*Es verdad.*" His glance slid past the shoulder straps and grommets of my corsetlike top and continued down my jeans. "So, what brings my lovely Goth here this morning?"

While trying to ignore his penetrating stare, I relayed my concerns about Stevie and Bionic's race, and when I was finished, Calixto frowned.

"I fear history is about to repeat itself."

"Not if I can help it. I'm going to his apartment this afternoon to, try and talk some sense into him before he throws his career away." I told Calixto my hope of steering Stevie toward Agent Turner.

"Don't tip your hand, Fia."

"No chance," I said as my cell chirped with an incoming message. I read the text telling me to check for a message from Brian at the TRPB. I called into the TRPB, using my passcode and read his encrypted message: "Connection between Gorman and Savarine found."

I showed the new text to Calixto, who leaned forward in Maggie's office chair. "Call him, Fia. Maggie already left for the day and most of the help is gone. It is safe." He stood and came around the desk, standing close so he could hear the conversation.

Brian answered immediately. "This is interesting, Fia. Richard Gorman has used a shell company to purchase a large number of shares in Savarine's SEA fund."

"What's he hiding?" I asked. "If he wanted a part of SEA, why not buy openly?"

"A good question," Calixto said.

"Oh, you're both there," Brian said. "Good. Gorman's shell company bought in for two hundred thousand dollars."

Did Joan know about this? "That's a big stake," I said. "What are most people paying?"

"Ten, twenty-five, as much as fifty thousand. Next to Savarine, Fia's stepfather will be the biggest shareholder."

Did Rich really think he'd get his money back out?

"I believe we need Fia to work her magic and find out what Gorman is up to," Calixto said. "This fund is beginning to have an unpleasant odor."

"Yep," Brian said, "that's exactly what Gunny wants her to do."

"Hello," I said. "I'm still here." It really annoyed me when the male agents talked about me like I wasn't there.

"Sorry, Fia," Brian said. "And I wish I had more for you. I have one last lead to pursue and if it pans out, you'll be the first to know."

I thanked him and ended the call.

"Time for you to visit the Gormans," Calixto said.

"I *know* that." I couldn't help frowning at him. "But first, I'm going to talk to Stevie."

With that pronouncement, I left Calixto and made tracks for my side of the barn. This was one more reason not to get involved with him. He had seniority over me, and if I were foolish enough to sleep with him, what was currently only a small annoyance could snowball into major resentment. Unless, of course, we both fell madly in love and lived happily ever after.

Yeah, like that was going to happen.

18

After grabbing a tuna salad sandwich at the track kitchen, I drove back to the side street off Lake Avenue to the brick ranch owned by the old man with the Jack Russell terriers. I parked the Mini out front, and walked behind the house to Stevie's garage apartment. His yellow Motobecane wasn't in sight, but I walked up the stairs and knocked on his door anyway, thinking as long as I was there, I could check on Lila.

No one came to the door, so I knocked again, listening for any human noise from within. There was no sound and the apartment felt deserted. Maybe Stevie had taken Lila somewhere on his bicycle, or the old man had driven them to go grocery shopping. I trod back down the wooden staircase, walked to the brick ranch, and rang the bell to see if the old guy was home.

Barking immediately erupted from inside, and I could hear the slow footsteps of Stevie's landlord.

"Hi," I said, when he opened his door. His body had sagged since I'd last seen him and his hands rubbed together repeatedly. I had to raise my voice so he could hear me over the dog chorus. "I'm the gal that came to visit Stevie last week. I was hoping I could find him?"

"Yeah," he said. "I remember you. Raymond, shut up!" he shouted. "Bosco, you, too. Damn dogs." His gaze came back to me and he took a breath as if steeling himself. "Stevie ain't here," he finally said.

I leaned over and let the dogs sniff my hand. They both shivered happily and Bosco fell over for a belly rub. I obliged, and he wriggled in ecstasy. My attention stopped their barking.

"I don't think I introduced myself last time," I said. "Fay Mason."

He extended a gnarled hand to grasp mine. "Lou Powzalski."

Raymond lifted his brown and white head and gave a low, plaintive moan.

"Cut that out," Lou said. "Dog hasn't stopped doing that since—" He sucked in another breath. "Since they took Lila outta here last night."

"*What?*" Fear coiled tightly inside me. "What do you mean, *took* Lila?"

Lou's rheumy blue eyes narrowed. "There was two toughs came by last night, see? Made her leave with 'em." He shook his head at the memory. "I told Stevie we had to call the cops, but the boy wasn't having any of that. Said it would only make it worse."

Where had I heard that before?

"So I ask him what's going on, and he just clams up and won't say nothing."

"Lou, what did these two guys look like?"

"Trashy Italians." He pronounced it "eye-tallions." "One

young guy, tough-looking, like a hoodlum. The other one was older. Had a ball cap, sunglasses."

"At night?"

"Yeah, like maybe he was in disguise. Had a big old mustache, too. Coulda been fake."

"Did they say anything?"

"I was in the TV room, looking out the window. I seen 'em drive up in this car, so I was keeping an eye on 'em. I saw them take her away from Stevie. Right off the landing. Dragged her down the steps. Terrible to see, but I couldn't hear nothing, and by the time I got outside they was driving off with her."

Jesus Christ, had to be Rico's people. "What did the car look like?"

"Was one of those SUVs. Kind of a blue-green, I think."

"Lou, where is Stevie now?"

"I don't know. He left early this morning and never came back. I don't like this one bit. I called the cops, but they said a family member had to report the girl missing, and then it had to be after she was missing twenty-four hours."

"But she was abducted! That's kidnapping. We could call the FBI!"

"Look, I'm ninety years old and I sound like it on the phone. I had to tell 'em I never heard what those thugs said. And you, you ain't even a witness, Miss Mason. Cops won't pay us no mind. They need to hear it from Stevie, and he ain't talking."

"Do you have any idea where Stevie might have gone?"

He shook his head. "Sorry."

The urgency in our voices had the two dogs following our words back and forth like they were watching a Ping-Pong match played with dog bones.

"Lou, I'd really like to see Stevie's apartment. See if he left any indication as to where he's gone. Maybe those thugs left a clue behind that might tell us something. If you have a key to the apartment, would you let me use it?"

He stared at me a moment, then seemed to make up his mind. He nodded. "I got a key, but I gotta go up there with you. I ain't letting nobody snoop in my tenant's residence without me being present."

"Fair enough," I said.

Lou went to small table near his front door, pulled out a creaky drawer, and held up a steel key. "Here it is."

With the two dogs bouncing alongside, we did a slow walk to the back and an even slower climb up the stairs to Stevie's apartment. Lou had to stop twice on the stairs to catch his breath. I tried not to feel guilty.

As soon as we got the door open, Raymond whined anxiously and bolted inside. The dog rushed past the battered couch and TV into a room. I followed him and found him sitting on what had to be Lila's bed. A big clue was the pink stuffed horse on the pillows. The flowered bedspread and ruffles at the hem were pretty good indications as well. The room had a small white dresser and a desk with hand-painted flowers on its legs. A poster of some tweeny pop star I didn't recognize was taped to the wall over Lila's bed. Raymond sniffed the pink horse and pillowcases and whined piteously.

"Dog's just about moved in with the girl," Lou said. "He's been over here every night. Lila told me he sleeps with her on that bed." His lips pressed tightly together as he shook his head. "This ain't right."

"No. It's not." I left Lila's room and walked around the rest of the apartment, feeling intrusive as I checked Stevie's bedroom. It was austere, with a single bed and the only adornment a framed picture of Lila. Judging from her appearance, it had been taken maybe two years earlier. She didn't look as happy. Strain showed in her eyes, and I knew it was a good thing Stevie had gotten her away from their parents. A good thing until now.

As I searched Stevie's dresser and desk, I could feel Lou's eyes on me, making sure I didn't do anything that would upset Stevie. The kids were lucky to have the old man.

I searched the entire apartment for something that could tell me where Lila or Stevie might be. I discovered no notes, maps, crumpled business cards, or telling matchbook covers. I sighed and my shoulders slumped.

Lou cocked his head to one side. "That was a real thorough search you just did, missy. If I didn't know better, I might think you were a thief."

"I was a patrol officer with the Baltimore Police Department," I said, hoping to allay his concerns.

"You don't say?"

I nodded. "Not that it's doing me any good now. We might as well leave."

Raymond was still sitting on Lila's bed, and refused to abandon it. Lou finally picked the little dog up and after closing the apartment's door, carried him down the stairs before setting him on the ground.

I don't carry a business card when undercover, so when we reached the house, I dug around in my purse, found a pen, and tore a piece of paper from my tuna sandwich receipt. I scribbled my number on the scrap and handed it to Lou.

"If you hear anything, will you call me?

"Sure thing," he said.

We shook hands, and I left, driving back to the track where I picked up a copy of the overnight. It listed the entries that would run in two days. I scoured the sheet and saw Bionic listed in the seventh race, going a mile-and-an-eighth, with Stevie named as jockey. I had to find Lila. But how? I crumpled the overnight into a tight ball and threw it into a nearby trash can. *Damn every-thing.*

When the afternoon chores were finished, I called the Adelphi and asked to speak to the Gormans. As I'd hoped, the desk manager told me they'd already checked out. Rather than call Joan and have her fob me off, I climbed into my Mini and drove north to her house.

Joan's red Maserati brightened the driveway, and the waxed paint of a silver caterer's van reflected rays from the late-afternoon sun. I assumed staff had come to finish cleaning up the mess from the party, probably accessing the kitchen through the open garage door. Rich's black Mercedes was absent. *Perfect.*

I rang the bell and a moment later I heard Joan's heels clacking across the stone foyer inside. The door opened partway.

Her face was drawn, her eyes half-closed with exhaustion. She appeared to have aged overnight. After producing a weak smile, she gestured in the direction of her kitchen.

"The caterers are here cleaning up, and I'm very tired, Fia. I don't really have time for a visit. You should have called."

"I wanted to see how you were. How 'bout I just come in for a few minutes."

Joan pulled the door wider. Her sigh was impatient. "All right." In old jeans and a much worn sweatshirt, she walked away from me.

"Could we sit in the living room?" I asked, noting the house smelled faintly of garbage.

"Let me check on these people first." She headed for the kitchen where a man was dragging a trash bag so stuffed it looked ready to split open. "Those *stupid* police! Forcing us to leave the shrimp shells and crab legs sitting in the kitchen. Now, the whole house *stinks*. The backyard is worse. This stuff should have been cleaned up by midnight!"

I bit my tongue not to say, "A man was murdered!" Instead, I said, "I'm sorry all this has happened to you."

Two women worked at the kitchen sink hand-washing and drying glasses.

"Those go in the upper right-hand cabinet. No, the upper *right* hand," Joan said. "Are you deaf?"

The man with the trash bag was struggling to wiggle his burden through the door to the garage. He glared at Joan, and tugged harder on his bag.

"Stop!" she yelled at him. "There's a hole. That stinking seafood crap is leaking on my kitchen floor!"

One of the women said, "Don't worry, Mrs. Gorman. We'll clean everything up and mop the floor. It will be like we were never here."

"I doubt *that*," Joan said. "Come on, Fia, let's go to the living room before I have a nervous breakdown."

She marched into her living room, made a beeline for the bar, and poured herself a few fingers of bourbon. "Fia?"

"No, thanks."

She took her glass and collapsed on the damask love seat. I took one of the velvet couches. The bronze statue of Behold the King stared at us from the credenza.

"How is Rich holding up?" I asked, tracing my fingers on the velvet and watching the beige color darken as I stroked the nap in a different direction.

"He's managing," she said, taking a large swig. The sweet smell of her bourbon drifted across the room mingling unpleasantly with the odor of rotten fish. In the kitchen, a glass broke on the floor.

"Oh, for God's sake," she muttered, before shouting, "Would you people be careful!"

"Yes, Mrs. Gorman."

She settled farther back in the love seat and took another large sip. I smiled pleasantly and waited for her to get tanked on bourbon. After she'd had a few more sips, I spoke.

"You had some interesting people at your party, Joan, like that Darren Onandi. Is he Rich's friend?"

"Onandi? They knew each other years ago. His bank invested in Rich's business back when it was a start-up company. I hadn't heard his name mentioned in ages. Apparently he was in New York City on investment business, so Rich invited him to come up."

So that was the connection. Maybe we hadn't found it because Brian and I hadn't searched far back enough through the records of Onandi's bank.

"His girlfriend was quite lovely," I said. "And I also liked that Al Savarine fellow. What do you know about him?"

She stretched, took one more sip, and said, "Almost nothing. Why are you interested? He wasn't very attractive."

I smiled and forced a giggle. "You're right. He looked like a thug." I paused a few moments, then said, "I don't want you and Rich running into trouble."

Her eyes narrowed. "What do you mean?"

"Did you know Rich bought into a questionable business deal with Savarine?"

"Who told you that?"

"A very reliable source at the racetrack," I said.

She paled and took a substantial sip of whiskey. "I knew something was wrong. Rich has been acting weird recently."

"How do you mean?"

"Even before that dreadful party. He's been secretive, and

he jumped on me for talking about his partnership with Percy. He told me not to talk about his horse businesses with other people. He's *never* been like that."

"Is that why you wouldn't talk to me on the phone when you were at the Adelphi?"

"Yes, he was very tense. But it's understandable after the ordeal we'd just been through. But what is this 'deal' you mentioned?"

I told her about the hedge fund.

Joan sagged deeper into the love seat. "This isn't like Rich. He's never kept things from me. He told me everything, including the close to shady moves he was forced to take to get his internet company sold." Her voice took on a pleading tone. "But he's never broken the law. Fia, you were a cop. Can you find out more about this Savarine?"

"I don't have connections with the police anymore." *I could lie with the best of them.* "But I'll see if I can learn anything new."

She sat up straighter, her shoulders tensing. "Just don't ask Rich anything."

"Why? Are you *afraid* of him?"

"No, of course not," she said, but her eyes skittered away from me.

I wasn't the only liar in the room.

19

The day before Bionic's race, Stevie was at the barn in the morning. He gave Bionic a long jog the wrong way around the track, rode him back to the barn, and avoided my attempt to talk to him. I wanted to tell him I knew about Lila, get him to open up. But he was so tense, I was afraid he'd implode if I pushed.

As soon as he finished his work, Stevie lit out of the barn like a chicken chased by a hatchet. Moments later, Javier handed me Bionic and I began walking him. The colt looked good, with tighter muscles and a belly that had drawn up nicely into the greyhound look of a fit racehorse. He had a good chance to win. *If* he was allowed to run.

After rounding the end of the barn, I led him down Maggie's side. Ahead, the bantam rooster perched on the outside rail, his glossy tail feathers iridescent in the morning sun. Apparently Becky Joe's threat to snuff the bird had been an idle one, and by now, Bionic was familiar with the rooster and ignored him.

As we drew closer, the bird made little chuckles of alarm and sidled away from us on the rail, before hopping down, ruffling his feathers, and stalking off. He was as self-impressed as Mars Pizutti and as hard to catch as Stevie.

When we rounded the next corner, Mars's shedrow stretched ahead of us, and I slowed to stare at a white Cadillac I hadn't seen before. A moment later, Rico Pizutti climbed out of the driver's seat. He headed toward Mars's office, his large nose jutting over his down-turned mouth. He wore dark glasses, gray slacks, and a white zip-up pullover—probably dressed for lunch at his mob restaurant.

When Bionic and I passed him, I nodded and said good morning, but he ignored me. When I glanced back, he was stepping into Mars's office. I quickened my horse's pace, hurrying around the barn, before slowing to a crawl as we neared the office. Fortunately, the sand and dirt of the aisle muffled the sound of Bionic's hooves. I turned my cell to record and slid it into my breast pocket, hoping it could catch their conversation over the thudding of my heart.

"Is she all right?" I heard Mars's whiny voice ask.

"She's a little *desolate*," Rico said, and laughed like he'd told a great joke. "Get it?"

"Yeah, I get it. But it's not funny. I don't like this, Rico. She's a little girl."

I stopped walking Bionic, my ears straining to hear the next words.

"Oh, for Christ's sake, Mars. Don't be such a softie. Your horse will be favored to win. Sefino's gonna give his long shot some electrical assistance, and we're gonna make a pile of money."

"I still don't like it," Mars whined. "Stevie's a good kid."

Rico's next words were so soft I barely heard them. "Yeah,

well, I told him if he doesn't pull that horse, his kid sister's gonna wind up in the bottom of the lake."

"You wouldn't do that!"

"The Pizutti family doesn't make idle threats, Mars. You should remember that."

Footsteps sounded on the office's wooden floor, and I encouraged Bionic to step up to a normal walk. We were almost past the room when Rico appeared in the doorway. He frowned at me, then shrugged. After all, I was a weirdo Goth and a lowly hot walker. Why would I be a problem?

He followed us down the shedrow, and as I went around the corner and headed up the other side, I heard the Caddy's engine turn over, signaling Rico's departure. As soon as I put Bionic away, I sent a text to Calixto asking him to call me *immediately*.

He did, and I told him what I'd heard.

"I am on my way. Did your recording come out?"

"I haven't had time to play it back yet."

"Let us pray you were successful. I will call my contact at the FBI now. Perhaps our friend Rico has just purchased a one-way ticket to Ray Brook," he said before disconnecting.

Ray Brook would make a nice home for Rico. A federal correctional institution conveniently located in the mobster's neck of the woods, it was just up the road in the Adirondack Mountains. As far as I was concerned, they could throw Mars in there, too.

I found Becky Joe in the tack room, cleaning Bionic's bridle in preparation for the next day's race.

She looked at me and frowned. "What's wrong?"

"Nothing's wrong, but something's come up. I have to leave. Could you get someone else to do the water buckets?"

"You done everything else?" When I nodded, she said, "Yeah, I'll do it."

We both looked out the tack room door as we heard the rumble of a muscle-car engine. Calixto's Jag.

"I'll say something's come up," Becky Joe said. "If that came for me, I'd leave, too. He's one fine package."

I didn't bother to correct her impression that I was out for a lark with Calixto. I just smiled, told her thanks, and climbed into the Jag's passenger seat, leaving her standing in the doorway with her arms crossed and a knowing look in her eyes.

Calixto drove off the backstretch onto East Avenue, found a parking spot, and cut the engine. I hit playback on my phone and turned the volume as loud as it would go.

We heard Mars ask if Lila was all right, Rico say she was a little *desolate,* followed by his laughter, then Mars saying it wasn't funny. Fortunately, the part about Bionic being favored to win his race and the "electrical assistance" planned for Sefino's long shot came through loud and clear.

I paused the playback. "Do you have any idea who this Sefino is?"

"Yes, the trainer Joe Sefino. He is training a horse for Rico's associate, Alberto Rizelli."

I remembered the old wiseguy from Rico's Italian restaurant, with his seamed face and nose slightly pushed to one side. "But Rizelli's a convicted felon," I said. "How can he get an owner's license?"

"Unfortunately, the New York State Gaming Commission does not consider a criminal conviction an automatic bar to being licensed."

"Well, that's special," I said and resumed playing the recording. We heard Rico talking about making a pile of money and Mars saying he still didn't like it, that Stevie was a good kid. I tensed waiting to hear Rico's words about putting Lila in the bottom of a lake, but there was silence.

"*No,*" I said. "It has to be on here!" Fuming with annoyance, I played the sound from the beginning again, but Rico had spoken so softly his words were lost. The next voice was Mars saying, "You wouldn't do that!"

I felt like throwing the stupid phone.

"Easy, *pequeña leona.* Tell me what Rico said."

I drew in a long breath and exhaled. "I don't remember his exact words, but basically, he said he'd told Stevie that if he didn't stop Bionic from winning, Lila would be drowned in a lake."

"What lake?"

"Don't you think I'd tell you if I knew, Calixto?"

His facial muscles were so hardened, his eyes so narrowed with anger, he almost frightened me. But I knew his wrath was directed at Rico.

Reminder to self. Never get on Calixto's bad side.

"Play the end again," he said. I did and we heard Rico's final words, "The Pizutti family doesn't make idle threats, Mars. You should remember that." Then his footsteps on the wood floor as he left.

I turned the phone off. "I'm trying to remember exactly what Rico said, and I can't!"

"It will come to you, Leona. In the meantime there is a burn phone in the glove box. Take it please and hand me your phone. The FBI lab may be able to enhance the recording and retrieve Rico's missing words."

I opened the glove box to find the burn phone and the first thing I saw was a Glock semiautomatic. I couldn't help but smile.

"You know, TRPB agents aren't supposed to carry guns."

"A ridiculous rule."

"Won't get any argument out of me," I said, grabbing the throwaway and putting it in my tote bag. I handed my smartphone to Calixto, then closed the glove box.

His fingers closed over my wrist. "I have the number of this phone and will give it to the Fair Hill office so Brian or Gunny can contact you. Don't go, how do you say, 'off the reservation' without telling me. You got in enough trouble in Florida."

"I won't. But what do you think Rico meant when he used the word 'desolate' in relation to Lila? It's got to be a clue, but I can't make anything of it. Unless it means she's out in the wilderness somewhere."

"I do not know. When you get back to your room, run the whole scenario by Brian."

He dropped me off by our barn, where a breeze had kicked up, driving bits of hay, straw, and trash along the path outside the shedrow. A bank of clouds thickened on the eastern horizon as Calixto drove away, blocking the sun and turning the bright red of his Jag to the color of drying blood.

Hoping he'd have good luck at the FBI lab, I went straight to my car and drove home to my room on Union Avenue, where I called Brian and relayed the conversation between Rico and Mars.

"Let me work on that and call you back, Fia. I doubt I'll come up with anything, but I sure as hell will try. That poor little girl."

I'd only met Brian a few times after I first landed at the bureau. He'd taught me the ins and outs of the agency, but even though we'd been in the same building, most of our contact had been through phones and computers. He was twenty-seven, thin with short, curly hair and wire-rimmed glasses. Not the most handsome guy I'd ever met, but a genius on the computer. I thanked him, hung up, and rummaged around in my freezer, glad I'd bought a frozen lasagna.

A nice Italian meal to eat while trying to figure where some not-so-nice Italians had stashed a frightened little girl. The whole thing left me with no appetite, but I knew if something broke,

I needed to be nourished. I poured a mild drink of Woodford Reserve. It made the food go down a little more easily as I forced myself to swallow the pasta and sauce.

Think Fia, think. Nothing came to me so I let my mind drift. No doubt Lila did feel desolate. I had to unclench my jaw so I could swallow my next bite. I thought about the little dog Raymond, Lila's clear, intelligent eyes, and felt more miserable and angry with each memory.

What lake? The title of Sir Walter Scott's poem drifted into my mind. "The Lady of the Lake." I sat bolt upright. *The* lake, not *a* lake. Rico had said Stevie's kid sister was going to wind up in the bottom of *the* lake.

I booted up my computer, furious with how long it seemed to take. Finally, I was able to google the words "Saratoga Springs, Adirondack Mountains, lakes, and desolate." Faster than you can say I hate waiting, Google asked, "Did you mean Lake Desolation?"

20

Lake Desolation? Had to be. At least I hoped it was the place they'd taken Lila. I clicked on the site, my eyes immediately sweeping over pictures and maps, soaking up the information on my screen.

In the foothills of the Adirondacks, Lake Desolation, curvy and long, wound through scattered cabins and was surrounded by acres of forest. According to the map, it was barely a half hour from the racetrack, in an area called Middle Grove, bordering New York's Lake Desolation State Forest. I studied the Earth map of the forest. It looked mountainous, wild, and lonely.

I called Brian and when he answered, I told him what I'd found.

"Can you search property deeds, see if Rico Pizutti or any of his associates own a cabin or land up there?"

"You got it, babe."

"Thanks, Brian. I'm going to head up there and have a look around while you dig."

"Be careful, Fia. No heroics."

"No *way*. I'm calling Calixto now, and leaving a message for Agent Turner, too, to tell them where I'm going, what I found out." I paused a moment. "Damn, I hope this isn't a false lead."

"Sounds dead-on to me," Brian said.

The excitement I heard in his voice matched the pulse racing in my veins. I disconnected the call, washed the Goth makeup off, and went to my tiny closet for my disguise kit. I yanked off my Goth T-shirt, and pulled on a plain, long-sleeved blue one, not bothering to change out of my jeans and paddock boots.

The vest I'd used in the past to hide my holstered Walther had been destroyed in a fight with two gang members in South Florida. I'd found a sturdy khaki replacement at Walmart and slipped it on in case I felt the need to wear my Walther. I packed the vest with extra bullet clips and a Buck knife.

Then I grabbed my Walther, a power bar, and a bottle of water and shoved them into my tote bag. I slung the bag over my shoulder and picked up the disguise kit. My waterproof jacket and flashlight were in the Mini. I was ready to go.

I drove to Lake Avenue and headed north on Church Street, making my calls to Calixto and Turner as I drove. For once, I was glad both attempts went to voicemail. I didn't want to hear admonishments about being careful or waiting for reinforcements. I was only scouting around, after all, not breaking into cabins or anything else that put me at significant risk.

The farther north I sped, the more the clouds thickened and spread across the sky. The afternoon grew dark and a threat of rain dampened the air flowing in my window. After reaching Middle Grove Road, I arrived at Lake Desolation Road barely four miles later, but the area was so secluded, it could have been a hundred miles from Saratoga Springs.

Outside my car, hemlocks and white pines formed a dense green wall. Deciduous trees, mostly beech and maples, added to the mix, their long trunks reaching to the sky as their branches sought sunlight. The forest crowded so tightly against the road, it felt claustrophobic.

For a long time, I didn't see the lake. It finally appeared ahead, with a rustic eatery called Tinney's Tavern on the left side of the road. Only one car was parked in its lot. So much for a late lunch crowd where I could scan the customers and ask a few questions.

The map had shown the road continued winding up the west side of the lake to the northern tip, before curving down back down the east side. I continued on at a snail's pace, hoping to get a sense of the area. Every so often a mailbox and a narrow dirt or gravel road indicated the presence of a cabin on the lake. A few boxes had names on them, but none with the name "Pizutti."

I must have been halfway around the lake when Brian called. There was no traffic on the road, so I stopped, and grabbed the little notebook I kept in my glove box, ready to jot down any useful information he might have for me.

"Fia, a Leonardo Pizutti owns a cabin on the lake. He's thirty-five years old, and though he has no outstanding warrants or previous convictions, he's probably a nephew or cousin of Rico's. But guess who owns a twenty-acre parcel farther north?" Brian sounded almost jubilant.

"Not in the mood to guess. Who is it?"

"Alberto Rizelli! He's got a cottage up there, on the edge of the state forest. Looks like there's a long gravel road leading to the property. It's called—you're going to love this—Isolation Lane. Branches off Lake Desolation Road just to the northeast of the lake."

"I'm on the northern tip of the lake now. I should hit that cutoff soon. Where is Leonardo's property?"

"It's south of you on the east side. Looking at the county property map, it's about six driveways after the cutoff to Isolation Lane."

"Okay," I said, "I'm going to drive up to Rizelli's. He's only—"

"Don't do that. It's a long dead-end road. You'll be trapped if anyone comes in behind you. Wait for Calixto and Turner."

"It's okay, Brian. Rizelli's only seen me once. As a blonde in Pizutti's restaurant. I've got my red Kate O'Brien wig and fake glasses. I can act dumb and lost if I run into him."

"I don't like it, Fia."

"I bet Lila Davis likes her situation even less!"

"Don't get hotheaded like that. You'll piss off Gunny."

As I drew in a long calming breath, the first drops of rain splashed against my windshield. A wet breeze blew into the car, chilling my face. "I'll be careful, Brian, I promise. Calixto is probably on his way by now." I didn't add that I hadn't heard from him or Turner.

"Okay." Brian's voice sounded resigned. "You've got a GPS tracker on that phone, and I'm not letting you out of my sight."

"Good. I'll call you if I learn anything."

I should have known Calixto would hand me a burner with tracking ability. He probably knew exactly where I was. The thought comforted me more than I cared to admit. I slid my window up against the cold rain and drove on, looking for Isolation Lane.

I found it and turned up the rough gravel road, stopping long enough to shrug into my waterproof jacket and pull out my red wig and glasses and put them on. *Just in case.*

Filled with potholes, wet leaves, and twigs, the bumpy road

wound up steep hills, down through a wet vale where my tires slid in black mud, before rising up a long incline with the light of a clearing visible through the trees ahead. I stopped the car, cut the engine, and opened my window so I could listen. The rain was light, but the temperature had dropped even more. I heard nothing but the patter of drizzle on the leaves and the drip of water coming off the pine needles surrounding my car.

I called Brian. "Hey," I said, when he answered on the first ring, "I'm near a clearing on Rizelli's land. Do you have me on live satellite?"

"I do. But I only get glimpses when your car is clear of the tree canopy."

"What's ahead?"

"A cabin, with smoke coming out of the chimney. Is it that cool up there?"

"It is today. How many cars do you see?"

"One. Looks like an SUV."

I remembered Lou telling me the kidnappers had been in a blue-green SUV. "Can you see its color?"

"It's satellite imagery, Fia, not magic."

"Yeah, okay. Anything else?"

"Not unless you want to count utility lines. What are you going to do?"

"Drive up and act lost. Brian, can you look at the county map again, and give me the owner's name on a nearby cottage? I'll say I'm looking for them."

A moment later he said, "If you hadn't turned off on Isolation, you would have come to Martin Scheinman's place. Try that on for size, but for God's sake be careful!"

"I will, Brian." I disconnected, cranked up the engine, and drove toward the clearing.

21

When I cleared the trees, the first thing I saw was a blue-green SUV. My anxiety level kept rising as I parked next to it, smoothed my red wig, and climbed out of the Mini. I hurried through the rain, across a rough yard of wet leaves, gnarled roots, and pinecones.

I climbed a few steps up to a wood deck, sheltered beneath a roof, before a cabin built from rough-hewn pine logs. A worktable with a chain saw stood near the door. Inside, an interior door slammed, then the sound of someone unlocking the front door. It opened, and a hard-faced man stared at me. He was probably midthirties with thin lips and cold eyes.

"You lost or something, lady?"

"You know, I think I am," I said, ducking my head and giving him a sheepish smile. "I'm looking for Martin Scheinman's place, and I must have made a wrong turn. Your road, it just goes on forever, you know? I was worried I'd made a mistake, but the road was so narrow, I was afraid to try and turn around, you know?"

His stare was stony, but he nodded. "You turned too soon. Scheinman's is the next drive over back on Desolation." He started to close the door.

"Listen," I said quickly, "I hate to bother you, but I could really use a bathroom?" As I spoke, I looked over his shoulder into the interior of the cabin. Behind a couch and a low book-case, I could see a closed door with a key in the lock. Was Lila behind it?

"Sorry, lady, you're not using my cabin. Use a tree on your way out." He shut the door in my face, and I heard the sound of a key turning and then a bolt slid home.

Jerk. Was he the Pizutti nephew, Leonardo? Or some goon attached to Rizelli? I marched back to my car, circled it around the clearing, and headed down the drive. I followed the road, looking for a place to turn off. About halfway to the muddy spot, I spotted a narrow trail that could have been an old log-ging road. It looked almost made to order, as a short way in, it curved and disappeared around a thick stand of hemlocks. But would the Mini fit on the narrow path? I eased my car past the opening, then started backing in slowly. No way I'd be able to turn around once I was on the narrow trail.

The rain suddenly hardened, pelting angrily on the roof of the Mini, and I was grateful for my waterproof jacket. As I re-versed along the path, the lacy needles of the trees scraped against the car. Then the rear windshield hit the solid wood of a long branch. I grabbed my Buck knife, got out, but discovered I could break the pine branch faster than I could cut through it. The rain pelted like ice on my head as I broke off a few more obstructive branches.

As soon as I climbed in the car, I turned the heat up full blast before backing far enough around the conifers that the Mini was hidden from anyone traveling on Isolation Lane. I hated having to shut down the engine and heat to avoid discovery, but by now the exhaust was pluming bright white in the cold air. I pulled out my power bar and scarfed it down with sips of water before calling Brian and telling him I thought I'd met Rico's nephew and that Lila was locked in the cabin.

"I don't like this, Fia. You've completely disappeared off my satellite picture."

He sounded frustrated, but I thought it wasn't directed at me so much as his inability to do anything but sit in a chair and stare at a screen. *It would drive me nuts.*

"Where the hell are you, anyway?" he asked. "You were heading out of there and then you disappeared."

"I hid the car behind some evergreens."

"That's *crazy*. Get off Isolation Lane and wait for backup!"

I could picture his thin face, anxious and worried, staring at his computer screen through the thick lenses of his glasses.

"Brian, I didn't know you cared."

"Don't be flip. You're on your own up there. Calixto and Turner haven't been able to leave because there was a bomb scare at the track."

"*What?*"

"Someone left a suitcase outside one of the simulcast parlors. They had to call in a bomb squad. See? This is why we don't go off on our own until we *know* we got backup."

Outside my car, a wind had risen, causing a branch to slap against the Mini's roof. As sheets of rain sluiced down my windshield, a sense of alarm filled me. Brian was right. I should leave while I still could. Yet I could almost feel Lila's fear and Stevie's despair.

"Fia," Brian said, "please tell me you're leaving."

"I will. But I've got to go back to the cabin—through the woods on foot, so that guy can't spot me. If I can see Lila through a window, we can call in the county police or the FBI, right?"

"Damn it. Don't do that."

I grabbed the discarded power bar wrapper, held it to the phone, and crinkled the foil against the mouthpiece. "I'm having trouble hearing you. I'll try again after I look inside the cabin."

I ended the call, removed my jacket, and buckled on my holster. After sliding in the Walther, I stuffed extra bullet clips in a vest pocket. Opening the zipper behind the jacket's collar, I pulled out the attached hood. After removing my wig, I shrugged into the jacket, slid the hood over my head, and pulled the drawstrings tight. I opened the car door, took a deep breath and stepped into the deluge.

I worked my away across the forest floor, circling past a deadfall and pushing away the branches that tried to slap my face and block my path. Some of the hardwood saplings grew so close together, I had to turn sideways to pass through them. It was rough going, but I was afraid if I walked on the road, the wind and rain would be too loud to hear the whine of an engine or the crunch of tires on gravel. I'd be a sitting duck.

By the time I glimpsed the cabin through the branches ahead, my lower legs were soaked, and I was surprised to see only fifteen minutes had passed since I'd left the car. My forced march had left me sweating inside my long jacket, while my wet legs and knees burned with cold.

Glancing through the forest into the distance, I shivered. A perfect place to commit murder and bury the body. *Shake it off, Fia.* I eased up behind the trunk of a large birch. Only a few saplings and scrawny pines stood between me and the clearing where the SUV was still parked.

Motionless, I listened for any sound besides the gusts of wind and rain. Nothing. Ahead, a dim glow from a lamp escaped through one of the front windows.

I receded into the woods a few feet, before circling around the edge of the clearing to reach the back of the cabin. I could see another dull glow leaking through one of the rear windows. This window was barred. I considered the short glimpse I'd had of the interior. This had to be the room behind the locked door.

I paused a few beats, gathering my courage, hoping my dark jacket and black jeans wouldn't stand out in the fading light. I crept across the yard, hurrying to reach the wall next to the window. Eyes and ears straining, I pressed against the pine logs and listened. Nothing. Hugging the wall, I stepped closer to the window until I could peek inside.

Lila sat on the bottom half of a bunk bed, her knees drawn up, her arms circled tightly around her shins. The sight of her wrenched my heart, and before I could sink out of sight, she saw me.

Her eyes grew large, she sprang from the bed, and rushed toward the window. Quickly, I shook my head, before putting a finger to my lips, and mouthing the words, "I'll be back."

Disappointment that her rescue wasn't imminent caused her to sag slightly, but she nodded that she understood. Staying close to the wall, I moved away from the window. Using the over-hang of the roof above as shelter, I pulled out my phone and sent a text to Brian.

"Lila locked in cabin. Leaving now." I knew he'd relay everything to Calixto and Turner. I hoped Calixto was on his way. I would call him as soon as I got to my car.

I made a beeline for the woods, entering the undergrowth a short distance from where I'd exited. Hurrying around a log that had fallen next to a clump of thick brush, I stopped abruptly. A baby moose lay at my feet. It must have been sleeping and I'd all but stepped on it. The calf raised its head in alarm and bleated.

Didn't think I could shush a moose, so I stood perfectly still as it clambered to its feet and dashed into the trees ahead. I had no time to think as a large hairy form with pinned back ears charged straight at me. *Mama moose.*

I tried to jump to the side, but she was too nimble. She changed course, knocked me down, and ran over me. Her big cloven hooves hurt like hell as they trampled me, the pain in one shin immense. I'd automatically covered my head with my arms, but a glancing blow struck me on one ear.

Scrambling to my knees, I looked up in time to see her reverse course and charge me again. I couldn't help it. I shrieked. This time I waited until the last possible second and half threw myself, half rolled out of her path. She missed me, but the sound of human footsteps running toward me were as frightening as the thump of her hooves. The cow snorted in fear and dashed into the woods.

Dazed, I glanced up. The man from the cabin loomed overhead, the ugly snouts of six bullets pointing at me from the cylinder of the revolver grasped in his hand.

22

"Get up," he said.

"I can't. I—I think my leg is broken."

"Bullshit. I saw you jump away from that cow. Didn't look broken to me. Now *get up*, or I'll fire one in your leg and you can see how that feels."

I was dizzy from the head strike and my leg hurt like hell, but he was right. It wasn't broken. I rolled onto my hands and knees and stood up.

"That's better. Now walk to the deck." He kept his gun trained on me as I stumbled up the wooden steps and stopped under the roof's overhang.

"Don't move," he said, as he edged around me to the work-table and lifted the lid on a metal box. Reaching inside, he pulled out a plastic cable tie, the type that serve in place of handcuffs when the police need to restrain criminals.

"Turn around. Put your hands behind your back."

I did. As he leaned in behind me, I kicked back and ran one boot down his shin as hard as I could, then finished by trying to stomp on his foot. But he was too quick for me, jerking away from the worst of it.

"Bitch!" he yelled, smacking my already bleeding ear with his revolver. I went down on my knees, gasping and fighting waves of dizziness. He drew the plastic tight around my wrists. "Don't move."

I could hear him pull something from his jacket and fear made me look up, which I instantly regretted as my head felt ready to crack open. His hand held a phone, not some further instrument of torture. His fingers tapped in a number, the call connected, and he spoke.

"Yeah, Al. It's me. I just caught some woman up here snooping around."

I'd bet my life he was talking to Alberto Rizelli. The old mobster evidently had a hearing problem, because I could hear him yell at my captor.

"What?"

"I said, I just caught some bitch snooping around up here. What you want me to do with her?"

"What do you think, Tony? Get rid of her! I ain't gonna be implicated in a kidnapping."

"Right," Tony said.

"And, Tony," Rizelli yelled, "not my place! Take her down to the lake."

"No problem."

Tony slid the phone back in his pocket. "Get up. I'm taking you for a little swim."

I had to stop him. Slowly, I staggered to my feet, then kicked as hard as I could at his family jewels. But in my dazed state, I was too slow. He'd seen it coming, and my solid strike turned into a glancing blow as he stepped out of the way.

"You fucker!" He clubbed my head again. Blackness closed in. For a fading moment, I heard the sound of rain and the wind. Then nothing.

When I came to, I was still lying on the deck's rough wood. I could still hear the rain. Hard to know how much time had passed, but it was getting dark. Trying to move, I discovered a second cable tie bound my ankles. Gingerly, I turned my head and looked around. My gun and cell phone lay on the wooden table. I didn't care about the gun as much as I cared about the tracking device in the phone. How would Brian or Calixto know where this lunatic took me?

Nearby, a car engine whined. Tony was backing his SUV to the steps. He opened the rear hatch, jogged up the steps to the deck, and slid my gun and cell phone into his raincoat.

"Don't worry, sweetheart," he said when he saw me staring, "you can keep these with you at the bottom of the lake."

His sick grin turned into a short laugh. Then he pulled duct tape off a roll and sealed my mouth shut, before dragging me down the steps like a bag of unwanted trash. He hoisted me inside the SUV and slammed the hatch closed. A moment later, I heard the driver's door open and felt the SUV sway slightly as he climbed in.

We bumped down the road, my head screaming with every jolt. I could feel the tires skidding beneath us when the SUV hit the low muddy spot, hear the engine whine as it climbed the hills on the way to the main road. I felt the car slow almost to a stop before making the left turn off Isolation Lane and onto Lake Desolation Road. The crunching sound of gravel beneath the SUV's tires faded behind us as we picked up speed on the paved road. Outside the hatch glass, it was dark.

I was shaking with fear, and desperately began coaching myself. *You'll find a way to stop this, Fia. Someone will see you. Calixto will come.*

The SUV rolled to a stop. The hatch opened. Tony pulled me out, and dropped me on the ground, before grasping the cable tie around my ankles. He dragged me across a stretch of wet ground, while sticks and pebbles struck my head and shoulder blades. Everything *hurt*. The rain still hammered against the earth, and it was dark, and so cold. *Who would see us on a night like this?*

We reached the edge of the lake. Tony grabbed a canoe lying on the ground, flipped it upright, and pulled it to the water's edge. He slid it partway into the lake before grabbing my ankle tie. I twisted, and wiggled like a bug in a spiderweb, until he smacked my face and heaved me into the canoe. For a moment, I thought I heard the whine of a car engine, and I raised up frantically. But there were no headlights. There was nothing.

He left me in the canoe and disappeared into the night. When he returned, his hands held a large cinder block. Seeing it, my teeth started chattering, but not with cold. He ran a chain through the hole in the block, then around my ankle ties, fastening it all together with another cable tie. He slid the canoe all the way into the water, not seeming to care that his shoes and pants became soaking wet. His thin lips formed the same sickly grin.

"Thing is, bitch, I *like* killing people. Oh, man, look at you shake. This is too much fun."

I tried to scream, but the tape covering my mouth turned the effort into a useless moan. Tony heaved himself into the canoe and picked up a paddle. He dipped it into the water. Lying on my back, I stared up, knowing we'd left the shore behind when the dim skyline of trees receded, then vanished.

Without any warning, he rolled my straining, twisting body up and over the edge of the canoe.

"Have a nice swim." He laughed.

I fell into the water like a stone, the cinder block pulling me down fast. I grabbed a last breath through my nose before I went under. As the water filled my ears, I thought I heard a splash somewhere. Then cold, heavy water closed over my head.

23

The pull of the block took me lower and lower. I held my breath. A useless action. There was no hope. But in my head, I heard my dad's voice. "Fia, the race ain't over until you hit the wire."

I tried to fight against the cinder block's relentless pull. Desperate for air, I got the crazy idea that once I hit bottom, I could spring back up, break the surface, and *breathe*. Except the block took me down like an elevator and there was no ground floor. I could no longer hold my breath. Precious air bubbled from my nostrils. My father's voice grew silent.

Something grabbed my head. Hands. They pulled me up. The water churned beside me as strong legs kicked viciously. We were rising, but I didn't care anymore and only wanted to hear my father's voice again. Wanted to be with him.

My next awareness was someone coughing. Then I felt hands on my chest, water spilling from my mouth. I rolled to one side, coughing up more water, choking and sputtering.

"*Mi corazón*." Calixto's hands grasped me, lifted me to a sitting position. "I will kill them. All of them."

The duct tape and cable ties were gone. I leaned into him, clung to him. "I'm all right," I said, then immediately burst into uncontrollable sobs of shock and relief until I stiffened and pulled away in fear. "*Where is he?*"

"The bastard? He is gone. Our friend here took care of him."

Confused, I looked up to see a man wearing night vision goggles, holding a rifle. He slid the goggles down.

"Agent Turner, ma'am. Pleased to meet you."

I'd never met Turner. He'd always been around, but I'd never actually seen him. To me, he looked like an angel.

"Thanks," I said, before easing back into Calixto's arms, loving the feeling of safety until my memory flashed back and I was falling through the water again, my breath bubbling out. Again, my body shivered and shook. Calixto put his lips close to my ear and softly said, "*Mi pequeña leona,*" repeating the words again like a lullaby. In that moment, I wanted to stay with him forever.

"Sorry we didn't get here faster, Fia," Turner said, his words speeding with excitement. "By the time we spotted Rizelli, that scumbag already had you over the side. Man, I wish you could have seen Calixto dive in and blast through that lake like a cigarette boat. Then I squeezed off my shot and put a bullet in that piece of shit. Man, one shot and I hit him. He dropped like—" He abruptly stopped his recital, as if realizing I was too shaken to listen, and perhaps there might be a better time to tell his tale. "Uh, you two are drenched. You guys need a blanket or something? It's cold out here."

In the distance, I heard a police siren. Then I remembered, and leaned forward.

"We have to get Lila!"

"*Una momenta, leona,*" Calixto said. "We must deal with the police first, then we will get Lila, yes?"

Within a half hour the county police had arrived in force. It seemed every cop on hand had a wool blanket in the trunk of his cruiser and Calixto and I were wrapped in all of them. They put us beneath a tent they threw up for shelter against the rain.

Turner went to his car and returned with a pint bottle of Maker's Mark. I was really starting to like this guy. I sipped the whiskey. Nothing ever tasted better to me. Probably to Calixto, either, since together we emptied the bottle in less than five minutes.

By now, I was fired up and ready to blast to the cabin to rescue Lila, but an unmarked police car bumped across the grass, stopped behind the squad cars, and detectives Clark and Ferguson climbed out. When a county cop spoke to them, Clark headed straight for us. The taller Ferguson motioned for Turner to follow him as he took long strides to the canoe that held Tony Rizelli's body.

I had no interest in seeing it.

"You two again," Clark said, shaking his head as he peered at Calixto and me through the round frames of his glasses. "What is it about you and murder, Ms. McKee?"

"You should be more worried about the kidnapping of Stevie's little sister. She's still up at that cabin!"

"What are you talking about?"

I explained. "So right now she's traumatized, terrified, and up there alone."

"We'd better go," he said. "Ms. McKee, are you able to walk to my car?"

"Yes," I said, rising unsteadily to my feet with Calixto's help. Between the head and leg injuries, the trauma, and the whiskey, my first step was more of a lurch. My shin throbbed like hell where the moose struck it, but though I'd probably have a terrible bruise, walking wasn't too bad.

Calixto grasped my hand, steadying me. He leaned close. "Go ahead, but don't worry. I'm not allowing you out of my sight."

I hated letting his hand slide from mine as I slid into the passenger seat of Clark's unmarked car. I hated being away from his warmth. I was worried about the severity of my head pain, too, but my desire to reach Lila outweighed everything.

Calixto slid into the backseat of Clark's car, and a county cruiser with two patrol officers followed behind us. Clark could see I was still shivering and turned his heater on full blast as he drove up Isolation Lane. The hot air hit the damp wool blankets still wrapped around our shoulders and the car began to smell like a herd of wet sheep.

Outside, the forest was black, the car's headlights working hard to penetrate the gloomy night as the rain drummed on the roof overhead. When we pulled into the clearing, Clark insisted that he and the county officers should clear the cabin before either Calixto or I went inside.

"No," I pleaded. "Let me go with you. Lila *knows* me!"

"All right. But you stay here," he said to Calixto, as if unable to relinquish all control.

"No *problema*," Calixto said, but his narrowed eyes told me he didn't like it.

There wasn't much space to "clear" inside the cabin. Two bedrooms, a bath, and the living room with a small kitchen against one wall. When I spotted the light glowing under the bedroom door with the key in its lock, I rushed to it, ignoring Clark's calls to wait, ignoring the pounding in my head, and the protests from my shin. As I turned the key, one of the county cops tried to grab my hand to keep me from opening the door, but the lock clicked open. I rushed inside.

"Fay," a small voice cried. "I *knew* you'd come back." She flew off the bed and wrapped her thin arms around my waist, pressing her face against my chest. She shuddered. A wail escaped her. Safe at last, her bravery abandoned her.

I knew the feeling and held her while she sobbed.

On the drive back, the rain finally stopped. We picked up my Mini, and Lila tried to reach Stevie, but his phone took her to voicemail. She left a message.

"Stevie, it's me! Fay came. She *saved* me!"

Not every day I got to hear words like that.

When we got back to the lake, Ferguson was watching the EMTs zip Tony's body into a black bag before loading it into an ambulance. We climbed out of Clark's car, and one of the crew, a woman with kind eyes, took Lila aside to check her over.

After watching the woman lead Lila away, Clark turned to me. "Ms. McKee, I need you to answer a few questions."

When did he ever not need me to answer questions?

Calixto gave him a hard look. "Ms. McKee has been through a terrible ordeal, Detective. She has a head injury, was almost dead when I pulled her from the water, and should be taken to a hospital with Miss Davis. She's wet and chilled. Allow me to answer your questions."

Clark was not intimidated. "I'll get to you in a minute, Coyune." But he paused, and I thought his eyes softened as he glanced at me. "You up to it?"

I nodded and he waved me back to his car, where I slid onto the bench seat. Calixto stood outside, his arms folded across his chest.

"So tell me what happened," Clark said. "Preferably from the beginning."

I did, and he seemed particularly interested in how Lila's

abduction and the murder attempt on me related to Alberto Rizelli.

"Never liked that scum moving to our town. We've been itching to nail these guys for a while. So, you believe Tony was talking to Alberto Rizelli on the phone? That it was his voice saying Tony should take you to the lake, right?"

"Yes."

"What about Rico Pizutti? You got anything for me on him?"

"No. I wish I did."

"Yeah, me too," he said.

"I still think Rico was behind the abduction. If Stevie will talk, you'll have a case, at least for the kidnapping."

"I'm more interested in the attempted homicide."

Of course he was. He was a homicide detective. Which reminded me it would be good to ease away before he thought to ask more questions about the murder of Matt Percy.

"So who will handle the kidnapping end of this," I asked. "The FBI?

"Yeah. I'd better make sure dispatch relayed the info."

I was willing to bet my next paycheck Calixto had already called his FBI contact. Clark pulled out his phone to make the call.

"So," I said, "you're done with me, right?"

"For now."

I slid from the car and made a beeline for Lila who was still with the kind-eyed EMT.

"I wanted to talk to you," the woman said. "Lila seems to be all right physically, but her family should get her in for psychological counseling. Just in case." She smiled and handed me a card with the names of several therapists. "And you," she continued, "need to get a CAT scan for your head and a lung X-ray. *Tonight.*"

One of the county cops offered to drive my Mini back to the Victorian on Union Avenue, and since nobody wanted to ride with Tony Rizelli's body in the ambulance, Turner drove Calixto, Lila, and me to Saratoga Hospital.

As we drove away from Lake Desolation, I was relieved I'd avoided more questions from Ferguson or Clark about Matt Percy's murder. I was too brain-dead to piece together the jagged pieces of a murder puzzle. Still, I couldn't quite let the crime go. Something about Percy's murder left me with a niggling unease, as if I'd forgotten something.

24

By the time we got to the hospital, it was well past midnight. After Lila and I went through triage at the front desk, a nurse led Lila through a set of swinging doors and they disappeared somewhere into the inner workings of the ER unit. Then it was my turn, and I was led through the doors to one of those curtained cubicles, where I waited to be seen by a doctor.

Calixto lied so smoothly and easily it alarmed me. He was so convincing when he said we were husband and wife, I almost expected him to produce a marriage license. But I was glad he followed me in. While we waited, I lay on the room's bed and listened as his repeated calls to Stevie remained unanswered.

A while later, a white-coated doctor padded into my cubicle in rubber-soled shoes. He whisked me off to a cold room, took a CAT scan of my head, then sent me back to my bed. A pulmonary specialist came by next and led me to a different machine in an equally cold room for a chest scan. Apparently, Lila hadn't needed any machines, because when I returned to my cubicle, she was waiting there with Calixto.

"Lila has been telling me about the two men that abducted her. One, of course, was Tony Rizelli. But," he asked Lila, "you never heard the name for the second guy?"

Lila's face paled, and her eyes seemed to focus on something far away.

"Just tell me what he looked like," I said, "and we'll be done, okay?"

She opened her mouth, but no words came out. I wrapped an arm around her shoulder. "You're safe now, sweetie. You can tell us."

"He was just some old guy." She addressed her words to the floor. "He never said anything."

"Old like parents, or old like grandparents?" Calixto asked.

"Like grandparents."

I looked at Calixto. "Sounds like one of the old Mafia guys."

He nodded, then tried for more detail from Lila, "What was he wearing?"

"A baseball cap and sunglasses. Old clothes. I don't really remember them."

"That's okay," I said. "Did he have a beard or anything like that"

"Yes," she said, her voice suddenly stronger. "He had a mustache."

"Good." I gave her a little squeeze. "Last question, okay?"

Still looking at the floor, she nodded.

"Did you see any marks on his arms or hands? Like a tattoo or a scar?"

"No. He had on long sleeves and a turtleneck."

"Thank you, Lila. We don't need to talk about it anymore."
I turned to Calixto. "The description matches what Lou told me.
But we still don't know who he is."

"Oh, we will find out," Calixto said. "And when we do, this
man will wish he'd never seen Lila."

"Will you shoot him?" Lila asked.

"Probably just put him in jail," I said.

"Good! That old guy belongs in jail."

Calixto smiled. I could tell he loved her flash of spunk as
much as I did.

"So," he said, "Lila received a clean bill of health from the
nurse-practitioner."

"But they want me to get psychological counseling," Lila said
with a trace of rebellion. "Do I *have* to?"

"I wouldn't hurt," I said. "And it'll make them happy. Then
they'll leave you alone, right?"

The last part made her smile. "Okay."

While we waited for my results, it occurred to me that Stevie might be holed up at Lou's house instead of his more vulnerable garage apartment. Though I didn't like calling Lou in
the middle of the night, I decided reaching Stevie was more
important, so I called. Lou answered on the second ring.

"Don't worry about it. I never sleep anymore anyways," he
said, when I apologized for disturbing him. "You got my message?"

"No." *Not likely when the FBI still had my phone.*

"You'd said to call if I saw Stevie."

"You *know* where he is?"

"Sure. He's asleep in my guest room."

I could feel my shoulders sag with relief. "Lou, I found Lila!
She's fine."

"Thank God! Where is she?"

"Right here next to me."

"Well, put her on the phone, for God's sake!"

Lila took the phone and I could hear Lou yelling, "Stevie, wake up. Come talk to your sister!"

I glanced at Calixto as Lila spoke to Lou and Stevie. There was a light in his eyes I understood. The light that comes when things work out, when heartache doesn't win.

Lila told Stevie we'd come over as soon as we escaped from the hospital. As she ended the call, my first doctor showed up.

"You received a mild concussion. But," he said with a smile, "there's no brain bleed."

Always nice to know your brain isn't bleeding. The doc left, and eventually the pulmonary guy came by and told me I had a little water in my lungs. He gave me an antibiotic shot, a prescription for pills, and said to come back in a week. Then we beat it out of the hospital. I can never get out of those places fast enough.

When we reached Lou's, the front door opened, and Lila was overrun by a squirming, crying Raymond. She clutched the little dog to her like she'd never let him go. Stevie crowded forward and managed to get his arms around both of them. With Lila, Stevie, and the dog all crying at once, Lou scurried off to grab some tissues. I could have used one myself.

Two FBI agents stood inside the living room. Calixto knew one of them, who he introduced as Special Agent John Meloy. Meloy was maybe thirty-five, short, but built like a fireplug— the kind of guy you don't take on in a wrestling match. I was content to know the agents were taking Lila and Stevie to a safe house for the remainder of the night and stayed out of their conversation. At least until Meloy told Lila she couldn't take Raymond with her.

"After what she's been through you'd deny her the comfort of this little dog?" I was furious.

"No, he *has* to come with me," Lila pleaded.

"For God's sake," Lou said, "that's her dog. They sleep together. You want her to cry all night?"

"And she will," I said. "Besides Stevie's got to rest. He's riding a race tomorrow. So take the dog, and put them all to bed."

Meloy threw his hands up in the air. "All right, all right. The mutt comes, too."

Calixto, who'd been watching the exchange, had a gleam of amusement in his eyes, and a not-quite-hidden smile.

"What are you laughing at, Coyune?" Meloy asked.

"Absolutely nothing," he said. Then his gaze shifted to me. "She is a force when she is angry, no?"

Meloy nodded. "Glad she's your problem."

After the two agents rounded up the kids and Raymond, we left right behind them in Turner's car. It was 3:00 A.M. as Turner drove out of Lou's neighborhood.

"Where to?" he asked.

Calixto, who looked dead-tired, rubbed at his forehead a moment. "Fia's rental is out of the question, and there is not enough room at our apartment."

"You guys share a room?" I asked.

"For the summer meet, yes," Calixto said.

Before now, he hadn't revealed one clue about his living arrangements in Saratoga, which was so typical of him.

"Drop us off at the Adelphi," he said.

Turner looked doubtful. "You plan to get a room in the middle of the night during racing season at the *Adelphi*?"

"They always have a room or two for VIPs," Calixto said.

Turner made a derisive sound. "But you're not a VIP."

Calixto gave him the hard stare.

"Right. Adelphi, next stop."

In the hotel lobby, I collapsed in a chair close enough to the front desk to see if Calixto could con a room out of the desk clerk at Saratoga's premier hotel in the middle of the night. With no reservation. Mud from the lake smeared his jeans and white shirt. A bit of dried pond scum stuck to his hair. *God knows what I looked like.*

"Good evening," Calixto said, his Cuban accent more pronounced than usual. "I am Calixto Coyune and I require a room."

The desk clerk's raised brows and skeptical stare were unmistakable. "Sir, I'm afraid I don't see your name on our reservations list. Do you have a confirmation number?"

"Tell me," Calixto asked, "what brand of coffee does the Adelphi serve?"

The clerk appeared confused, then said, "Coyune, of course." Sudden understanding lit his face. "Are you—"

"Yes. Marquise Coyune is my father." He pulled what must be his Florida driver's license from his wallet.

The clerk studied it a moment. "Oh, yes, Fisher Island, of course. I've heard your father has lived there for years." He stared at his computer screen. "Would a suite with a balcony suffice?"

By the time I dragged myself into the hotel room, I could hardly stand up, let alone appreciate the splendor of the two-room suite. I staggered into the marble bathroom, cranked the shower and let the hot water wash away the remains of Lake Desolation. If only it were that easy. The water stung the heck out of my ear where the cow moose had struck it with her hoof, not to mention that Tony had repeatedly clubbed the same spot before knocking me out.

After stepping from the shower, I gingerly patted the side of my head and the damaged ear with a hand towel, before wrapping myself in a terry cloth hotel robe, and drying my hair. Then I zombied toward the bedroom.

"Fia," Calixto said, as I passed through the parlor, "try to get some rest. I will stay on the couch tonight."

I nodded, and entered the bedroom where a damask coverlet of pale gold lay between me and the sheets. After tossing throw pillows onto the floor, I tugged the coverlet back, climbed between the sheets, and passed out.

Sometime later, I woke with a start, thinking I'd heard someone crying out. Calixto sat next to me on the edge of the bed, one hand on my shoulder.

"*Corazón,* you were having a nightmare."

The dream still gripped me, causing me to gulp in air. In the dim light that spilled through the bedroom doorway, I could see the worry in Calixto's eyes.

"I was sinking through that cold, black water . . . in the lake."

"You are safe now, *querida.*"

"Did I thank you, Calixto, thank you for not letting me drown in that water?"

"It was nothing. See if you can go back to sleep."

Eventually I did, and when I awoke in the morning, I found his note on my night table.

"Stopped at your apartment to get you some clothes and your laptop."

What, you broke in? Went through my underwear drawer? I kept reading.

"Breakfasting in the palm court downstairs. You need to eat, please join me."

Glancing around the room I saw jeans and several of my tops folded on a chaise lounge in the bedroom. On the floor next to it, I spotted my carryall that held my disguises. Investigating the clothes, I found a small pile of my inexpensive, embarrassingly functional underwear under the first top. Hidden beneath that was the diamond bat wing necklace he'd given me. He must not have wanted to leave the two-carat stone in my room. I stowed it in the room's small safe, then I got dressed. Carefully.

Bruises and strained joints from Lake Desolation slowed me down and caused me to wince more than once. In the bathroom mirror, my damaged ear reminded me of a red cauliflower. I thought about putting my wig on, but headed to the elevator instead. I found Calixto in the palm court, wearing a black blazer and perfectly creased slacks. He was working on a plate of ham, eggs, and potatoes.

"I'll have what he's having," I said when a waitress arrived. "And coffee."

"What are your plans for the day, *querida?* You should rest upstairs. I like to think of you being safe. At least for one day, no?"

"Uh, no," I said. "I'm going to watch Stevie's race. I'll wear the blond wig."

"And your *track* clothes?"

"I may have to pick something up."

The waitress came back with my coffee and a small pitcher of cream. The first hot sip was like a gift from heaven.

"You mean go shopping, yes? You can't go to your apartment."

I drank more coffee, then set the mug down. "I thought I might go to Violet's."

"Excellent choice." He pulled his billfold from his inside jacket pocket.

"I have a credit card," I said quickly. "You don't need to do that."

"I insist." He slid a thumb and forefinger into the wallet, withdrew a thick wad of bills, and reached over to set them before me on the white tablecloth.

Two women at a nearby table, who'd been having trouble

keeping their eyes off Calixto, became almost bug-eyed. Their gaze flitted from him to the money, then to me.

"Oh, great," I said, "Now those ladies think I'm a call girl."

He glanced at the women and smiled. "You do look as if you were ridden hard and put away wet."

"Thanks a lot. You'll *pay* for that."

"I certainly hope so."

This man was going to drive me crazy.

25

With eight hundred dollars in my wallet, I took a cab from the Adelphi to the rental on Union. I scanned the avenue, but didn't see any bad guys sitting in parked cars or loitering on the street.

Still, I paid the cabby quickly, scrambled into my Mini, and put the pedal to the metal, keeping an eye in my rearview mirror to make sure no one was tailing me.

I drove to Violet's boutique, where I purchased a short white cotton dress, a pair of white and gold sandals, and a little gold bag to use instead of my battered tote. The boutique had some exquisite lace bras and panties in assorted animal prints, so I bought those, too, along with a pair of designer sunglasses. Amazing how fast you can whip through eight hundred bucks.

It occurred to me Joan would approve of my selections, which reminded me I needed to call her. But after the stress of Lake Desolation, I decided to give myself a day off.

Then I remembered I'd left her in a pretty bad way, dumping the information about Rich's questionable deal with Savarine the way I'd done. What if something new had happened to upset her and she'd tried to reach me? *Am I starting to care about her?*

At any rate, she couldn't reach me on my cell, currently in Calixto's possession. Though he'd said he'd bring it to the races, I was anxious about waiting that long to call her. I left the boutique with my purchases folded in lavender tissue inside a purple shopping bag and headed back to the Adelphi. Once in the room, I grabbed the ivory-colored phone, designed to look like a model from the previous century.

I dialed Joan's number and got her voicemail. When the leave-a-message indicator beeped, I said, "Joan, I left my cell at the track, but will have it later this afternoon, if you need to reach me. I hope you and Rich are okay. I'll call again."

Since Stevie's race didn't run until four, I crawled back into bed, sank into a quiet and dreamless sleep, and didn't wake up until one. I ordered a sandwich from room service and almost corrected the man on the phone when he said, "Will there be anything else, Mrs. Coyune?"

I'd forgotten Calixto had registered us as husband and wife, a plan to thwart predatory Pizuttis who might be on the hunt for Fay Mason, Kate O'Brien, or Fia McKee.

I took a hot shower before the food arrived, and after eating, I lay on the gold coverlet in my new animal print underwear watching a rerun of *Burn Notice*. I could get used to this. Not the Mrs. Coyune part, of course. But the pleasant benefits that came with money.

I left the hotel at three, in my blond wig, white dress, and new sandals, reaching the paddock as Becky Joe was leading Bionic in. After buying a program, I stood well back from the rail, relying on my disguise to hide me. I used the program to partially cover my face. Even so, I started with alarm when Mars and Rico Pizutti entered the paddock. Why wasn't Rico in jail?

What a pair. Mars, as usual, resembled a rooster, and Rico, a third-rate actor impersonating Marlon Brando in *The Godfather*. Why did he even show up? He knew his scam was broken. Did he plan to offer Stevie a bribe?

I'd lay money the pair had hoped to take Bionic out of the race, but track stewards frown on late scratches, and Mars knew he was already under a microscope. It bugged me to know Bionic would likely win the race, and those two pricks would still receive the purse money. But they'd lose the big payoff they'd planned with trainer Sefino. *Serve the assholes right.*

Inside the paddock, Sefino's horse, Stay the Course, had arrived and was prancing behind Bionic. The new horse was a chubby little guy, and I could see why his odds were long. Aside from being overweight, his legs were so short it was unlikely he had much stride. His past performances indicated he was in over his head. What he needed was a teenage girl to ride him in amateur shows, adore him, and feed him bags of carrots.

Ahead of Stay the Course, Bionic's muscles rippled with health and strength. The veins popped out on his skin as his heart rate increased with excitement and anticipation. He *knew* what was coming.

Stevie strode in with the other jockeys, and I felt like cheering. The shadow of fear had left his face. He looked positively jaunty. Mars and Rico scowled at him in unison.

A moment later, the paddock judge called for "riders up," and when Mars gave Stevie a lift onto Bionic, Rico's hand rose like a claw and grabbed at Stevie's knee. The old mobster's mouth was twisted, his expression threatening. He said something to Stevie, and Stevie gave him the finger and laughed. Becky Joe, grinning like a Cheshire cat, led him and Bionic from the paddock. Still grinning, she handed them over to their pony escort who ushered them out of sight under the grandstand.

I knew Calixto was watching events unfold on the monitor in the racing office. Earlier at breakfast, he'd said he planned to remind the stewards and Stevie about the planned scam with Stay the Course. Though this last warning was probably unnecessary, there was still a chance Stay the Course's jockey carried an electrical device. He could fire his horse up like a rocket and achieve blastoff down the stretch.

I figured Rico and his mob buddies had laid down a ton of money on overseas bets the day before. But with Stevie riding to win, they stood to lose it all. I wanted to march over, point a finger at them, and laugh. I settled for imagining it, and failed to stop the resulting grin.

When the horses disappeared in the tunnel, I walked through the grandstand, came out trackside, and watched as they paraded before me. Some of them pranced sideways, their heads turned to stare apprehensively at the metal gate that loomed over them at the finish line.

Two big tractors, engines running, were on the track. One was hitched to the starting gate and would whip the metal contraption out of the way before the horses came back around. Racetracks usually keep a second tractor nearby, in case the first one stalls. A metal gate blocking the finish line is not conducive to successful racing.

The race would run a mile-and-an-eighth, the exact circumference of Saratoga's dirt track. Once the horses warmed up, loaded into the gate, and burst free, one time around would do it.

The crowd on the track apron cut off some of my view, but I was able to see Stevie and Bionic on the huge video board that stood in the infield. When the horses began to load, my heart beat faster. I had to remind myself to breathe.

On the loudspeakers, Larry Collmus took the call. "Stay the Course balks slightly at the gate. And now he's in. Bionic goes in, and we are waiting on Jenny's Boy."

There was silence for a moment, then some jockeys yelled, "No, no, no," when their horses thrashed in the metal stalls. Then silence.

A loud clang as the metal doors flew open, the shrill sound of the bell, the roar of the crowd as the horses exploded from the gate.

"And Jenny's Boy goes for the early lead with Stay the Course running second. On the inside, Paisley Tie runs third, with Running Fool just to his outside in fourth. Behind these, Bionic sits comfortably in fifth, with Bravery just to his inside, running sixth."

I tuned Larry out, watching Stevie on the video board. He sat chilly, waiting for the race to unfold. I'd bet he had his eye on Stay the Course's rider. *I* would if I were riding that race.

The field was already through the first turn, entering the backstretch. Paisley Tie was starting to move and drew even with Stay the Course. Stevie let Bionic out a notch, and his colt's stride lengthened.

"Into the far turn now," Collmus cried, "Jenny's Boy starts to falter. Paisley Tie goes by that one and draws even with Stay the Course. Bravery is making a move, and Bionic is flying on the outside. And oh! Stay the Course makes a *huge* move, surging to the lead as the field reaches the top of the stretch!"

Damn it. The rider had zapped Stay the Course. Stevie went for his whip.

"Stay the Course is opening up. Bravery passes a tiring Paisley Tie. Bionic is *coming*. Stay the Course has the lead with a furlong to go. Bionic passes Bravery, and takes aim on the leader! Just strides to the wire! Stay the Course is *not* staying! Bionic is coming, and it's Bionic with Bravery second, Paisley Tie third, and Stay the Course fading to fourth!"

I had to stop myself from running out on the track to greet Stevie when he rode Bionic back. The scam had totally failed! I wanted to scream and jump up and down. Instead, I stood still, like I had no particular interest in what had just happened, like I was just a blond bimbette with a nice wardrobe. Undercover work can be *so* restraining.

Out on the track an official's car whizzed past and I spotted Agent Turner inside with a track security guard and a man in a business suit. The car stopped near the sixteenth pole and the men scrambled out. Striding forward, they stared down at the dirt as if looking for something. The guard took three fast steps, leaned over, and picked up a small object. Grinning, he held it in the air like a trophy. Though I couldn't make it out, it had to be the zapper.

No doubt, the stewards had been on the alert, had already reviewed the race on tape, and probably seen the jockey toss the evidence. They had him on film. He was in big trouble, and I hoped he'd rat on the rest of the scumbags. Get them all ruled off.

Stevie rode Bionic to the winner's circle, and I wanted to be in there with him. His win photo should be placed in the dictionary next to the word "triumphant."

But I'd seen enough, and didn't want to risk hanging around just to get my phone back from Calixto. I decided the smart thing was to leave before the last two races and the inevitable traffic.

Driving away from the grandstand my euphoria ebbed. As I navigated the streets leading back to the Adelphi, the bright colors of the shops on Broadway seemed to fade. Maybe it was stress about Joan or the murder at her home. Worrying if I should contact Detective Clark to see if there was news.

And what had happened to Julissa? I could still picture her

look of defeat as she walked back to Onandi and his Rastafarian sidekick the night of the murder. Once again, I wondered why so many good women end up in the hands of bad men.

Thoughts like these were not helping my mood, but I couldn't seem to stop its descent. In an effort to lighten up and get with it, I turned on the radio. Except, I landed on an oldies station with Gordon Lightfoot singing "The Wreck of the Edmund Fitzgerald." I snapped the radio off, feeling cold and adrift.

Lake Desolation was still with me.

26

When I entered my room at the Adelphi, a vase filled with red roses stood on the gilded table in the sitting room. A small card tucked into the fragrant blooms read, "For Leona. Calixto."

My fingers stretched to touch the velvety texture of the rose petals. I breathed in their sweet scent, and the darkness of Lake Desolation began to break up and drift away. It was time to live in the present.

Prowling around the suite, I saw the bed was made, and two clean robes hung in the bathroom along with fresh towels. The French doors to the bedroom balcony, which I'd closed that morning, had been reopened, and the air that drifted in had a faint smell of bread and chocolate from the bakery next to the hotel.

Using the room phone, I dialed Joan's number, and this time she answered.

"Fia," she said, "I've been trying to reach you." Her voice sounded strained.

"Are you all right?"

"No, I'm not. I'm really worried. I feel like something bad's going to happen."

"Are you at home?" She didn't answer right away and my anxiety deepened. "Tell me where you are, Joan. I can drive to your house right now, or meet you somewhere. *Talk* to me."

"No." Her voice sounded urgent. "Rich has someone here. I don't want you to come now!"

"Then when?"

"Tomorrow, Fia." She paused a moment. "Do you know where the Racing Hall of Fame is?"

"Yes."

"Can you meet me in the lobby there at nine tomorrow morning? Wait, you'll still be at work. I—"

"I won't be at work, Joan. I'll be at the Hall of Fame, at nine."

"Thank you. I have to go," she whispered. "Someone's coming."

She disconnected, and as I set the ivory receiver back in its cradle, I realized the fear I'd heard in her voice had left me white-knuckling the hard plastic gripped in my hand. So much for a day off from stress. I was about to try to reach Detective Clark, when the phone rang. I grabbed it.

"Joan?"

"No. It is Calixto. You sound upset."

I explained about the abrupt conversation with Joan.

"So, you will see her in the morning, and there is nothing you can do about it now, correct?"

"No," I said.

"Good. Then you should have an early dinner with me. And a drink."

"Yes," I said. "That is *exactly* what I need."

"*Muy bueno.* I am in the lobby."

"Five minutes," I said, before heading to the bathroom, where I fluffed my blond wig, reapplied lipstick, and sprayed on a light touch of perfume.

When the elevator arrived in the lobby, the door slid open to reveal Calixto, wearing a black linen suit, his pants' cuffs draped perfectly over polished leather shoes. A square of red silk gleamed from his breast pocket. At his wrists, the gold of his double-C cuff links winked from beneath the sleeves of his jacket.

I was blindsided by the heat that flashed through me. For a moment, I stared at his strong cheekbones, his thick lashes. Those damn lips. The growing warmth inside me slid south. I hoped I wasn't blushing.

The corners of his mouth twitched ever so slightly. "*Querida,* let us have a drink at the bar and decide where to dine, yes?"

"Sure," I said, surprised my voice sounded normal.

We sat in red damask chairs in the lobby bar, and ordered drinks. The atmosphere seemed almost magical, but then Calixto got right down to business, and it broke the spell.

"You have stirred up a swarm of hornets. Our friend, Meloy, speaks of fierce activity and anger among the Pizuttis. It might be amusing to visit their nest."

"*Why?*" Was he crazy? "How do you propose to do that?"

"Have dinner at Zutti's Café."

Our waiter came back with our drinks, and leaning forward, I clutched my glass of vodka and took a sip.

"You're *kidding.*"

He spread both palms in a classic Latin shrug. "You are disguised, obviously rested, and what better time to observe the enemy than when they are distracted?"

He'd turned into a cop. Suddenly on the job and more interested in the Pizutti family than me. The realization was like a cold shower. I would never know where I stood with this man. I opened my mouth, closed it, and took another sip of liquor.

"So, *querida,* are you game?"

"Of course."

We finished our drinks, left the hotel in fading daylight, and walked along Broadway to the green awning of Zutti's Café. Inside, the same dark-haired maître d' greeted us and led us past the refrigerated cases filled with pastries, cheesecakes, and chocolate concoctions layered with whipped cream. This time, they didn't appeal to me.

The high heels of my gold sandals clicked on the glossy wood floors as we were led to the same table, set with a starched white cloth and a vase of fresh-cut flowers. Like before, Calixto ignored the chair on the opposite side of the table and slid onto the upholstered banquette, close enough that I felt the heat of his thigh near mine.

While he ordered wine, I glanced around the restaurant and then to the back, where the latticed screen partially hid the table where I'd seen Rico with Alberto Rizelli the last time we'd come.

I grew quiet. Rico was hunched over the table, smoking a cigar. I felt my lips compress. "Why isn't Rico Pizutti in jail? Please, at least tell me that Alberto Rizelli is behind bars?"

Calixto's gaze sought the secluded table where Rico, who remained as free as a bird, was polluting the atmosphere with his smoke.

"Yes, *querida.* Meloy told me they picked up Rizelli today. The FBI has him on tape telling Tony Rizelli to get rid of you.

They have taped conversations between him and Tony about abducting Lila."

"The FBI had their phones bugged?"

"Yes, of course. Which reminds me . . ." He reached into his pocket, withdrew my cell, and placed it next to me.

I was glad to see it. After dropping the phone into my gold bag, I turned back to him. "So Rizelli's finished?"

"Yes. He has violated his parole, broken many federal laws. He will be imprisoned for life."

"Good. But why is Rico free? He was at the races today. *Look* at him back there, drinking wine and enjoying a cigar."

"Unfortunately, the FBI did not catch Rico with their phone taps. He is very clever, and now, Alberto will not give him up."

"Too bad the FBI didn't have that table bugged," I said, staring at Rico. I was not surprised that a mobster like Alberto Rizelli would not give up a family member. We were both silent a moment. Calixto's steady gaze on me was slightly unnerving, and I cast about for something to say.

"What about the jock today that used the buzzer on Stay the Course? No way he can slide out of this one. *Right?*"

"Absolutely not. And after he was caught, the rider told track officials that the trainer, Sefino, paid him to do it. But though Sefino is in deep trouble with the racing commission, he refuses to admit any connection to Mars or Rico. The man has a family and is not a fool."

"You're saying, he's willing to go to jail for a Pizutti so that he and his family won't be murdered?"

"Exactly. And his family will be taken care of financially."

"Why am I not surprised?" My stomach growled, and I wondered how I still had an appetite after talking about these people and the lives they lived, and what Rico had tried to do to me. But I was alive, and I was hungry.

Our waiter arrived with a bottle of red. After Calixto tested it, I took a sip. Elegant, earthy, and full-bodied. We ordered poached lobster and salad, as another server placed Italian bread and a dish of olive oil on our table. I broke off a piece, dipped it, and bit into the warm flaky crust. I was not disappointed.

Though the wine was excellent, I sipped slowly, determined not to drink too much. Chugging wine with a man as electric as Calixto was a good way to get scorched.

"So, who is left in this gang of mobsters?" I asked.

"There are four or five of them up here." He stared toward the kitchen. "It would appear a new one has arrived. If you look now, you will see him."

I glanced past Rico and his cigar. The swinging door was open, as a waiter, carrying a large tray of dishes, followed in the wake of a busboy with a pitcher of ice water. Behind them, I saw a thin, older man in a sleeveless T-shirt. He had ropy muscles on long, powerful-looking arms.

"Who is that?" I asked, not liking the man's hard face or the long jagged scar that disfigured his neck.

"Gio Rizelli. He was an enforcer for Alberto back in New York."

"He looks like he still is." The door swung shut and it was fine with me I could no longer see him. "I wonder why he came to Saratoga. You'd think they were under a bright enough spotlight they wouldn't bring anyone new into town." I paused a minute and an idea surfaced. "Maybe he's been here a few days," I said. "Maybe he's the guy who helped Tony abduct Lila?"

"He could be," Calixto said. "The man was wearing a turtleneck. No one would have seen the scar on his neck."

We were silent a moment, thinking about Gio. Then Calixto said, "I wonder who else is back there?"

Right on cue, the kitchen door swung open again and Gio

Rizelli and another man, also dressed as kitchen help, stepped out. I grabbed my bag, held it up as if rummaging for something. I lifted my phone, just enough to snap pictures, as Gio leaned over the table and spoke to Rico. The third man gestured excitedly with one arm. Rico rose from his chair, pointed his cigar at them and herded the two men into the kitchen. The door swung shut.

"Got 'em!" I said, placing my bag back on the banquette. "Hopefully Lila can identify him."

"If he's the one," Calixto said. But he raised his glass to me. "A beautiful woman is a dangerous thing."

"And so were those guys. Did you recognize the newest one?"

"No. But send the pictures to me, and I will forward them to Meloy. If he doesn't know, he will find out."

"No doubt," I said as our waiter brought dinner.

The meal was excellent, but I stiffened halfway through when Al Savarine walked into Zutti's. He stood near the front door, talking to the maître d'.

"Interesting," I said, "that the owner of Ziggy Stardust and the questionable hedge fund is here. He appears to be dining alone."

"I don't think he's here to dine," Calixto said.

The maître d' left Savarine up front, passing by our table quickly. As he went through the swinging door to the kitchen, I looked, but didn't see Rico.

"It appears," Calixto said with an amused glint in his eye, "that the owner of a hedge fund is searching for a member of the mob."

I nodded, realizing I'd been so distracted by Stevie and Lila, and the Pizuttis' role in their torment, I'd stopped concentrating on the hedge fund as Gunny had ordered me to do. I hadn't focused on the murder at my mother's house, either. Not the way I should have.

My thoughts slid back to the night at Joan's house. Closing my eyes a moment, I let my memory drift through that evening. I'd seen Joan in the kitchen, the Rastafarian, Onandi, Percy, and Rich. Something clicked into place.

"I *heard* him on the phone!"

"What are you talking about? Heard who?"

"Matt Percy. That night, before he was murdered. He was talking to the *FBI*. He had something he wanted to tell them. Said he was trying to do the right thing. Whoever he was talking to, insisted he come into the office the next day, and Percy wasn't happy about it. Of course . . . he never made it."

I couldn't suppress the image of Percy's slit throat. The red spatter on the wall, his blood pooling slowly down the drain. I had to force myself to breathe.

"Fia, what is it?"

I inhaled once more and was able to continue. "Did Meloy ever say what that was about?"

A frown crossed Calixto's face. "No. I don't believe Percy told them why he was concerned. Only that it was something about the hedge fund. Something he didn't dare discuss on the phone or write in an e-mail."

"But Rich bought into that fund. Isn't it possible that Percy provided investment money, too? Brian and I couldn't find any connection between Percy and the hedge fund. But it could have been hidden."

"Go on."

"And if Percy bought in as a silent partner, he had access to information, maybe even finding something dirty. Isn't it possible that whatever Percy knew, Rich knows?"

Calixto stared at me. "*Sí, es posible.*"

I paused for a small sip of wine, glad he'd chosen to sit so close to me. We could talk quietly, not be overheard. Besides, he made me feel safe.

"Something was going on at Joan's earlier this evening. Someone was there that made her afraid, and when I see her tomorrow I'm going to try and find out who. And why."

"No more risks, Fia."

"Who? *Me?*"

Calixto's eyes narrowed, and I thought I was about to receive a lecture. Before he could speak, the kitchen door swung open and the maître d' reappeared, motioning for Savarine to approach. He did, moving quickly through the restaurant. As he passed by us, he still looked like a thug to me. But now, worry lines tightened his narrow face and lips, making his overbite seem more pronounced.

"The man is wearing twelve-hundred-dollar shoes," Calixto said.

"Only you would know that."

The slightest twitch appeared on Calixto's lips. Whatever his thoughts, they were interrupted when Rico emerged from the kitchen and Savarine stepped behind the latticework to join him at the table. They both sat, and the maître d' spoke to a busboy before returning to his station.

The busboy disappeared into the kitchen before coming back with an empty bus cart covered by a white tablecloth. He parked it on our side of the screen, making Rico's table harder to see.

I slid the chain of my little gold bag over my wrist, put my palms on the table, and stood, crab-stepping to get out of the confined area. "I'm going to the ladies' room."

"More likely, you are up to no good. *Recuerde,* Fia, no risks."

"Of course not. Would *I* take a risk?"

27

The restrooms at Zutti's Café were located at the back of the restaurant, down a hallway that opened a few feet to the left of where the busboy had parked his cart. Rico's cigar smoke curled through the lattice and drifted into the room as I headed toward him. I could hear his low voice and Savarine's, but not what they were saying.

I walked to the back, stumbling slightly as if I was a bit tipsy. When I reached the entrance to the hallway, I stopped, blinking as if my eyes were bothering me. I lifted a finger to one eye and touched my lower lid.

"Stupid contact lens," I said, dropping to my knees in the direction of the bus cart and searching the wood floor as if looking for a lost lens. Scooting to the cart, I slid my phone, already set to record, under the cloth.

Listening, I heard Savarine say, "I need your help, Rico. I had no idea—"

"Stop!" Rico's voice. Savarine had his back to me, but Rico had seen me before I disappeared behind the cart.

"Found it!" I said, rising to my feet with a goofy smile, before heading for the ladies' room, my hand closed around an imaginary contact lens. For good measure, I stumbled again and said, "Stupid shoes."

When I returned to Calixto, he looked like he wanted to strangle me. "How do you propose to reclaim your phone this time, *leona*?"

No flies on Calixto. "When we're ready to leave, a last drunken trip to the ladies' should do it," I said, ignoring his irritation. "They shouldn't leave those bus carts around where people can stumble over them."

"Then you might as well play your part." He took my full glass and slid his empty one before me, making it look like I'd already drained a glass. His hands moved so deftly, he could have been a magician.

He signaled our waiter, and my new glass was quickly filled. I grinned foolishly at the server and took a big sip. By now, he and the rest of the Zutti's staff surely had pegged me as a lush.

With an occasional sidelong glance, I kept watch on Rico's table. Savarine was leaning toward the mobster. The bus cart hid his lower body, but the muscles of his neck and shoulders appeared bunched with tension. After about ten minutes, he threw one hand in the air as if frustrated, then slammed it on the table. He stood abruptly, bursting from behind the lattice, before turning back to Rico, his words just loud enough to hear.

"If I go down, you go with me, Pizutti!"

He strode past us, his hands clenched into fists, his overhanging front teeth pressed hard into his lower lip. Behind the screen, Rico tapped a number into his phone. A moment later he stood and disappeared into the kitchen.

"Showtime," I said, scrambling off the banquette, moving quickly, but unsteadily, toward the ladies' room. Moments later I stumbled wildly and dropped my bag on the floor by the bus cart. Sinking to my knees, I giggled and leaned toward the bag, managing to knock it under the cart. I crawled forward, slid my hand under the cart, and groped until I found my phone and slipped it inside my bag. Clutching the bag, and standing slowly, I straightened my dress.

"*Sorry*," I said to an appalled waiter and the people who stared from a nearby table. "Little too much vino." Giggling once more, I disappeared into the ladies' room.

When I returned to Calixto, he couldn't help himself. He was grinning. "You are a real . . . *cómo se dice?* Oh, yes, piece of work. You are a real piece of work, Fia."

"I am, aren't I? Can we get out of here? I want to get to the hotel and play this recording."

We left the café, and when we stepped into the dark street, a sudden chill hit me. I began walking quickly down the sidewalk toward the Adelphi.

Calixto put a hand on my arm. "I am as anxious as you to hear what they said. But short of running like maniacs to the hotel, we have to wait a while longer. Remember, you've had too much to drink, and," he said, releasing his hold on my arm, "we should maintain the leisurely pace of lovers."

Did he have to use that word? It was unnerving. I swallowed my impatience, and zeroed in on another question. "These additional mobsters coming to town makes you believe something's up, doesn't it?"

"Yes, *pequeña leona*, it does." He surprised me then by closing his warm hand over mine. He stopped walking. "You are chilled." He slid his jacket off and put it around my shoulders.

It was filled with his heat and his scent. I pulled it close around me, and was suddenly more apprehensive about being alone with him at the hotel than the discussion that had taken place between Rico and Savarine.

When we entered the foyer of our suite, I caught sight of myself in the mirror, almost startled to see I was still wearing my wig. Slipping into the bathroom, I removed it and tousled my short hair, careful not to touch my ear. I looked so different from the blond bombshell I'd played all evening. The wig's removal left me feeling more vulnerable, but clean and authentic.

Calixto was sitting on the parlor's gold and beige couch. I settled next to him, put the phone on speaker, and fingered the keys to bring up the recording.

"You ready to hear this?" I asked. Glancing at him, I almost flinched from the intensity in his eyes.

"I like you better without the wig." He dropped his gaze to the phone I'd placed on the coffee table before us. "Yes, I am ready."

I hit the Play button and Savarine's voice filled the room.

"You had to have known about this guy and the money behind him. I feel like you've gotten me in bed with the worst kind of criminal."

"You came to me, Savarine. You aren't stupid. You know the kind of connections I have."

"I need your help, Rico. I had no idea—"

"Stop!"

Rico's voice, when he'd seen me disappear behind the cart.

There was a moment of silence, the only noise the background clatter of the restaurant. Then we heard my voice. *"Found it!"* followed by more silence, then, *"Stupid shoes."*

"Yes," Calixto muttered, while we waited for Rico and Savarine to continue. "A true piece of work."

Rico spoke. *"You guys are all alike. You want the money, but you don't want the dirt. Or maybe you're simply a fool."*

"I am not a fool." Savarine's sounded furious. *"But I didn't expect to be threatened by the business partner you set me up with. The stuff he's doing is going to bring this whole thing down on us!"*

"There is no us. You walked into this with your eyes open. I got nothing to do with it."

"Rico, please, this guy has to be stopped. I need your protection. I can't control him!"

"And you think I can?" There was silence for a moment, then Rico said, *"For the sake of my father and the friendship he shared with yours, I'll think about it."*

More silence, and the sound of ice rattling in a glass, as if one of them was drinking. Probably Savarine. For courage.

"What should I do now?" he finally asked.

"Give me a minute. Let me think."

It seemed like Rico was dragging it out, enjoying Savarine's discomfort through the long silences. Finally, he continued. *"Tell you what. I'll get back to you on this. It's complicated."*

I heard an exasperated sound, then Savarine's hand slamming the table, his chair scraping the wood floor, his footsteps, and finally, *"If I go down, you go with me, Pizutti!"*

Calixto and I exchanged a look. We waited, hoping to hear the phone call Rico had made afterward, but it must have been a text. There were no words. Then we heard him leave the table, and a sudden clatter from the kitchen as the door swung open for his exit.

Leaning forward, I picked up the phone, turned it off, and asked the obvious question. "Who's Savarine afraid of?"

Calixto stared at the floor as if it might hold the answer. "I don't know, but I suspect it's a person or group who fronted the hedge fund money."

"He seemed to be talking about one person, a partner. Could it be *Rich*? Is that why Joan's afraid?"

Calixto didn't answer. We were silent a minute as we thought about Savarine's conversation with Rico.

"Brian and I both researched that fund," I said. "On paper, it appears to have been formed by a number of individual investors. There was no indication of one person or entity fronting the initial funds. I asked you about Rich because he's the only one close to the role of single investor." I grew silent.

It seemed more likely that Savarine was afraid of someone else in the mob. Someone younger, more powerful than Rico. Maybe someone operating in New York?

Next to me, Calixto's focus was internal, his eyes hooded. He exhaled slowly, as if coming back from far away. Turning, he stared at me with an intensity that sent heat to my core. I straightened, shifted away from him. I needed to think through Savarine's conversation, not get sucked in by this man's dark eyes.

"Except," I said, talking fast, "the fund is worth many millions. Rich's contribution was two hundred thousand. That wouldn't provide him with the kind of controlling interest Savarine was talking about. Right?"

"Unlikely," he said. "Though Rich does not strike me as a good man, he doesn't seem the type to incite the fear we heard in Savarine's voice. There is someone else. Someone evil."

The chill that shot through me had nothing to do with desire. "That's what I think, too," I said, my voice barely above a whisper.

Calixto's jacket lay on the couch between us. I picked it up, slid it back over my shoulders, and stood. Lithe as a panther, Calixto rose and stood next to me. I glanced outside the French doors of the balcony. We had never closed them. The night air flowing inside hinted of places farther north.

Truth be told, I could use a shot of cold air. I stepped outside. He followed, standing close as we looked at the streetlights on Broadway and the people and cars passing below.

With a purr of barely contained power, a red Maserati flashed past beneath us. "That could be Joan," I said.

"Don't fret about Joan. You will see her in the morning. Hopefully find out what troubles her, and maybe Savarine as well. I will talk to Meloy. Between the three of us, we may learn something useful. But for now, we should let it go, yes?"

I nodded. "Sometimes, when I do that, the answer floats to the surface."

He closed his hand over mine. "We make a good team, Fia."

"Yes, we do." I smiled, but looking up I got lost in his steady, insistent gaze. Its intensity suggested he was not thinking about Joan, Meloy, or Percy's murder.

Turning to face me, he grasped the lapels of his jacket that wrapped around my shoulders. Slowly, he pulled me against his chest. His muscular thighs were warm and hard against mine, but not as hot as the growing erection that pressed against me.

"Oh, God," I mumbled, "I'm in *so* much trouble."

"*Sí, pequeña leona. Es verdad.*" He almost laughed, then he kissed me, the electricity instant, overwhelming.

I don't remember how we got to the edge of the bed, his jacket on the floor, the buttons on my white dress undone, the sheen of my silk lingerie reflecting in the glow of his eyes. *What am I doing?* With a ragged breath, I put my hands on his shoulders, stopping him.

"You told me before, we should stay at the Adelphi one night. But only as part of our romance cover. Is that what this is?"

"No, Fia, that is not what this is. But if you don't want this, tell me. Unless I stop now, the decision will no longer be yours."

I let out a breath I didn't realize I'd been holding. My hands dropped from his shoulders and slid down the hard muscles of his chest and stomach. When had his shirt been unbuttoned? Had I done that?

I gasped as his desire and physical strength engulfed me. Yet, this was more than just desire. A sweet and powerful emotional connection drew me to him, and I'd bet my life he felt it too.

My control slipped away as his strong hands, determined fingers, and knowing tongue sparked an electrical connection between every hot spot on my body, exploding me over the edge, leaving me astonished, sated, and breathless. His body covered mine. He thrust inside me, rough, hard, and relentless, yet I'd never felt safer in my life. I loved that his long pent-up desire overwhelmed him as much as it did me. That his eyes glazed over. That he called my name.

He collapsed next to me, and happier than anyone has a right to be, I lay next to him in a kind of afterglow, the night air drifting in and cooling my heated body.

Time passed. He propped himself on one elbow, watching me. "You know, *leona*, I have wanted you since that first moment I saw you at Gulfstream."

My finger traced the ragged scar where a bullet had entered his shoulder months earlier in Florida. He'd saved my life that night. I rose up and gently kissed the jagged circle of flesh.

"And what now?" I asked.

"*Now?* I want you more than ever." His hands closed over my wrists, and pinned them down on either side of my head as he shifted over me. Rigid, he slid inside me again. My legs locked around his hips, straining to pull him closer. Wild and ferocious, his love carried me over the edge again.

We fell asleep in a tangled heap of legs and sheets. I woke up sometime later, when he rose to shut the French doors. The outline of his hard body against the ambient light coming from the city beyond the balcony stirred me again. But he slipped back in bed, pulled the comforter over us, and lay still. Content, I snuggled against him and drifted away.

28

Sunlight, streaming through the balcony doors, along with the rich smell of Coyune coffee, awakened me the next morning. Beneath the gold comforter, I enjoyed a long, delicious stretch.

"Good morning." Still naked, Calixto sat on the edge of the bed and handed me a steaming mug. "You are happy, yes? I would hate for you to have regrets."

"No." I grinned. "No regrets."

"*Bueno.*" He had ordered croissants and fresh fruit, and while sitting in bed we ate breakfast from the tray the hotel had sent up. Room service had added a small vase of wildflowers.

I felt like a lazy cat with a bowl of cream. But before I'd finished my second cup of coffee, he had a text from Meloy at the FBI, followed by a call from Gunny at the TRPB office in Maryland. On the night table next to me, the clock ticked relentlessly toward nine, when I had to meet Joan.

I looked at the hard muscles of Calixto's abdomen as he spoke to Gunny. Oh, *hell*, I was falling in love with this man.

Get a grip, Fia. You'll be fine.

I left the bed, disappeared into the shower, and after drying off, armed myself with a fresh pair of jeans and a hoodie with deep, kangaroo pockets. I could stuff my hands inside if my fingers were seized by an uncontrollable urge to touch him.

At nine, I walked up the brick path to the Racing Hall of Fame, slowing to gaze at the statue of Seabiscuit. The almost life-size sculpture stood on a polished stone slab, and for a moment, I let my fingers touch the cool cast metal of one hoof.

The Howards had bought the future racing legend out of a *claiming* race. And they'd done it here at Saratoga. I walked on, pulled open one of the heavy glass entry doors, and stepped inside onto smooth stone tiles. Across the lobby, next to a display case of gleaming silver trophies, a woman stood with her back to me.

Keeping my voice low, I said, "Joan?"

She turned, her gaze darting about the room, restless as a housefly. She finally focused on me. Her breath rushed out, her shoulders sagged slightly.

"Fia, you came. Thank you."

"Of course I did," I said, moving closer.

She looked a little rough, her makeup applied hastily, her eyeliner wandering beyond the corner of one eye, her lipstick blotchy. Even her blond highlights seemed dull.

"Tell me what's wrong."

Again, her eyes flitted about the room. But it was so early, no one was there to worry about, except the docent who was walking toward us.

I spotted a window bench, and glancing at the approaching museum guide, I put a hand on Joan's arm. "Why don't we sit by the window so we can talk?"

The docent backed off as we settled ourselves on the wooden bench.

"Joan, what's going on?"

Her lips pressed together as her gaze skittered away from me before drifting to the floor. "It's Rich. He and that man, Savarine, are in some kind of trouble. I heard them talking."

"Okay. Tell me. "

"Something about that damn hedge fund. The one you told me Rich put two hundred thousand into."

"It's having money problems?"

"No. Money's not the problem. It sounded more like Rich and Savarine were tricked into something illegal, that Rich could go to jail!"

Somewhere inside the museum a deafening pounding erupted, accompanied by the roar of a crowd.

Joan let out a little scream.

The docent hurried over, gesturing at a nearby hall. "That's just a video playing in the contemporary racing gallery," she said. "In the exhibit room."

Joan scowled at the woman. "Does it have to be so *loud*?"

"*Most* people like it," the docent replied, her voice chilly. "It's designed to give a sense of really being at the races."

"Thank you," I said. "We were just startled." *Hell, if I'd had my gun, I might have shot someone.* I turned back to Joan as the docent retreated.

"Last night, Joan. Exactly what did they say?"

"It's more about how Rich has been acting, Fia. I told you already. He's so weird. Secretive, like he's afraid. He's *paranoid*. That's why I couldn't talk to you last night. Savarine was there.

I was walking on eggshells, trying to stay out of their way. But *I heard* them." She stopped, swallowed, and grew silent.

I didn't say anything, waiting her out.

She took a breath and finally looked at me. "They were in the library. I stood outside the door. They were talking about someone who had taken money, taken it illegally, and used it to start the fund."

"You mean like, stolen money? Cash, transfers, what?"

"I don't know! They both sounded scared to death, and Rich said they had to get out. But Savarine said it was too late. He said they were in too deep. Then he accused Rich of letting whoever this person is talk him into investing the two hundred thousand. That made Rich furious. It was awful to hear him." By now, her lips were drawn so tight, her teeth showed like a small cornered animal. I put a hand out to touch her but she shrank away from me, her words tumbling out. "Rich was yelling, 'You brought that fucker into this. I'm not going to jail!' And then they started *fighting*. I could hear them punching each other. I ran down the hall. Outside to my car. I had to *leave*."

So it was her car I'd seen on the street below our balcony. Mental note, if in danger, do not rely on Joan to watch your back.

"But you have no idea who this man is that they're so worried about?"

"No."

"Can you make a guess?"

"*No*. I told you, I don't know!" She dropped her forehead into her hands. "First that man was murdered in our home, and now this. I don't know what to do."

I stared at her. So much for money and the perfect life with the man she'd left her family for. I didn't want to feel sorry for her, but I couldn't raise the old anger to override the compassion

that flooded me. Whatever else she was, she was in trouble. I
had to help her. I rose from the bench. She stood up, facing me.

"I still have some cop friends in Baltimore," I said, ashamed,
but a little proud of how easily I lied. "I'll see if I can learn anything that will help you and Rich."

"Thank you, Fia." She hugged me. When I immediately
stiffened, she dropped her arms and stepped back. "Do you have
a gun?"

Her question reminded me of our first meeting in Saratoga,
when she'd asked me about the man I'd killed in Baltimore. When
she'd wanted to know how hard it was to kill someone.

I stared at her. "Why do you want to know if I have a gun?"

She gave me that look, the one that asked how she'd ever
produced such a stupid daughter. "For God's sake, Fia. A man
was killed. In my home. Rich is scared to death, fighting with
another man. Under the circumstances, I'd think you'd understand why I might like to have a gun around."

"I don't have one." I didn't have to lie since mine was somewhere on the bottom of Lake Desolation. But, if I'd still had my
Walther, I would have lied anyway. I trusted Joan with a gun
about as much as I trusted an armed monkey.

I told her again I'd do what I could to help. We parted a few
minutes later, and after I climbed into my Mini, it occurred to
me I had done nothing about replacing my gun. I decided to wait
until I got back to Maryland, then I sent a text to Calixto.
"Where are you?"

"At the track, Maggie's barn. Spoke to Meloy."

"On my way," I typed back.

I didn't want to wait to meet him at the hotel. If I met him
there, we'd have trouble keeping our hands off each other. At
least, I knew I would. *Stop thinking about him.*

After I parked near the East Avenue entrance, I was careful

to approach the barn from Maggie Bourne's side. I didn't need Mars spotting me. When I was close enough, I looked at the end where he usually parked his SUV, but didn't see it. Still, I used trees and a storage shed to partially hide me as I walked toward Maggie's shedrow.

By now, it was after ten, the track was closed, and it was possible Mars had gone for the morning, which suited me just fine. Glancing left and right, I stepped onto Maggie's shedrow, then poked my head in her office, where she sat at her desk studying a condition book.

Lifting her head, she smiled. "Hey, stranger, where have you been?"

"Long story," I said. "How are you, Maggie?"

"Not bad. You looking for Calixto?"

"I am."

With a mischievous smile, she said. "Turn around."

I was startled to find him standing right behind me. I think I blushed. I wanted to drink in every inch of him and fought to keep my eyes on his face. He looked at me without expression, his body language in formal mode. *How did he do that?*

"*Querida*, I'm glad you stopped by. We should talk, yes?"

Maggie rose from behind the desk. "I was just gonna take this book with me to the kitchen. Office is all yours." Without waiting for our response, she slung her leather bag over her shoulder, dropped the condition book inside, and left the office.

"Tell me," Calixto said. "Did you learn anything? What did your mother say?"

Still in formal mode. All business. I shook it off and walked around the desk to sit in Maggie's squeaky office chair. I told him about the scene Joan had described and how much the fight between Rich and Savarine had disturbed her.

"I've never seen her like this. She's always been in control.

Confident, poised. Always certain of what should and shouldn't be done. She certainly told *me* often enough."

"So," Calixto said, "she has been . . . humbled."

I stared at him. "Yes. And then," I said, spreading my palms, "she asked me if I had a *gun*."

"Watch your step with her, *querida*. A woman like her is dangerous when cornered. I've seen it in her eyes."

I'd seen it, too. "I will. But we need to find out who this man is. The one Rich and Savarine were talking about. He's . . . he's the puppet master."

A flicker in the doorway caught my attention. The calico stable cat from Mars's shedrow stood on the threshold, her white whiskers brilliant in a shaft of late-morning sun. She stretched, than seated herself and began to wash a front paw. She probably preferred Maggie's side of the barn. I sure did.

I turned from the cat to Calixto. "You've seen Meloy. Did he tell you anything?"

"Only that when Percy first called him, he sounded as apprehensive as Rich and Savarine. We know Percy was worried about the fund. About where some of the money was coming from. About where it was going. But Percy was planning to give Meloy names and dates, and most important, a document he said Meloy would find *very* interesting."

"A document? Have they—"

"No," he said. "They searched Percy's car and the house he rented for the summer. They have found nothing."

I'd been twirling a pencil I'd grabbed off Maggie's desk. I stopped, my fingers gripping the yellow wood.

"And now," I said, "the document is missing, and he's dead. He was going to blow the whistle, so someone killed him." His death had been so violent.

Calixto nodded. "That is what Meloy thinks, but unfortunately, he doesn't know any more than we do. The fund has been examined over and over again. They've followed the money through every database, through every computer program, and found nothing. Whoever's running this thing hid his tracks well."

I'd been gripping the pencil too hard. I let it drop to the desk and rubbed my sore fingers. Somewhere down the shedrow a horse whinnied, and in the distance another one answered his call. I could hear salsa music and someone singing in Spanish from the barn across the way. I missed the track. When the morning chores were done, and the horses bedded down, the place could truly soothe my soul. I pulled my thoughts to the present.

"Calixto, do you think another mobster, maybe one from New York, is behind all this? The way Savarine begged Rico to rescue him from this man I think of as the puppet master. It's got to be someone Rico has influence over."

"That sounds reasonable."

But there was something about the tone of Calixto's voice. "But you don't think so, do you?"

"Fia, I don't know. Meloy suspects a money-laundering operation is behind this and that would suggest Mafia involvement. But they are not the only criminals."

Sudden memories of the men who tried to kill me in Florida made me shudder. They had wanted me dead, had planned a horrible ending for me. No, mobsters were not the only criminals. Not by a long shot.

"But," Calixto said, "the Mafia is probably our best bet."

Damn, we knew so little. Between Calixto, Meloy, and myself, we should run for champion know-nothings. We'd probably win.

Calixto's phone pinged. He answered, listened, and said, "Gunny, yes."

They started talking. I stood, pointed at myself, and then the door.

"Gunny, hold on a minute," Calixto said, before turning to me. "You are leaving?"

"If Mars isn't here, I want to see Becky Joe and the horses. Stevie might be over there, too." I needed a break from the maze of questions.

He nodded, turned away from me, and continued his conversation with Gunny. When I reached the door to the shedrow, the cat circled my legs like a furry little submarine. With each pass, she rubbed against my shins, her tail straight up, like a periscope. When I leaned over to pet her, she was purring so loud, the vibration almost torpedoed my hand. I picked her up and carried her down the shedrow with my nose buried in her fur.

Halfway down the aisle, despite the comforting presence of the cat, the thorny question pricked me again. *The unseen puppet master.* Who was he? Had he killed Percy?

"He must have!" I said out loud, startling the cat, who twisted her head to stare at me. "Who the hell is he?" I asked.

The cat wasn't talking.

29

As I approached the end of Maggie Bourne's shedrow, I scanned the grassy area and dirt paths beyond. A man crossing the grass near the next barn stopped me cold.

Mars? No, only a guy with the same body type, not Mars. Though his SUV was still absent, I inched slowly around the corner to his shedrow, just in case. Rounding the corner, I found the groom, Javier.

His eyes widened when he spotted me. "Fay, *cómo estás?*"

"*Muy bueno*, Javier. Good to see you." I glanced up and down the shedrow. "Mars, *está aquí?*" I said.

"No. He is not here. You are happy to know this, yes?"

"*Sí*," I said, setting the calico down in the shedrow. "It's very good to know." We exchanged a partners-in-crime palm slap. After giving me a nod, he walked to the barn hose and got busy topping off the horses' water buckets.

"Holy shit, look what the cat dragged in!" The voice belonged to Becky Joe.

As she drew close, the cat who was still at my feet, glared at the woman, lashed her tail, and stalked off.

"That cat doesn't like me."

I felt myself smiling. "Becky Joe, how are you?"

"Not as good as you," she replied. "Look at that grin on your face. When a woman looks like that, and there's a man around like Calixto, it can only mean one thing. You *slept* with him, didn't you?"

Was it that obvious? I tried to deny it, but felt my grin grow even wider.

Becky Joe shook her head. "You were just over there, weren't you?"

"I might have been," I said, feeling my cheeks flush with warmth.

"Oh, lordy. If a man like him gave *me* what he gave you, I'd light up like a Christmas tree. And honey, you look like Rockefeller Center on Christmas Eve!"

Smirking, she pointed at a long bale of hay a few yards down the shedrow. "Sit down and spill. How was he?"

"Becky Joe!"

"Oh, come on. Give an old lady a vicarious thrill."

I burst out laughing. "Becky, you're incorrigible."

"Don't I know it!"

I'd been cut off from people since I'd joined the bureau. I hadn't spoken to my two cop girlfriends since I left the Baltimore PD. Except for my mother and my niece, I'd been surrounded by men, hardly candidates for relaying life's intimate details. But I liked Becky Joe and knew she wasn't big on gossip. God knows she'd been tight-lipped about Stevie when I'd first arrived.

She settled herself on the hay bale, and I joined her, leaning my back against the old wood of the barn wall.

A little sigh escaped me. "He was . . . he was just like I'd hoped he would be."

Becky Joe groaned. "That good, huh?"

"Better." We grinned at each other.

A small breeze stirred up the smell of dust from the dirt aisle. I relaxed on the improvised bench, resting the back of my head against the wall, loving the sweet scent of hay that drifted up from the bale below.

"He's a rare one," she said, "Quiet on the surface, but still waters run deep. You'll have your hands full with that one. That's a fact."

I nodded, and we sat quietly, simply enjoying the luxury of being at the backstretch on a Saratoga morning. Though I'd re-laxed, talking about Calixto had sent a heat wave to my core. No one had ever left me breathless and so consumed with desire.

My memory drifted back to the past when my father's un-solved murder had left me filled with a burning anger and a need for revenge. To seek justice. Maybe it was the wrong reason to become a cop, but that's what had happened.

There had been a guy at Towson University where I'd stud-ied criminal justice for two years and obtained a degree. Mike had studied there, pursuing the same degree. Our romance had lasted almost two years, but when his cop uncle got him a job on the Cincinnati police force, the long-distance relationship hadn't worked for us. I hadn't been the easiest woman, anyway. I had too many issues with my father's murder and the lingering effects of Joan's abandonment.

A couple of years later, I'd become close to a cop named Ben on the Baltimore PD. That one had lasted six months, until he got shot in a domestic violence call. When he got out of the hospital, he'd changed. Without a word to me, he'd transferred up to Rising Sun, Maryland. He'd called from there, saying he needed to be where it was safer. Hell, any place was safer than West Baltimore, and I couldn't blame him. Both Mike and Ben had been good men, but I'd always known I could live without them. Now, a man like Calixto . . .

I hoped he wasn't some kind of fantasy. And then there was that nagging question—how do you ever know when a professional liar is telling the truth? I mentally brushed these thoughts away and turned to Becky Joe.

"So how are the horses? What's Ziggy Stardust up to?"

Becky Joe had fallen asleep and jerked awake. "What? Ziggy?" She rubbed her eyes a moment. "Mars is gonna enter him in the Travers."

"I figured he would, after that last work. Is he as ornery as ever at feeding time?"

"He'd like to take the handle off my rake the other day. Pulled the whole thing into the stall with him. I had to get Javier to help get it out before the damn horse killed himself!"

"That rake wrestling is dangerous," I said.

"Don't joke about it. He could've flipped that thing upright and impaled himself, or maybe put an eye out."

"You have a point," I said, mentally pushing away some of the things I'd seen go wrong on Pimlico's backstretch when I'd worked for my dad. Sometimes it just seemed if things could go wrong for a horse, they would.

I stood up and stretched. "I should visit your nags. I've missed them."

"Help yourself," Becky Joe said. "I'm gonna set here awhile."

I walked down the shedrow, stopping to see Bionic. His dappled bay coat gleamed with health, and next door to him, the gray filly, Wiggly Wabbit, pushed her head over the stall door toward me. I leaned forward until we touched noses. I blew gently in her nostrils, a sort of universal horse greeting.

"Broken any phones lately?" I asked her.

She didn't answer, just wiggled her ears at me.

"That how you got the name Wiggly Wabbit?"

She snorted and withdrew her head.

"And now for the big guy." I moved to Ziggy Stardust's stall. Since it wasn't feeding time, he was calm, even friendly, nodding his head up and down at me, letting me pet the large star on his forehead. My fingers traced the little spangles of white that cascaded down his face.

"That's some trademark you got there, Ziggy. You going to win the Travers? I bet you will." He nodded his head up and down more vigorously, making me smile. "Thanks for the tip. I'll put some money on you."

At the last stall, I stroked Dodger's neck, before deciding I'd counted on Mars's absence long enough. He could show up any minute. As I started to head back to the other side, I heard Stevie's voice.

"Hey, Fay, wait up."

I turned to see his skinny form hustling past Becky Joe, who'd fallen asleep again on her hay bale.

"Are you still working for Mars?" I asked. I'd hoped he'd find a job with another trainer. My wish must have shown on my face.

"It's not so bad," he said.

He stood before me, his eyes about level with my nose. I'd almost forgotten how small he was. It was one of the things that had made me even angrier when Rico had been so brutal with him.

"Look," he said, "it was Alberto and Tony Rizelli who grabbed Lila. Not Mars. And Rico leaned really hard on Mars to get me to help with that betting scam. Alberto's out of the picture, in jail, and I'm *telling* you, Mars didn't want any part of it. He's been good to me."

If he was determined to believe that, there was no point in arguing with him. I'd learned to keep quiet when someone locks themselves in the denial cage. Stevie held the key. I hoped one day he'd use it.

"At least," I said, "he's got some good horses, and you've done well riding them."

"That's what I'm saying. I made money on Bionic and Wabbit. People *noticed* me."

"Yeah, they did. I think you've got a good future ahead of you, Stevie."

"Thanks."

Wabbit thrust her head into the aisle next to Stevie and he rubbed the side of her cheek. She pushed harder against his hand as if to say, "Don't stop."

"So, how's Lila?" I asked.

"Pretty good. She's seen some therapist woman a couple of times, and her nightmares aren't as bad."

I didn't say anything to that. I worried about the extent of damage done to her. None of what had happened was good, but at least the two of them were in one piece.

"We're back in our apartment at Lou's," Stevie said, "and Lila has the dog. She loves that dog. I figure we're lucky."

"You are," I said. "You riding a race anytime soon?"

"Mars has a couple shipping in to run, and I get the rides. So it's all good."

"Sure," I said. "I'd better be going." I left him there at Mars's barn, wishing I could make him see reality, but knowing in the end it was up to him.

When I reached the other side, Calixto was gone, but checking my phone I found a text asking if I'd meet him for dinner at the Brook Tavern at seven.

"Absolutely," I texted back. I was not one to pass up a free meal at a nice restaurant on Union Avenue. Especially with Calixto. I could get used to the life I'd enjoyed the last two days. No dirty chores at the track, meals out, an opulent suite at a five-star hotel. But on my drive back to the Adelphi, I got a call from Gunny, a reminder that my job with the TRPB was far from over and my life of luxury would end soon.

"You feeling okay?" he asked.

"Yeah, Gunny. I'm fine." In the background I heard a familiar sound, like dice rattling in a cup, and I knew he was taking his antacids. "Don't worry about me, Gunny, I'm tough."

"So you say. Listen, I've been talking to my contact at the FBI. You're still keeping an eye on your stepfather and Savarine, right?"

"Of course."

"Okay then. A huge deposit was made to the hedge fund this morning and the FBI is trying to trace it back through overseas shell companies. Somebody has gone to a lot of trouble to cover their tracks."

"You got that right. I want to know who it is as much as you do. I'd bet a year's paycheck this person is behind Matt Percy's death."

He was silent a moment, then, "Not necessarily. It could be anyone. You be careful. You got that?"

"Of course." We disconnected, and after finding a parking spot on a side street, I walked into the Adelphi. Three feet inside the lobby, I stopped abruptly. Talking to the hotel's concierge was a tall man with curly hair. His profile was visible, and I recognized the light cocoa skin and large hooked nose of the Jamaican, Darren Onandi.

30

Why was Onandi back in Saratoga? At the Adelphi? I drifted to a nearby couch, sat down, and pretended to search for something in my tote bag. The last time Onandi had seen me, I was at Joan's party. I'd worn makeup and was dressed to the nines, so I doubted he'd recognize me now as Joan's daughter.

So why was I afraid that he would? I glanced up from my tote. Onandi nodded at the concierge, turned, and when his small, piercing eyes swept over me, a little spider of unease crawled down my spine. He turned away, and walked through the potted palms marking the entrance to the courtyard, probably intent on a late lunch.

I abandoned the couch and made for the elevators, not wanting to be around when he returned to the lobby. He might not recognize me, but I didn't particularly want him *noticing* me, either. As soon as I was in the elevator, I called Calixto, but was sent to voicemail. I left a message.

"Onandi's here at the Adelphi. I'll be in our room on my laptop. I want to talk to Brian about digging deeper into Onandi's bank records. See you at the Brook Tavern."

I ended the call and suddenly felt like kicking myself. Joan had revealed the connection between Rich and Onandi. Why hadn't I run with it? Any momentum I'd had in that direction had stopped abruptly with my trip to Lake Desolation. Afterward I hadn't even thought about it. *Damn.*

If Onandi had invested money in Rich's start-up company way back when, maybe they still shared business interests. In retrospect, it seemed ridiculous that Onandi would have traveled from New York City to Saratoga with his entourage just to attend a garden party.

By now, the elevator had reached my floor. The doors slid open, and I stepped into the hallway that was lit by the subtle glow of antique wall sconces. Sudden movement caught my attention. Down the hall, a woman peered around the door of her hotel room, before snapping her head back inside and quickly shutting the door.

I knew that face. *Julissa.* I strode down the carpeted corridor to the door that had just closed and rapped my knuckles on it.

"Julissa, it's Fia McKee. Open up."

I was answered by silence, but I could almost feel her presence just inside. "Julissa, please, let me talk to you."

I heard a slight rustling sound, then the knob turned, and the door opened.

"*Fia?* You look different."

"I was totally dolled-up at the party," I said, staring at her face. She had a black eye. The cheek next to it was swollen and horribly bruised. Her stale sweat smelled of fear. But the hopelessness I saw in her eyes hit me the hardest.

"You have to leave," she said. "You'll get me in trouble. What do you want?"

"For starters," I said, "to get you away from the animal who did this to you."

"*No.* I've told you. I have no money. There's nowhere to go. Darren's spies are everywhere." With these last words she began to shake. She glanced up and down the hall, and the fear in her eyes made my gut contract.

"You *can't* help me," the words came in a soft wail.

"Bullshit! I can. I'm taking you out of here."

"No, if he sees me trying to leave, he will kill me. He could be on the elevator now. He could—"

"*No,*" I said. "He isn't. He just went into the dining room for lunch. About four minutes ago. I *saw* him. Come on, Julissa, this is your chance!"

A flicker of hope lit her eyes. Seeing it, I grabbed her wrist, and tried to pull her through the doorway.

She dug in her heels, resisting. "I won't make it through the lobby."

"You're not going through the lobby. I have a room about ten doors down." I held up my key card.

Seeing truly is believing. She darted across the threshold and into the hallway. Together we ran to my room, where I barely got the door unlocked, before she lunged inside. I slammed the door shut and locked it.

Restless and panting, she wandered about the suite. She finally sank onto the gold and beige upholstery of the parlor couch, her arms wrapped protectively around her stomach. She looked so thin and weak. The lustrous, curly black hair I'd so admired in Violet's boutique had grown dull, almost matted.

"When was the last time you ate?"

Lost in her own nightmarish thoughts, it took her a moment to respond. "I don't remember."

"Well, *I'm* hungry. Let's get some lunch from room service. What would you like?"

"I don't care."

"Fine, I'll order for you." I got room service on the phone and ordered a BLT for me and a New York strip, fries, and salad for Julissa.

"I tried to run," she said. "But Dajon saw me."

"Dajon?"

"The Rastafarian," she said. "Dajon told Darren, and Darren was so angry with me. You can see what he did."

Oh, I saw, all right. The *bastard*. So, the Rastafarian had a name. Dajon. What was I going to do now?

I walked from the telephone desk to the couch and sat next to Julissa. "You'll be safe here, until we can find a permanent solution for you."

She continued, almost as if I hadn't spoken. "I took some clothes to the consignment shop, got some money. I bought a bus ticket to New York, but Dajon had followed me. He took the ticket, the money. Then he called Darren." She shuddered.

"This was yesterday?" I asked.

She nodded. "I have a friend in the modeling business in the city. I thought I could hide there, get work. But look at my face now. I *hate* him." Carefully, she lowered her head into her hands, whimpering as her bruised flesh pressed into her hand. "He used to be so good to me . . ."

I so wanted to help this woman. I needed a plan. But sometimes it's the little things that help the most. Sitting next to her, smelling her, I knew she hadn't bathed in a while. Who would want to remove their clothes in a suite inhabited by Darren Onandi and a leering Rastafarian?

"Would you like to take a hot shower while we wait for room service?" I asked.

She considered it, started to shake her head, then appeared to find a bit of resolve. "You will stay here, keep the door locked?"

"I will."

"I have no clothes."

She was taller than me, but skinny through the waist and hips. "I have some stretch pants that will fit you, and you can wear one of Calixto's shirts."

The mention of Calixto startled her. She drew back, putting space between us.

"He's a good guy," I said. "He's staying here with me. He will protect you."

Her shoulders relaxed slightly, then she nodded. "Okay." She stood and headed for the shower.

By the time she came out, lunch had arrived, and after tentatively eating a few bites of steak, she begin to eat faster and faster, plowing through the crisp french fries like a starving woman. No doubt, she was starved for a lot of things—like freedom, love, and security. God only knew what Onandi had done to her sense of self-worth.

When she was finished, I insisted she lie on the bed for a while. She did, and as I expected, she went out like a light. I used the time to power up my laptop and send a secure e-mail to Brian.

Once we opened a secure link, Brian worked it so we had an audiovisual feed.

"We should do this more often," I said. "It's like having you in the room with me."

Brian's brows lifted above the top rim of his glasses. "Careful what you wish for, McKee." He blushed slightly, as if embarrassed by his words. "So, what's up?"

I explained how Onandi figured in Rich's past. "I'm sorry I

didn't tell you about it earlier, but things got crazy right after that, and to be honest, I didn't even think about it until now."

"Are you saying the daring McKee was daunted by her near-death experience?"

He was in a rare mood today. "Anyway," I said, "we didn't go back through Onandi's bank records far enough. My mother hooked up with Rich *seventeen* years ago. His company had already made him wealthy as sin. So if Onandi's bank did invest in Horizons Unlimited, it could have been twenty or more years ago."

I'd given him something to chew on. The creases around his eyes puckered as he thought. "First thing, I'll find out if Gorman's company was always called Horizons Unlimited. Then I'll track *any* business associated with him back to the first mention of Onandi or his bank. The nature of their connection might prove interesting."

"That's what I'm thinking." I remained silent a moment, and allowed my mind to drift back in time. Back to when Joan had left us for Rich. Part of me still hated the man. I remembered Joan saying how Rich was forced to make "shady moves" to get Horizons Unlimited sold. I had no doubt he was capable of shady moves and dubious associates, like . . .

I grew still as a piece of the puzzle dropped into place.

"Onandi," I said. "The hedge fund! There's a connection."

"Of course," he said, his face flushing with excitement. "That makes perfect sense." He grinned at me. "Our intrepid detective, undeterred by her dip in the dell."

"Shut up," I said. "Just find something."

"Yes, master." He disconnected, and my screen went blank.

By 5:00 P.M, I'd updated Gunny on our suspicions about Onandi's connection to the hedge fund. As I shut down the computer,

Julissa wandered into the parlor. She looked better, her almond-shaped eyes less shadowed. Even her lips looked fuller, her mouth more relaxed. Food and sleep have a tendency to restore, something I needed to remind myself sometimes.

"Fia," she said, "you've been so kind to me. Thank you."

"We girls have to stick together, right?" I said.

She smiled for the first time. Damn, she was beautiful. Then the brightness that had briefly touched her face dimmed. She folded her arms across her middle. "You should know Darren has another man up here. Someone worse than Dajon."

I didn't like the sound of that, or the way her voice rattled as she spoke of this man. "Who are you talking about?"

"Kamozey."

Why was this name familiar? I closed my eyes. It was the night when Calixto, Turner, and I had driven away from Lake Desolation. I'd been so exhausted, but even so, I'd started thinking about Percy's murder. Something had bothered me that night, leaving me with a prickle of unease, as if I'd forgotten something.

It finally came to me. At the garden party, I'd overheard Onandi threatening Dajon, with the name Kamozey. What was it Onandi had said? "You want me to tell Kamozey you screwed up?" His words had left the Rastafarian's voice weak with fear.

And there was something else. Something Onandi had said to Rich, but it still wouldn't come to me.

"I've heard that name. Who is he?"

"He is a horrible man. A killer. He makes Darren's enemies disappear."

"He's *here*? In Saratoga?"

"Yes, he came yesterday. Dajon is not a nice man, but he is a puppy next to Kamozey. Kamozey is why I risked running."

"Okay," I said, not liking the way her fear was mounting. No one knows you are here, Julissa, and Onandi didn't recognize me without the makeup and clothes. Only Calixto will know you're here. They *won't* find you. Just don't leave this room!"

She wasn't going to like me disappearing to have dinner with Calixto, but I needed to talk to him without her present. The less she knew about us going after Onandi, the safer and less worried she'd be. But when I told her I had to leave, her eyes widened with alarm.

"The restaurant's close by," I said. "I won't be gone more than an hour." I grabbed an Adelphi notepad and pen. "Here, this is my cell number. If you need me, you call me, okay?"

"All right."

I hated leaving her. She'd been through so much, but my conversation with Calixto needed to be private. "I'll bring you back some dinner. There's a bar inside that cabinet"—I waved toward an ornate marble-topped chest—"you should make yourself a drink, watch a movie or something. Relax."

Yeah, that was going to happen.

31

Just past seven that evening, I entered the Brook Tavern, a wood-frame, Victorian-era establishment on Union Avenue. Inside, polished floor planks and walls paneled in warm-toned wood glowed from the soft light of overhead lamps.

Standing in the entryway, I spotted Calixto sitting in a high-backed booth in a far corner of the dining room. One look at him and I could feel the blood rush inside me.

How could I keep reacting like this? I was thirty-two years old for God's sake. Not to mention there was an abused woman hiding in my hotel room, or that I moved beneath the oppressive weight of an unsolved murder. Either one should dampen anyone's libido. Except, they didn't.

Seeing me, he rose and waited until I reached his booth. He put one arm around me in a brief hug, then touched his lips to my cheek, letting them linger a moment too long.

"It's a big table," he said. "Sit next to me."

His side of the booth backed against an outside wall, making it unlikely we'd be overheard. I sat, careful to keep my thigh from pressing into his and quickly launched into my news that Onandi was in town. I related his suspected connection to the hedge fund, and what had happened with Julissa.

When I described her condition, his face darkened. "No woman should be treated like that."

"Maybe we can get her to New York," I said. "She has a friend there, a model. That's Julissa's world. But Onandi has her passport, and she can't get a work permit without it."

"Hold off on that for now, Fia. You did the right thing, giving her a safe hiding place, but let's take one thing at a time. Let's nail down the relationship Onandi does or does not have to Savarine's hedge fund."

He paused, his gaze meeting mine. "You have good instincts. I am inclined to agree he may be your 'puppet master.' "

"And I'd bet the farm he murdered Percy," I said.

I told Calixto about the new player in town, and the little I knew about Kamozey. "I sent a message to Brian before I left, asking him to run the name. He's studying Onandi's bank records from seventeen years ago, as well."

Calixto nodded. "*Muy bueno.*"

"I'd suspect Kamozey's the killer, but he wasn't here in Saratoga that night. I think Julissa would have known if he was. Of course, there's always the Rastafarian, Dajon. Just because he was stoned out of his mind doesn't mean he didn't take a knife to Percy." I felt my lips curl at the memory.

Just then, our waitress showed up, and Calixto told her we were a bit rushed.

"We would like to order drinks and dinner now," he said, before turning to me. "May I order for you?" When I nodded, he glanced back to the waitress, "Did I see Whistle Pig on the bar when I walked in?"

"Excellent choice," she said, her smile revealing a lot of white teeth. Her eyes were practically gleaming with dollar signs.

How expensive was this stuff? For that matter, what was it?

"Two," Calixto said, "on the rocks."

After he ordered the scallop special, the waitress left, and a short time later the bartender delivered two highballs filled with amber liquid the color of bourbon. I took an exploratory sip.

"This is wonderful. Is it bourbon?" I asked Calixto.

"Rye whiskey."

Growing up in the Baltimore area, being a horsewoman and a cop, I thought I knew a lot, but I realized more and more, my knowledge of the finer things was lacking. Of course, when your mother takes the money and leaves you behind . . .

"It's really good," I said. "I've never heard of it before. Guess I know a lot more about feed grain than grain alcohol."

"You have everything you need," Calixto said. "You have the perseverance of a bulldog, the tracking ability of a bloodhound, and the heart of a Thoroughbred. I wouldn't want my partner any other way."

I was half-stunned by the compliment. It meant so much more than if he'd said I was beautiful or clever.

"Thanks," I finally said. "You're not too shabby, either." I took a large swallow of my drink and focused on the tablecloth. I could feel his eyes on me.

"Meloy called this afternoon. He received a copy of the coroner's report on Percy."

Straightening, I twisted slightly and stared at him. "Tell me."

"Percy was knocked out by a blow to the head *before* his throat was cut open. The coroner's take on the murder weapon is revealing. Apparently, the cuts and incisions into the skin, bone, and cartilage indicate a combat knife was used. One with a fully serrated blade, about four-and-a-half-inches long. The entire knife was probably ten inches."

"I'll keep that in mind in case I find a stray knife in my mother's garden." I said, trying to lighten my mood. But I couldn't keep my fingers from touching my throat.

"I know, *querida,* it was a terrible death."

He paused a moment and we both took a healthy swallow of whiskey. "But even more telling," he continued, "is the way the wound was inflicted. The coroner believes the killer was either amateurish or enraged. The way the neck was sawed open was excessive and unnecessary."

I thought back to my cop days. "I can understand why he'd say that. If Percy was unconscious, the killer could have simply turned his neck to expose carotid artery and given it a quick slice. That would have done the job faster, and a lot more easily."

I took another sip, set the glass down, and began to think out loud. "Even if the killer was a novice, he still had the sense to cover himself and his clothes with plastic. Of course, he could have seen serial killer movies. Or read that type of novel. He'd know they're always carrying plastic bags and sheeting in the trunk of their cars." *And duct tape, rope, and handcuffs.*

"Or," Calixto said, "the killer was a professional, but filled with rage and a desire to inflict the worst possible damage in the shortest amount of time."

I flashed on Percy's flopped-back head, all but severed from the neck. *Don't go there, Fia.*

With exquisite timing, the waitress showed up with our food. It wasn't rare meat oozing with blood, but still, after the details of Percy's death, I had to pause a moment before I could take a bite of the scallops. We got through the meal, ordered coffee, a takeout for Julissa, and were out of the tavern by eight.

On the sidewalk Calixto said, "I'd like to talk to her."

"You should."

Since I'd come in a cab, I climbed into Calixto's XK for a ride back to the Adelphi. As the Jag powered away from the restaurant, I thought about the three thugs currently residing in the hotel.

"When we get there," I said, "it might be better if Onandi or his men don't see us together. One of them could be in the lobby. The less they know or think about Mr. and Mrs. Coyune, the better."

"You're right, of course. I will drop you off, then park. And, since someone could be watching from the lobby, you will take the elevator to the wrong floor, yes?"

"Of course. I'm not leading anyone to Julissa."

After climbing the steps from the third floor to the fourth floor, I opened the stairwell door, and looked left and right. The long corridor was empty. As I passed by Onandi's suite, I heard male voices and smelled cigar smoke. So much for the hotel's nonsmoking rule. I sped down the hall, and when I reached our suite, was glad my key card wouldn't open the door. It meant Julissa had turned the bolt from the inside. This erased the vague, but nagging fear I'd had that Julissa might have disappeared.

I rapped gently and called her name. "It's Fia," I said, keeping my voice low.

She let me in, quickly closing and bolting the door behind us. I handed her the plastic bag holding her take-out dinner from the tavern.

"Scallops," I said. "Eat them while they're hot. Then we'll talk."

She did, and a few minutes later, Calixto arrived. After they exchanged a brief greeting, he remained standing, and I knew by the way his eyes darkened, and the vein in his temple pulsed, he was inventorying the damage to her face. One of his hands closed into a fist.

If I'd been Onandi, I would have left town.

"I am sorry for your trouble, Julissa," he finally said. "Fia tells me you have a friend in New York you were hoping to contact."

"Yes, I used the room phone to call her while Fia was gone." She threw me a worried look, as if she might have made a terrible mistake. "I thought it would be safe?"

"It's fine," I said. "Onandi doesn't know you're here."

"But, what about the maid? She knows someone else is staying in the room. If Onandi asks . . ."

"He won't," I said. "He's bound to think you ran away."

Though Julissa had eaten less than half her dinner, she stood, slid the container of food back into the plastic bag, and dumped it into the hotel's hand-painted trash can.

"I'm sorry. I can't finish this."

"Don't worry about it," I said. Damn, she was tense.

Calixto settled into one of the room's upholstered chairs, and smiled at her, his relaxed body language suggesting she do the same.

"Tell me," he said. "Who is this friend?"

"We went to school together in Jamaica. She knows about Onandi. She wants me to stay with her in the city, thinks she can get me work."

Except you have no papers.

"But," Julissa said, "I don't even have the money to get there, and Onandi has my clothes."

Calixto gave her an open palm shrug. "*No problema.* We will take care of that."

Julissa's lower lip quivered and she grimaced like she was trying not to cry.

"I'll have a car and a driver take you to New York tomorrow.

I will give you cash, and," he said when she started to protest, "you can pay me back once you have work, yes?"

He sat with his long legs crossed, his Lucchese boots gleaming with polish, a half smile on his lips. Julissa nodded, fingering tears away from her eyes, while I restrained an impulse to throw myself on Calixto.

"*Bueno,*" he said. "It is decided. Fia, could I talk to you on the balcony for a moment?"

I rose from the couch, walked through our bedroom, and after opening the French doors, I stepped outside. Resting my hands on the railing, I watched the street traffic below. In the bedroom, Calixto cut the light, probably not wanting us silhouetted on the balcony.

The air outside was cool, and held a trace of exhaust, and cooking from nearby restaurants. The painted wood on the railing beneath my hands was as smooth as enamel. I leaned forward to look at three men who had left the hotel entry below, but Calixto slipped up behind me, put his arms around my waist, and pulled me against him.

"*Querida,* I cannot stay with you tonight. Not with Julissa here." His warm breath touched my neck. "I find this to be . . . *painful.*"

My own disappointment was sharp, and the heat from where he pressed against me, almost overwhelming. I started to speak, but something about the three men walking away from the hotel stopped me cold. Dreadlocks. A brightly colored hat shaped like a popover.

"That's the Rastafarian! The other two have to be Onandi and Kamozey."

Seeing them, my desire wilted like a spring blossom in a sudden freeze.

32

Calixto moved to the balcony railing and stood by my side. His gaze followed the three men walking on the street below. They crossed Broadway and entered a bar a half block away.

As he pulled his cell from his pocket, a mischievous glint appeared in his eyes. "An opportunity has presented itself." He entered a number, and said, "May I have security please?" A beat later, he said, "This is Calixto Coyune, I spoke with you earlier? I need immediate access to room four-ten. Mrs. Coyune will be going inside. Yes, that's right. Thank you."

"Am I about to do what I think I am?" I asked.

"Yes, *querida,* you are. I will go to the bar, keep an eye on them, and text if they head back."

"Got it," I said, opening the French doors and walking quickly into the living room to where Julissa had remained on the gold and beige couch. "Where does Onandi keep your papers?"

"*What?*"

I explained that I was about to have access to his room.

"The last time I saw them they were in a briefcase he has. It's made of plate steel, always locked. You won't be able to open it."

"Oh, I'll get it open."

Calixto appeared from the bedroom, making a beeline for the door.

"Wait a second," I said. "I need your gun."

He sent me a questioning look, and I explained my plan. When he handed me his gun, I slipped it into my tote bag. He made a hurry-up motion with his hand.

"The man is on his way to open the suite." He paused a second, his eyes suddenly worried. "You will ask him to make sure no one else is inside, yes?"

"You can bet on it."

After making sure no thugs were lurking in the corridor, we left. Behind us, I heard Julissa bolt the door. Calixto caught an elevator, and I stepped into the stairwell near room 410, leaving the fire door ajar so I could see the hallway. I reminded myself that if anyone did see me enter Onandi's room, they wouldn't know who I was. Calixto would have been a different story, so it made sense for me to be the thief.

A moment later the elevator dinged. A man, with a hotel security badge, stepped off. He paused outside 410, glancing around as if expecting someone.

I slipped into the hall, quietly introduced myself, and asked if he'd check the room.

"Of course," he said. "I'll make sure it's clear." He knocked on the door, saying, "Hotel Security." He said it once more, and when no one responded he unlocked the door and stepped inside, continuing to announce himself as he moved through the room and out of sight.

I wondered what he'd say if one of the thugs was in there,

but, no doubt, he had a list of clever excuses. I also wondered why the hotel was letting us into Onandi's room. Maybe Meloy had intervened on Calixto's behalf, or maybe the Coyune family was just that well connected with the hotel. Whatever the reason, it certainly made my job easier.

The hotel detective appeared in the doorway. "It's clear. You'd better get in and out fast. I can't stay here to keep watch."

"Mr. Coyune's taking care of that," I said. "Thanks for your help."

"You understand," he said, giving me his best hard-cop stare, "I never saw you. I was never here. The hotel will deny complicity."

"Of course," I said, walking past him into the room.

I wasn't here, either. If bullet holes appear, or a document goes missing, it'll be a mystery to me.

After the security guy glanced left and right, he hurried toward the elevator. I walked into Onandi's suite and bolted the door. The setup was larger than ours. A two-bedroom with a sizable sitting area. I wanted to find Onandi's room—the obvious place for him to hide things. The first bedroom I stepped into had two double beds. On one of the beds was a brightly colored dashiki, similar to the one worn by Dajon on the night of the murder. Dajon and Komozey must be staying in this room.

I left, slipped quickly across the sitting area and entered the bedroom on the other side. The sight of the king bed and the thought of Julissa sleeping in it with Onandi turned my stomach. As I moved farther into the room, I was stopped by a gleam of metal on the floor by a nightstand. The briefcase.

I closed the distance and grasped the case's handle, surprised by how heavy it was. I hoped its heftiness wasn't caused by something small and dense inside, like boxes of ammunition. Surely, the thick metal construction caused the weight? I set the case on the bed, then pulled Calixto's Glock from my tote.

I stared at the lock. It looked solid and tough. Blasting it with the Glock could mangle the lock mechanisms and they might never give way. I wasn't keen on firing straight at the case, either. Who knew what was in there? I turned it around. Hinges are usually weaker and easier to breach. Why fight the lock when I could blow off the hinges?

I grabbed one of the big foam pillows, folded it over the Glock to dampen the sound, and fired down on the hinge so the bullet would enter the mattress. The hinge flew off. I did the second hinge, then pried the case open. Papers. I pawed through a pile of them, wishing I had time to read them all. Even if I did, I couldn't use any of it as evidence. My mode of obtaining them was illegal and totally unauthorized.

I found Julissa's Jamaican passport near the bottom, dropped it and the gun into my tote, and got the hell out of there. There was no one in the hallway when I cracked the door open, so I sped down the corridor, rapped on the door to our suite, and Julissa opened it immediately.

"Here," I said, thrusting the passport into her hands. I was panting and could feel sweat beading on my forehead. I shook slightly from the adrenaline that coursed through me when I fired the gun. The timeless fear of getting caught had pumped even more of the hormone into my system.

Yet somehow I felt myself grinning. It had been so *easy*, and gone so well! I sent a message to Calixto relating my success. Julissa had been watching me, and when I put the phone back in my tote, she hugged me, her enthusiastic squeeze making it hard to breath.

"Thank you so much!" she said, stepping back before staring at the passport clutched in her hand, like she didn't believe it was really there.

"And tomorrow," I said, "you go to New York City."

"You have been so kind. I'm indebted to you both."

"You needed a break," I said. "We were happy to give you one."

The passport retrieval had gone so smoothly. I only hoped her escape would be as painless.

That night, Julissa and I shared the huge king bed. Though my heart longed for Calixto, with all that had happened in the last week, I was still glad that I wasn't sleeping alone. There had been too many alarming events. There were way too many scary people in this town.

Sometime in the middle of the night, I was awakened by whimpering and muffled cries. I tensed until I realized Julissa must be caught in the throes of a nightmare. Listening to the fear in her voice, I was more determined than ever to help this woman escape. I put a hand on her shoulder.

"It's okay, Julissa. You're safe now."

She murmured something unintelligible and settled back into a deeper, silent sleep. I lay awake for a while, staring at the ceiling that was lit by the ambient light sifting through the glass of the balcony's French doors. My stay in Saratoga had been so strange, so unlike what I'd expected.

I was in a wonderful vacation spot. In a city whose focus on horses, racing, and the arts made it "the place to be" in the summer. Soon, the Fasig-Tipton sale of blue-blooded yearling Thoroughbreds would be held. Sheikhs, billionaires, and movie stars would sprinkle the pavilion as million-dollar colts and fillies brought down the auctioneer's hammer.

But somehow I'd discovered a different Saratoga and spent my days on the dark side of this town.

33

In the morning, we ordered croissants, fruit, and a large pot of coffee. I would have preferred to eat outside on the balcony with Julissa, but she couldn't risk being seen from the street below or from one of the balconies that flanked ours.

So instead, we sat cross-legged on the carpet near the open French doors, enjoying the shaft of morning sun that pooled around us. We both uttered little groans of pleasure with our first sips of hot, fragrant coffee.

About the time we finished eating, Calixto showed up wearing a leather vest over a crisp shirt, jeans, and the inevitable, perfectly polished boots.

"Julissa, I have a town car picking you up at ten and driving you to the city. And I'm giving you this"—he pulled a wad of hundred-dollar bills from a vest pocket—"so you can get the clothes you need and pay your room and board until you get your own income."

He turned back to me. "You have a plan for getting her out of the hotel, yes?"

"I do. And you should take your gun back." I pulled the Glock from my tote and handed it to him.

"*Bueno.*" After he slid the gun into an inside vest pocket, he turned to Julissa. "I think you will like your driver. He is a former New York State trooper, and, of course, has a license to carry. The car is furnished with heavily tinted windows. You will be safe."

When tears welled in Julissa's eyes and she pressed fingers to quivering lips, I suspected she was about to launch into more declarations of undying gratitude.

"So, about sneaking you out of here," I said, "what do you think of wearing my blond wig, some fake tattoos, and a piece of jewelry you ordinarily wouldn't be caught dead in?"

"*Querida,* you are not giving away your bat wings?"

Calixto's lips were doing the twitch-that-is-not-quite-a-smile thing and his comment served as an excellent distraction for Julissa.

"No," I said. "I don't give away diamonds. It will be a loan. But you've got to admit, if Onandi sees her with tattoos, a blond wig, and wearing a tacky piece of Goth jewelry, he will never believe it's her."

"The black diamond is not tacky," Calixto said.

"You're right, and I have plans for that diamond. The bat wings, maybe not."

His face became expressionless. "As you wish, Fia."

Had I offended him? I started to backpedal, but as Calixto turned away from me, I saw the grin he was trying to hide.

"I love being around you two," Julissa said. "There's so much energy surrounding you."

Not to mention desire.

As if reading my mind, Calixto nailed me with a glance so penetrating, I flushed. I could almost read his thoughts, and they were fixated on us being alone together, in this very room, during the coming night.

"All righty then," I said. "Let me get that wig."

"Yes, do that, *querida,* and I will head to Maggie's barn."

Calixto left, and after Julissa and I headed into the bath, I grabbed a tube of gooey hair product and went to work on Julissa's thick, curly hair. I slicked it back and pinned it up, then settled the wig onto her head. The wig's long, straight bangs hid a few stray curls determined to spring forward from her crown.

We studied the result in the large mirror. Julissa's cafe-latte skin, dark brows, and almond eyes looked sensational beneath blond hair. From my undercover kit, I pulled a package of stick-on dragon tattoos. I pasted one on each of her biceps, and one beneath her collarbone.

"Now for the pièce de résistance." I got the bat wing necklace from the room safe and clasped the skeleton hands behind Julissa's neck.

I stood back and examined her. Calixto's oversized shirt and my too-short stretch pants didn't do much for the look. I doubted she wanted to arrive in New York City wearing that stuff, no matter how relieved she was to be escaping Onandi. She was, after all, a poster girl for style and femininity.

"Tell me," I asked, "did Onandi open any other accounts for you in Saratoga—besides Violet's?"

"He did, but why . . . oh," she said, as a gleam of mischief lit her eyes, "I see. Yes, Saratoga Saddlery. I bought a beautiful pair of cowgirl boots there and they have terrific casual clothes."

"I'll ride with you in the limo, keep watch while you charge everything you could ever want or don't want to Onandi, and then the limo will whisk you straight to the Big Apple." I was beginning to feel like I was weaving a Cinderella story. I hoped Onandi hadn't thought to close the account when Julissa disappeared. But Calixto had given her enough cash to get the essentials.

As my thoughts spun, Julissa glanced at her image in the mirror and touched the bat wing necklace.

"This *is* dreadful. But I see why you have plans for the diamond. It is a magnificent stone. But why would he give you such a tacky setting?"

"Long story. And Calixto has an odd sense of humor."

"True," Julissa said. "But he is a man as rare and beautiful as this diamond. Hold on to him."

I didn't want to go there. "Let me check the street, see if your limo has arrived." I hurried through the French doors onto the balcony and took a deep breath of cool morning air. Could I hold on to him? *Think about it later, Fia.*

I focused on the traffic below, and a few moments later, a Lincoln Town Car arrived at the curb before the hotel's entrance. It remained there idling, waiting for its passenger. I went back to Julissa. She stood in the bedroom, rocking from one foot to the other, one hand worrying with the necklace around her neck. I didn't blame her for being nervous.

"Time to go," I said.

Instead of taking the elevator we walked down the stairs, hurrying into the lobby, just as Onandi stepped off the elevator. Julissa froze, but I laughed.

"Can you *believe* she said that to me? I mean I just about died!"

Onandi's gaze passed over us with no sign of recognition.

"Come on, Patty," I said, clasping Julissa's wrist. "Let's go see her. You won't believe where she lives. I mean, wait until you *see* this place."

We walked quickly through the lobby, out the entrance, and climbed into the limo, where we were immediately hidden behind the darkened windows.

"Worked like a charm," I said.

She didn't answer, but I could feel the trembling that was radiating from her across the Lincoln's leather seat. We made it to the shop without further incident, and it turned out Onandi hadn't closed the account.

The Saratoga Saddlery's manager thought she'd died and gone to heaven when Julissa bought a suede vest, a leather vest, two pairs of Frye cowgirl boots, a tweed riding jacket, a leather coat, and . . . I finally lost count.

I picked up a huge, gorgeous tooled leather tote, then grabbed another one for good measure. After Julissa got dressed in some of her new purchases, we stuffed everything else into the totes and her driver stowed them in the trunk.

We stood on the street next to the waiting limo, both of us in tears as we said good-bye.

"Go on," I finally said. "Get out of here."

She did, and I felt strangely bereft as I watched her car disappear down Broadway. But I had helped another human in need, and a warm satisfaction overpowered my feeling of loss. Instead of taking a cab, I walked along Broadway to reach the Adelphi. People smiled at me, probably responding to the irrepressible grin on my face.

Then my phone rang. I stared at the caller ID, answered, and said, "Joan, is everything okay?"

"No. Rich is behaving even more oddly. He seems consumed by dread. I don't want to leave him here alone. Can you come?"

If I'd believed she was simply overreacting, I would have told her no. I did not want my feeling of contentment ruined by Joan.

But with Onandi and his thugs in town, and an unidentified murderer on the loose, I sucked it up.

"I'll come now."

"Can you bring a gun?"

"I told you, I don't have a gun," I said through clenched teeth. "Don't ask me again. I'll be there as soon as I can."

I walked on toward the Adelphi to retrieve my Mini, suddenly wishing I'd kept Calixto's Glock.

34

I drove the Mini north past the signs for Skidmore College, until I reached the heavily wooded lane leading across the bridge to Joan's development.

Outside the stone mansion, her perfectly manicured roses bloomed profusely. I parked on the flagstone drive next to Rich's large black Mercedes, and climbed from my car. No one would suspect a brutal slaying had occurred here only days ago.

A cool draft worked its way to me from the woods beside the house. It, or memories of the murder brought a sudden chill to my arms. The windows I'd found so tall and elegant on my first visit to this house, seemed blank, like eyes with no soul. I forced myself to exhale slowly.

Joan must have heard me drive up, because the front door opened, and she stood there pale and somehow shrunken.

"Thank you for coming."

I nodded and followed her inside to the living room. The huge vase of red roses was absent, but the statue of the horse, Behold the King, reared defiantly on the credenza. I didn't see Rich.

"Where is he?" I asked.

"In the library. Whatever has him so worried, he goes in there and just dwells on it. When I try to talk to him, he snaps at me. Tells me to leave him alone."

"Hey, Rich," I called. "You have company."

"Fia," Joan hissed, "I don't know if that's a good idea."

"You want him to snap out of it or not?"

I raised my voice a little more. "Rich, I came all the way here to see you guys. Come on out."

"Who is that? Damn it, Joan, who'd you let in here?"

The anger in his voice prickled the hairs on the back of my neck. His sudden steps toward us were rapid and hard.

"It's just Fia," I said. "I'm sorry if I came at a bad time. I was hoping I could have a drink with you guys."

He entered the room, his face drawn, deep shadows under his eyes. His jaw was tight, a pulse ticking on one side beneath a bruise. Joan had said he and Savarine had fought. The evidence was obvious.

Joan rushed to the bar on the credenza. "That's a terrific idea, Fia. I'll get us drinks."

Rich's lips compressed in annoyance, then he waved a hand in resignation. "Oh, all right. Make me a scotch."

"I'll have a little bourbon, with a lot of water. Wouldn't want to drive under the influence." I grinned, like I'd just made a terrifically amusing comment. Joan managed a weak smile and handed me my drink. Rich's glare was so acidic, I was surprised my bourbon didn't turn into a whiskey sour. As I tasted the bourbon, his cell chimed.

"Can't people leave me alone?" But he took the call. "Al? You've got a lot of nerve, buddy. *What?* Now?"

He must be talking to Al Savarine. I walked to one of the beige couches, sat down, and listened.

"No, I've got people here. You can't expect me to . . . no, my stepdaughter, Fia. I—"

Whatever he'd intended to say, Al cut him off. As Rich listened, his face grew thoughtful. He nodded a few times before speaking.

"I don't like that he's in town, either. Maybe we should meet with him. But what do we say?"

He listened a moment, then, "Okay, you'd better get over here." He ended the call, but was so nervous that when he tried to slide his phone into a pocket he dropped it on the floor.

"Who was that?" Joan asked. "What's happening?"

He glared at her, his lips compressed. "Al Savarine."

After that one response, his stare seemed to cut through us, like we weren't even there, like he was seeing something else entirely.

I stood, grabbed his phone from the floor, and handed it to him. "What's wrong?"

"Nothing's wrong. Savarine just wants to come over and talk, is all."

"But you two were *fighting*!" Joan said. "Why would you agree to see him?"

It was clear to me that Joan didn't have a clue what was going on. I raised a palm toward her. "Hold on a minute," I said, before turning to Rich. "*Really?* Nothing's wrong? Then why do you look like somebody's got a gun to your head? Savarine told you Onandi's in town, didn't he?"

I was almost amused by Rich's astonished expression.

"How the hell do you know that?"

"Didn't Joan tell you I used to be a cop?"

"Oh, God," Rich said, before backing away from me and collapsing onto the other couch. "It's all gotten out of control."

"What's gotten out of control?" Joan's voice was so shrill and demanding, I wanted to cover my ears. "What are you *talking* about?"

"Joan, will you please just sit down and shut up! Savarine will be here in a minute. I need to think."

Instead of thinking he upended his scotch, then lifted the empty glass to her, his teeth protruding as he smiled. "Fix me another one, sweetie?"

Joan made a snort of disgust, grabbed the glass from his hand and walked to the bar. She poured herself a stiff bourbon before making his scotch.

"I'm curious to know what's going on myself," I said.

Rich gave me another sour look. "He's not gonna talk in front of you. You should leave."

"She stays," Joan said. "She's my daughter and an ex-cop with connections. Fia could help us."

"Damn it, Joan. Cops can't be involved in this!"

"Remember," I said, "the operative word is 'ex,' as in no longer a police officer. I just want to help." *I was such a liar.*

The room grew quiet as we sat on the beige couches and waited for the arrival of Savarine. Though no one spoke, I could almost hear the thoughts whirring inside our heads.

The sound of tires on the driveway pavers and the soft purr of an engine reached my ears. Clutching her drink, Joan rushed from the living room, through the front hall, to look out a window.

"It's him."

A minute later, she led Savarine into the room. His cologne smelled fresh, his suit was crisp, but he appeared to have gotten the worst of the fight with Rich. Several purple bruises blossomed on his narrow face, and he'd pasted a bandage above one eyebrow. It made him look more like a thug than ever.

He stiffened when he saw me. "Why is she here?" Then he waved a dismissive hand, as if I wasn't really important enough to worry about. "Rich, we need to talk . . . in the library."

"No." Joan moved closer to Savarine. "I've been kept in the dark too long. I have a right to know what's going on."

Savarine shook his head. "No way. Absolutely—"

"Sit down, Joan!" Rich said. She shrugged and sat next to him.

I glanced at Savarine. "I already know you're worried about Onandi."

Savarine, who'd been standing on one of Joan's silk carpets, whirled to face Rich. "You son of a bitch! Are you crazy? What did you tell her?"

Before they resorted to fists again, I rushed on. "Rich didn't tell me anything. I used to be a cop. There was a murder in my mother's home, okay? So I did a little investigating on my own. You can understand that, right?"

He stared at me, then nodded slightly. "Yeah . . . but forget about talking to the cops."

"Don't worry, they aren't involved in this. They're too busy investigating Percy's murder. And by the way," I said, leaning back on the couch, watching their faces closely, "I heard the knife used on Percy wasn't a household item, like a regular kitchen knife. It was a combat knife. Had a serrated blade and was about ten inches long. Ring a bell?"

Savarine's expression never changed, and if Rich knew anything, he was a master at not showing it. Joan paled slightly, and looked away from me. But she might only be lost in the remembered horror.

Rich bared his bucked teeth in a disdainful smile. "You're just a world-class detective, aren't you? So, who told you that?"

"Someone who knows someone with the Saratoga PD."

"Big deal. Who doesn't already know a knife was used?"

Joan was staring at Rich. An odd expression I couldn't read crossed her face, then her gaze dropped to the floor.

One of Savarine's legs started shaking, like maybe the reality of Percy's death was taking a hold on him. He lowered himself carefully onto the other end of my couch. "I don't care what was used. I don't want to be next. That's why we have to work this out with Onandi. He's got to let us step back from this thing."

Joan glared at Rich. "Step back from what?" When no one answered, her hand clawed at Rich's sleeve. "Whatever it is, why can't we just get on the next flight to California?"

"It won't make the problem go away, Joan."

"He's right," Savarine said. "Right now, we have to work out some sort of exit strategy with this guy."

"Goddamn it, Rich. Tell me what it is you need to exit from!"

Rich responded by taking another swallow of scotch.

"This is all linked to the hedge fund, isn't it?" I asked.

Savarine's hooded eyes slid from me to Rich. "She knows too fucking much."

Joan jerked upright. "I *knew* it! That damn thing you bought into. Oh, yes, I know all about that, Rich. Fia told me!"

If looks could kill, Rich and Savarine would have dropped me dead where I stood.

Joan's cheeks flushed with anger. "You morons! You got us into this mess! Maybe you're lucky Fia knows stuff. Maybe she can help."

I didn't comment on that one, and for a few beats, nobody said a word. But I could almost see the men's animosity swelling like a balloon in the space between them and me. Still, I had to ask.

"Onandi's the money behind your fund, isn't he?"

Savarine's eyes widened in surprise. His gaze dropped away from me, and he seemed to grow smaller. His shoulders sagged, and when he spoke, he sounded weak, defeated.

"I didn't know what he was doing! You have to understand, he *lied* to me." He dropped his head into his hands, making his next words harder to understand. "How was I supposed to know he was running a pyramid scheme in Jamaica? That he'd bilked millions from his clients."

Joan gave a little gasp. "My God, Rich!"

Then the words tumbled from Savarine's mouth, as if once he'd started talking, he couldn't stop. "And now, that son of a bitch has funneled the money through *my* hedge fund. He's suckered us into running a money-laundering operation for him!" He stopped, as if temporarily spent.

I glanced at Rich. "So why did *you* buy into the hedge fund? Surely someone with your business expertise suspected something? And you knew Onandi years ago. You knew what he was."

Rich just looked at me, but Savarine started in again.

"Percy found out. He was going to the *feds*." Savarine's elbows pressed into his sides, making him appear to shrink even more. "Do you think Onandi killed him to keep him quiet? Oh, God," he moaned. "And we're in the middle of it." His last words were so low I had to strain to hear them. Clearly, the man was terrified.

"I bet that's what happened," Rich said. "I bet Onandi killed Percy, or maybe that Rastafarian that works for him."

"At least we've kept quiet about this," Savarine said, "and Onandi knows it."

"What do you mean?" Rich asked.

"I told you! I told you on the phone I'd talked to him.

Remember? He wants to see us this afternoon so we can work this out. I told him we'd meet at my cousin's restaurant, Zutti's Café. Rico's expecting us."

"Yeah," Rich said, "I remember. When?"

"Around three thirty. So we should get going."

I remembered listening to the recording of Savarine talking to Rico. He'd asked for the mobster's protection, and now he probably felt safer meeting at Rico's restaurant. I glanced at my watch. It was approaching three. I doubted the café opened before six, so this was a good time for them to meet.

Joan rose from the couch. "I'm going with you, Rich. If you don't let me, I'll just follow."

Rich scowled at her. "Oh, for God's sake."

"I don't like this," Savarine said.

"Too bad, I'm coming."

I didn't say a word. I had my own plans.

I stood, walked into the kitchen and set my tote bag next to Joan's purse, where she habitually left it on a small counter used as a telephone desk. I fished inside a zippered pocket of my tote and found the device I wanted. After switching it on, I dropped it into Joan's purse, making sure it disappeared into the bottom beneath her wallet, cell phone, and makeup bag.

I hurried back to the living room, almost bumping into Joan as she came to collect her purse. The men had their car keys out, ready to leave.

Rich gave me a sour look. "Don't try to follow us."

"Why would I do that? I'm just heading into town."

35

As I sped over the stone bridge, I reached Calixto on his cell, and explained what had happened at Joan's house.

There was a short silence before he spoke. "Fia, I don't think you should follow them."

"It's just a meeting at a restaurant. I might learn something useful by tagging along."

"You aren't thinking this through. The restaurant will be empty at this time of day. You can't possibly go in there without being noticed. They will simply escort you out."

Calixto was starting to annoy me. "I'll think of something."

"*Querida*, from what you have told me, these people are becoming desperate. Don't do this."

"I'll be fine, and besides, I feel like I should keep an eye on Joan. Just in case."

"So, you admit that something could go wrong?"

"No. I just want to watch my mother's back a little."

"Fia, you are not a police officer, you do not have a gun. Stay out of this."

"I'm not abandoning my mother!"

"Like she abandoned you?"

I had no comeback for that. Holding the phone away from my ear, I glared at it, brought it back, and said, "Let me think a minute."

Calixto didn't respond, leaving the line open with an empty feel to it.

On either side of the road the woods were thinning as we drew closer to Route 9. I accelerated the Mini until I could just make out the tail end of Rich's Mercedes in the distance.

It wasn't in my nature to leave Joan to fend for herself. I could see Rico and his affiliates protecting Savarine. After all, Savarine was "family." But my mother? If something went wrong, why would they care about her? She'd be considered collateral damage.

Besides, I wanted to know what was going on. Okay, I admit it, I couldn't bear not to know.

"Calixto," I said, "have you forgotten that we were directed by Gunny to keep an eye on Savarine and his hedge fund?"

He had no comeback for that, so I continued.

"I'll be careful. Don't *worry* about me."

"Fia—"

I shut the phone off, and focused on Rich's Mercedes barely visible ahead. I knew where they were going, but I felt better keeping them in sight. Things happens. Plans change. Who knew what underlying agenda men like Rich, Savarine, and Onandi might have?

Face it, my mother had married a crook. He and Savarine could play the we-didn't-know card all they wanted, but I wasn't buying it. Serve them right if they both went to jail.

Far ahead, Savarine, who led the pack, hit Route 9 and sped recklessly down the highway. Fortunately, when the road merged onto Broadway, he was forced to slow down for traffic and I didn't lose them completely.

As I drove, I remembered Savarine's complaints to Rico that night at the restaurant. He'd accused Rico of hurting him by connecting him with a man like Onandi. Had Savarine been so stupid as to think his mobster cousin would set him up with a trustworthy partner?

I bet Rich had never bothered to warn Savarine about Onandi, either. And now, Onandi was making a fortune using Savarine's racing fund. Did Rich and Savarine really think the Jamaican would give them an easy out? For all I knew, Onandi and Rico might have some unholy alliance about which the other two men were clueless.

I had no answers. All I knew was that tangling with the Saratoga mob had almost cost me my life. And now, Joan was running to Rico with Savarine and Rich. In spite of my reassurances to Calixto, the whole thing gave me a really bad feeling.

Get a grip, Fia. It's only a business meeting.

I dropped even farther behind as we drew close to Zutti's. When Rich and Savarine's cars pulled in to the restaurant's lot, I drove past the entrance, and steered the Mini into an alley on the far side of the restaurant. I eased to a stop next to a Dumpster, then sardined the Mini into a spot between it and a metal fence. I'd always loved this about my little car, that I could squeeze it in almost anywhere.

I climbed out and walked down the alley to the rear of the restaurant. A man in a white tank stood on a rear deck outside, finishing a cigarette. He squinted at me through the curling smoke, stubbed out the butt, and went inside. Before the door closed, I caught a glimpse of a tile floor and shelves laden with supplies.

I kept walking behind Zutti's and glimpsed around the back edge of the building in time to see Savarine, Rich, and Joan hurrying around the front corner. I sped forward and watched Rich enter Zutti's behind Joan. She was carrying her purse.

I turned my phone on and texted Calixto, "I'm fine. They are in Zutti's."

His words came right back. "I know, I am watching."

I scanned the area, but saw nothing.

"Do you and Brian have me on satellite?"

"Of course."

I waved at the sky, just as a long black limo nosed its way down the street and stopped in front of Zutti's. It looked like the one Onandi had brought to Joan's garden party, the one Detective Ferguson had said was bulletproof. Did Onandi have a private jet he carried the thing around in?

The windows were heavily tinted, and I couldn't see inside as Onandi and the Rastafarian climbed out the opposite side before heading into the restaurant.

I glanced across the street, scanning up and down the block. I walked to the curb, turned around, and studied the storefronts on both sides of Zutti's. A current of air brought the scent of chocolate to my nose. Two doors to my right was a bakery.

I zipped back down the alley to my car, dug around in my carryall, extracted a different jacket and my only other wig, a red one. I changed jackets, pulled the wig onto my head, and using my makeup bag, darkened my eyes and applied black Goth lipstick. For good measure, I put on a pair of tortoiseshell glasses with fake lenses. I'd used them and the red wig in Florida when I'd adopted the role of Kate O'Brien. I realized I hadn't played Kate since I'd first met Calixto.

I jogged back to the bakery, hurried inside, and stared at the selection of cakes, pies, and cookies inside the glass counter. Nothing looked as good as what they sold in Zutti's. At least, not until a stout woman appeared from the back bearing a tray of cannoli.

"Oh," I said, "those are just what I need!"

She tilted her head up enough that she could look down her nose at me. "You'll have to get in line, miss. Let Rudy help you. When he's free."

I assumed the guy behind the case with a line of three customers was Rudy. I pulled out my wallet, withdrew a wad of bills, and waved them at the woman.

"I'll pay extra if you'll sell me that tray right now."

Her eyes slid to Rudy, who shrugged. The other three customers shuffled impatiently, one of them throwing me a dirty look.

"You want the whole thing?" she asked.

"Yes."

"It'll cost you."

"Fine. Just tell me how much."

She did. I winced, pulled out my credit card and paid. Two ticks later I was heading back to Zutti's with the tray wrapped in plastic. I paused at the entrance and set my face to dumb, leaving my mouth slack, and my posture lazy.

I struggled to get through the door with the tray of sweets until the maître d' pulled it open for me.

"What are you doing?" he asked.

"Uh, delivery."

"We're not expecting one. Where is this from?"

I gave him the name of the shop two doors away.

He frowned. "We don't order from them."

"Yeah, I know you don't. But someone from the kitchen

called and said it was an emergency order or something. Look, I just do what I'm told. You want these or not?"

He gave me an exasperated sigh. "Take them through to the back. But next time, use the *kitchen* entrance."

I winked at him. "Sure, pops."

I slouched my way toward the kitchen with my cannoli, looking at the floor ahead of me, ignoring the large table near the back where a group of people sat. One sideways glance as I passed them—Rich, Joan, Savarine, and Rico were at the table. My quick look also assured me no one cared about a delivery woman lugging a tray of cannoli.

The Rastafarian stood behind the table with his back to the wall. Standing beside him was the man Calixto had identified as Gio Rizelli. I recognized the hard face and long jagged neck scar of the former enforcer for Alberto Rizelli. It looked like Onandi and Rico had their thugs on display, probably to impress each other.

As I kept going, a waiter laying tables with silverware gave me a questioning look. He stopped long enough to help me by pushing open the swinging door to the kitchen. Inside, the room hummed like a beehive. Guys in white shirts and aprons tended large pots of boiling pasta or meat sauce. A couple of the men wore tall chef's hats. The odor of rich tomato sauce, raw seafood, garlic, and oregano assailed my nostrils. Steam rose from the pots, and trays of uncooked bread lined a counter under a big wall oven.

The man I'd seen outside in the tank top was chopping vegetables on a long cutting board. He glanced up with no sign of recognition in his eyes. As I stood there, my tray of cannoli grew increasingly heavy.

"Hey," I yelled, "where should I put these?"

A man with a chef's hat set down a huge fish he'd been scaling. With a scowl, he headed my way.

"Where did those come from? We didn't order no cannoli."

"Look, I just do what I'm told. You want these, or what?"

Another man joined the chef, looked over the cannoli, and read the ticket on the tray. He spoke in rapid Italian. They argued a little, then the first guy opened a huge refrigerator and motioned me to put the cannoli inside. I did, then gave them my best bimbo smile.

"You guys sell takeout?"

"Sure," the chef said.

I gestured toward the swinging door. "Any chance I can see a menu and maybe get a cup of coffee out there?"

"Yeah, we can do that. Benito, show the lady where to sit."

Benito, the second man, grabbed a menu from a stand by the swinging door, handed it to me, then ushered me into the dining room. I hid my face in the menu and sat at the table he indicated, straining to hear the conversation three tables away.

At first, I only heard a murmur, with no distinct words. Then a man raised his voice, making me glimpse quickly over the top of the menu. Onandi was speaking, his harsh and abusive words aimed at Savarine, whose face was whiter than my menu.

"You fool. You think Rico and his buddies can protect you? Let me show you how much."

He pulled a revolver from his jacket and shot Rico in the face. Without hesitation he shot Alberto as the mob enforcer tried to pull a gun from his jacket.

Rico sagged in his chair, half his face missing. Rizelli slid down the wall as a gush of blood painted the long jagged scar on his neck. He started crawling toward the kitchen door, only getting halfway through before Onandi shot him twice more. Rizelli lay still, his body leaving the kitchen door propped open.

As I fought a wave of nausea, Joan was screaming like she'd never stop. The front door burst open, and four or five dark-skinned men in long raincoats stormed inside. One had dreadlocks, but the others had shaved their heads smooth. A coat flapped open, revealing a waist belt and thigh harness. Strapped inside it, I saw the dull steel of a machine pistol.

36

I'm no coward, but I'm not stupid, either. I dropped from my chair and under the table in one beat, pressed 911 on my phone. A female dispatcher answered, I whispered, "Shots fired. Two victims. Zutti's restaurant on Broadway."

The dispatcher started to question me, but I kept going. "Multiple armed assailants." I didn't want her voice calling attention to me. I disconnected.

How long would it take the cops to arrive? Best case scenario— five to seven minutes. Sometimes longer. How far away was Calixto? Had he seen the men come into Zutti's?

A rapid glance from under the table showed the last of the men slamming the front door closed, followed by the sound of a bolt sliding home.

Joan had stopped screaming. She, Rich, and Savarine sat stiff and unmoving in their chairs. At the wall, the Rastafarian stood smirking as he examined a fingernail. His absurdly casual stance told me he was probably high on something, and that the men who'd just come in were Onandi's thugs.

How could I possibly get myself and Joan out?

Sit chilly and wait for an opening.

The first moments after the shots were fired, the kitchen was silent, and I wondered if the staff had fled out the rear entrance. But now I heard banging and thumping.

I looked to my left, into the kitchen, the staff was ripping open drawers and cabinet doors, pulling out *weapons*. They had handguns, machine pistols. One guy had a Taser. I heard magazine clips sliding home, saw men putting extra bullet clips in their white apron pockets.

The guy in the tank walked out, holding a submachine gun. He came forward, stood over Rizelli's body, and began spraying bullets at the men in raincoats.

Onandi's men, their machine pistols already out, fired back. The frighteningly rapid, deafening explosions from the automatic weapons enveloped me like a nightmare. I risked another look to see that Onandi had run toward the front door, putting his men between himself and the kitchen mobsters. He crouched behind the maître d' stand.

I heard glass breaking. Pieces of cake and pie from the dessert case flew through the air, mixing with glass shards and blood on the floor. Shaking, I was on my hands and knees, under the table. A man from the kitchen fell in front of me, his blood spreading on the floor, almost reaching my hands. He'd dropped his machine pistol. I slid my hand out and pulled the gun under the table.

It was an FN P90. I'd never fired one, but knew about it. One of the best. Its magazine lay along the top of the gun, transparent, revealing its owner had been dropped before he'd fired all of the weapon's fifty bullets.

A quick study of the FN P90 showed a selector switch near the trigger. The gun was set to fully automatic. I changed it to single shot, flinching as rounds of gunfire pounded my ears, and I heard men screaming. The sour smell of vomit reached my nostrils.

Joan, Savarine, and Rich had either fallen or sought refuge under their table. The Rastafarian had crawled under there, too. My fragmented view of Joan through the tablecloth showed her on the floor, her hands covering her ears. When I saw no blood, I felt myself gasp with relief.

Suddenly a brief moment of partial silence, the only sound the reloading of weapons and a horrible ringing in my ears. The stink of gunsmoke, blood, and human excrement filled my nostrils as I looked left and right from my hiding place. Two of the men in raincoats were down, and I realized the dead mobster next to me was the man in the wifebeater. Two other men lay on the floor inside the kitchen. Their white shirts and aprons were splattered with red.

This was insane. Was Onandi doing this to show Savarine and Rich he owned them? Hadn't he realized what could happen in a restaurant owned by the mob?

I didn't know how many armed men were still in the kitchen. One of the men in raincoats crouched behind a table he'd flipped on its side by the banquette. As far as I could tell Onandi's other two remaining men were behind the bar. Shattered bottles dripped liquor and wine down the display shelves. Shell casings littered the floor.

Benito appeared briefly in the kitchen door. He unleashed a round of machine-gun fire aimed at the table on its side by the banquette. The barrage of bullets moved the table and the man hiding behind it cried out once and was quiet.

A glance to my left showed Benito had disappeared, but two other men carrying FN P90s, charged into the dining room, firing rapid rounds at the bar. I felt the blast as much as I heard it. They didn't stop when they reached the bar. If Onandi's men were still alive behind it, their life lights went out as the mobsters shoved their machine pistols over the bar and kept firing.

It was too horrible. Spinning away from the gun in my hands, I threw up on the floor. Shuddering, I wiped my mouth on my arm, then grabbed the FN P90 again. A rapid scan of the room. Joan under the table, alive. The Rastafarian next to her, Savarine and Rich close by. Onandi must still be hiding behind the maître d' stand.

One of the mobsters in front of the bar yelled at Onandi's hiding place, "Get out from behind there. Now."

"Don't shoot," Onandi called, and stood behind the stand with his hands up.

Without hesitation, the mobster riddled him with bullets. A new wave of dread hit me. Were Rico's men going to kill us all?

But the mobster lowered his weapon, and the other one rushed to the table where my mother and the men hid.

"Mr. Savarine," he said, "it's safe for you and your people to come out now."

There was a scuffle under the table and the Rastafarian pulled Joan out and stood up with her. He had a gun to her head.

For one beat, nobody moved. Joan was about to be collateral damage. I aimed the FN P90, sighting on the Rastafarian's hip, on the side away from Joan. I squeezed off the shot. He screamed, and dropped to the floor. As Joan scrabbled away from him, one of the mobsters finished him off.

At that moment, there was an explosion that burst open the front door. Flash grenades were thrown into the restaurant. I had trouble seeing and couldn't hear anything, but was able to identify the figures busting through the front door as an FBI SWAT team. Additional movement in the kitchen told me more

FBI or the Saratoga County sheriffs must be breaching the back as well.

I saw my mother crouching next to Rich, then a sudden wave of dizziness hit me, the room swayed, and I slid into a black hole.

37

The FBI SWAT team member who helped me out from under the table told me I'd only been unconscious for a couple of minutes. I felt like I'd lived a year of my life in that restaurant.

Once he got me steady on my feet, he glanced about the bloody, shattered restaurant and shook his head in disbelief. "I don't blame you for shutting down. This is the nastiest scene I've ever encountered."

I didn't see Joan, Rich, or Savarine. Only bodies, crime scene cops and FBI agents. The smell of death mingled with the liquor and wine from shattered bottles behind the bar, and blood pooled on the floor with splattered cake, fruit pies, and whipped cream. Nausea rose in my throat until I forced myself to breathe. The Saratoga County homicide detectives, Clark and Ferguson, arrived, their stoic expressions almost hiding their shock. Thankfully, they ignored me.

A few minutes later, a medic looked me over. As he checked my vitals, my brain was completely fogged, and I was content to remain that way while a police officer drove me to the Saratoga Springs PD on Lake Avenue. Once he assured me that Joan was safe, he seemed to think he could ask questions. But I wasn't ready to talk about what had just transpired, at least not until I was forced to.

When I stepped into the four-story brick police station, I escaped into the ladies' room, avoiding the detectives that must have been waiting to question me. I needed a moment to breathe. I ripped off my bloodstained wig, threw it in the trash, and scrubbed my face and hands. I only wished I could wash away the blood that flooded my mind.

An FBI agent named Townsend and Detectives Clark and Ferguson took me into a room for my statement. By the time they were finished drilling me, the long day had faded to dark.

When I saw Calixto waiting for me outside the interrogation room, tears burned my eyes. When he put his arms around me, I held him like I'd never let go. When we finally broke apart, Calixto handed me his starched cotton kerchief, and I wiped away the tears that had spilled down my cheeks.

I realized Joan was standing behind him. As much as I'd wanted to keep her out of harm's way, I had no desire to embrace her. But she stayed close, positioning herself next to me when I sat on a metal bench with Calixto. I was grateful that for once, she had nothing to say. The three of us were quiet as we waited to see if the field office agents were going to release Rich.

Agent Meloy had told Calixto that Savarine wasn't going anywhere. The FBI had enough on Savarine, his hedge fund, and its relationship to Onandi's pyramid scheme, to hold him over until his arraignment.

When Joan finally spoke, her voice was so weak, I barely recognized it.

"How could Rich put us in such a terrible predicament? Will he go to jail?" Her volume morphed into a small wail. "What will I *do*?"

"From what I have been told," Calixto said, answering her second question, "United States Attorney Hartman and the Special Agent in Charge of the Albany Division, Zale, will both be here early tomorrow. They will likely be focusing on Savarine. I do not believe they have enough on Rich to arrest him."

Personally, I thought this was a shame.

The minutes ticked on, and the big electric clock on the station wall moved slowly forward. At some point, an officer brought in boxes of pizza and sodas. I sipped some Coke, unable to look at the gooey red sauce on the flesh-colored pie dough. The sight of it made me nauseous again.

When they finally released Rich, Calixto and I walked him and Joan outside to a cop waiting in a cruiser, who would drive them to their car, still parked in the lot outside Zutti's.

While we stood in the cooling air beneath the streetlights, I breathed in and felt my nausea recede. As I watched the cruiser's taillights fade into the distance on Lake Avenue, Calixto touched my arm.

"*Querida,* allow me to drive you to the Adelphi. You can get your car tomorrow."

"It's only a short drive," I said. "I'd rather have the Mini close by. I may need it in the morning."

He gave me an exasperated shrug. "As you wish. I will drop you off now, but I must come back here briefly to speak with Agent Meloy. I will see you at the Adelphi."

I don't recall ever being more exhausted and spaced out than I was that evening when Calixto dropped me off in the alley by

Zutti's. But as I cranked the Mini's engine and wheeled onto Broadway, my mental fog started to clear. Even that small sense of regained control seemed to lessen the pounding in my head, and suddenly, I realized I was starving.

I didn't want to wait for room service at the Adelphi. Besides, I had a craving for the best instant gratification for hunger—french fries. I drove to the McDonald's on South Broadway, got a double order and a Diet Coke at the drive-up window. Then I parked in the lot and wolfed down the crisp potatoes. Between the caffeine, grease, and potatoes, I felt my energy returning, and my head began to clear.

I also felt a familiar, protective wall building inside me. From past experience, I knew it would help shield me from the emotional damage of the events I'd witnessed, and help me mentally organize what had happened.

Rico and Onandi were dead, and if, as we suspected, Onandi had killed Matt Percy, he could no longer be questioned. We might never know if he was the murderer.

The Rastafarian was dead, and I was pretty sure that every single one of the other imported Jamaican thugs had been killed. In the end, Onandi had been a fool. Had he really thought he could go up against the New York mob and win?

I didn't know how many of the kitchen staff at Zutti's had perished.

I stared out my windshield at the cars zipping by on South Broadway, grateful to be alone to think, content to sip my Diet Coke. I almost felt bad for Savarine. Stuck in jail, he'd been duped and used. Rich and my mother, however, were safely on their way home.

No one should tangle with Joan. She always comes out on top.

I thought about that first time I'd gone to visit her at her lavish stone house. She'd been so curious that I'd killed a man, had asked me if it was hard. Next time I'd seen her, she'd asked if I had a gun. She'd asked on more than one occasion. She was not a stupid woman and probably had suspicions about Rich. But as long as the money poured in, she hadn't cared.

That night at the party, she'd been as shocked as anyone by Percy's murder. I took another sip of Coke, reliving that night, remembering how I'd eavesdropped on Onandi and Rich when they'd been talking inside the house. Something I'd been trying to remember finally came to me.

Onandi had said, "You'd better have a plan to fix this, Rich."

Rico may have put Savarine together with Onandi's money and helped to instigate the racing hedge fund, but Rich went along with the plan because he already knew Onandi. He'd been in the thick of it, and in my opinion belonged in jail with Savarine.

If my job was to protect the integrity of horse racing, anything I could do to provide evidence that could revoke Rich's owner's license would be a good thing. So what if I had personal reasons to detest the man? He was still no friend to horse racing.

I considered Joan and Rich. They had to be exhausted and in shock from the day's events. I'd been through this kind of trauma before and believed I had the advantage. Rich's guard would be down. Who knew what incriminating files he might still have in his office, files that he would soon shred?

I called Calixto, and left a text. "Feeling better. Going to check on Joan. C U at Adelphi."

I put my trash in a nearby waste barrel, drove back onto Broadway, and headed back north.

38

As I pulled in to the Gormans' driveway, only a few lights were visible inside the house. After parking beneath the outdoor lighting next to Joan's Maserati, I was dismayed that the car's slick red paint brought the image of Percy's blood circling the drain. Didn't I have enough horrific pictures in my head for one day?

Walking to the front door, I heard raised voices inside. As I rang the bell, the voices escalated into a shouting match. If Joan and Rich were going at it, they apparently couldn't hear the bell, or my subsequent rap with the door knocker. Just for the hell of it, I tried the knob. It wasn't locked. I eased the door open, and stepping into the hallway, I remained perfectly still.

My mother and stepfather stood with their sides to me in the living room, facing each other. Their legs were planted wide, their chins held high, and Rich's face was red with anger. He had a gash on his neck that was bleeding. They were too intent on each other to notice me.

Joan held a wicked-looking serrated knife. She was yelling.

"Who but a bumbling *idiot* would cut themselves with their own knife? And you lied about the knife. Telling me your brother sent it to you as a gift. Why would he send you a knife? You don't even hunt!"

Was she holding the murder weapon? For one confusing instant I imagined she'd killed Percy. Then I remembered her expression when I'd described the knife to her, Rich, and Savarine. She *had* known something. She'd known the knife belonged to Rich.

One of them was likely the killer. If it was Rich, Joan was oblivious to the danger she was in. Or was she too angry to care? I stared at Rich, suddenly focusing on his hands.

A spider of fear crawled on my skin as I saw he was wearing rubber gloves.

He took a step toward her. "Of course, I don't hunt. I make money. And all you do is *spend* it. You silly cow! You and your tennis courts, decorators, and cars. Swallowing up the dough like you're at a feeding trough."

His nostrils flared like a bull, his buck teeth were bared. And when he spoke again, his voice was deadly quiet.

"You are so *stupid,* you don't even realize you've put your fingerprints on the knife that killed Percy. How fun it will be to say *you* killed him. That *you* attacked me tonight. Tried to slit my throat like you slit Percy's." He touched a gloved finger to the gash on his neck and smiled at the blood staining the rubber. "I'll be forced to hit you in self-defense."

Joan's eyes widened as she realized what he had planned for her. He saw her fear and laughed.

"The only thing you've ever wanted is my money, right?

Who won't believe you wanted to kill the goose that laid your golden eggs?"

He twisted suddenly, lunged at her, hand-chopping her wrist. The knife flew from her hand. Before she could move, he slammed his fist into to her jaw. She went down fast, sprawling onto the floor.

Rich lifted his foot in the air, raising it over Joan's neck. He would crush the life out of her.

What could I use?

I darted across the carpet to the credenza. At the sound of my footsteps he whirled in my direction, finally aware of my presence.

Grabbing the heavy bronze statue of Behold the King, I said, "Behold this, asshole."

I swung the statue into his face. The blow reverberated up my arm to my shoulder. It knocked him flat. Blood spurted from his nose, pooling onto Joan's carpet, staining it red. I stood over him, panting. I suddenly felt *invincible,* as if I'd been injected with a large dose of speed.

I got a grip on myself, called 911, and dropped to my knees on the floor next to my mother. She was coming to, starting to move.

I pressed my hands to my temples, tried to breathe normally, and waited for the distant sound of police sirens.

39

I was so sleepy and relaxed, I didn't want to wake up. With my eyes still closed, I stretched. Instead of the endless expanse of the Adelphi's king bed, one arm fell off the edge of the mattress, and my hand touched cold metal.

Something wasn't right. I opened my eyes. I was in a hospital room? The light streaming through the window told me it was morning. The previous day rushed back to me. The gunfire, the blood, the bodies. Rich and Joan. What had happened after that? I couldn't remember.

I sat up, pushed the covers back, and started to swing my legs off the bed.

"Easy, Fia. Take your time."

I recognized the voice and stared at the source in the corner of the room. *Gunny.*

"How do you feel?" he asked.

"Drugged."

"I'm not surprised. They had to sedate you last night."

"Why?"

"Your doc and I think you had a flashback from your Dermorphin episode."

I was starting to remember. I'd felt that invincible high, felt like I wanted to laugh and never stop. Like I could take on the world.

"Oh, my God," I said. "Did I hurt anyone?"

"Let me see," he said, "the last normal thing you did was to pull the voice recorder from Joan's purse. That was a great move on your part, getting everything on tape. You handed the recorder to the first cop to arrive at the scene. Then you went berserk and tried to hit him with a statue. Of course, there was no Dermorphin in your system. After the day you'd had, it's not surprising your brain pulled up the memory and took you there. Fortunately, you were weak as a kitten, easily subdued."

I pulled my legs back onto the hospital bed and lay my head against the pillows. Months earlier, I'd been injected with the drug that was up to a hundred times stronger than morphine. While on the Dermorphin, I'd felt no pain, experienced tremendous strength, and fought my way out of a terrible situation. Afterwards I'd had flashbacks for a while, but they'd stopped. I was not happy to hear I'd had a reoccurrence.

"What time is it?" I asked.

"Just past nine. It'll be fine, Fia. You just relax and take some time off for a week or two."

He was such a liar. He didn't think it was fine. I could tell by the way he pulled out his plastic bottle of antacids, rattled two out, and popped them into his mouth. How was I supposed to take it easy? I didn't know who was dead, who was alive, the status of Rich or Joan, and I wanted to see Calixto.

"Okay, okay," he said. "I can see by the look on your face

you're not gonna relax. So here's the rundown. Your mother is fine."

Of course she is.

"Calixto's buddy, Special Agent Meloy, and some agents from the United States Postal Inspection Service, found enough information in Rich's office last night to put him in jail for a long time. He helped Onandi with that Jamaican pyramid scheme. They defrauded Onandi's wealthy clients. Funneled more than $120 million of those people's money to Savarine Equine Acquisitions in exchange for millions in bogus fees. Almost two million of that was drained from SEA."

As he spoke, I got a whiff of his spice cologne and found both the familiar scent and his presence wonderfully comforting.

"Turns out," he said, "the boys from the U.S. Post Office and the investigators for the United States Attorney's Office have been jointly investigating Onandi for a while. With a little help from the Securities and Exchange Commission, your Mr. Gorman is going to federal prison."

"Good," I said. "And he's not *my* Mr. Gorman." How long, I wondered, would it take Joan to find another sugar daddy?

"So, you don't have an inclination to leap from your hospital bed and throttle anyone, do you, Fia?"

"No, I'm okay. I appreciate you coming up, Gunny."

"Had to check on my girl."

I didn't respond. I was too busy fighting an urge to cry.

"You know," he said, "Calixto was here all night. He was pretty worried about you."

"Oh." I felt a surge of happiness, but refrained from asking where Calixto was and if he was coming back. It seemed unlikely that Gunny would appreciate an ongoing affair between two of his agents.

There was a knock on the door. It swung open about a foot

and Becky Joe Benson stuck her weathered face, wispy gray hair, and beat-up Stetson into the room.

"Heard you was shooting up the town yesterday, taking out the bad guys." She pushed the door wide and came in. "If that don't beat all, Fay. Only now I hear your name is Fia. You are something, girl. How you feeling? I can see you ain't dead yet."

Gunny had risen from his chair and was fast approaching Becky Joe. "Hold on a minute. Miss McKee needs to rest, and you need to—"

"It's all right, Gunny," I said. "Becky Joe is a friend."

Gunny backed off, and Becky Joe called to someone in the hall. "It's okay, kid, you can come on in."

Stevie Davis walked in, his steps hesitant, but his face was free from fear and the tension that had plagued him.

"I'm glad you're all right, Fay. Story was all over the track early this morning. I heard you was shot, then I heard Rico is dead. Not that that's a bad thing. Then they said all kinds of people were shot and killed. I'm . . . I'm so glad you're all right. You are all right, aren't you?"

"I'm fine, Stevie. It's good to see you. Are you still riding for Mars?"

"No, ma'am. I quit that job, I'm riding for Linda Wheat. Besides, Mars quit. He said NYRA was breathing down his neck, and his days as a trainer were numbered anyway. He wanted to get out before he got more charges or fines."

"Good, and Wheat is a fine trainer. What happens to Ziggy Stardust?"

"His owner, Savarine? He sold the horse to a Kentucky stud farm and they are going to race him in the Travers."

"Who has him?" I asked.

Stevie's mouth creased into a grin. "Just so happens Linda Wheat has him. 'Course I won't ride Ziggy in the Travers, but she puts me on him in the mornings and has a couple of nice ones she plans for me to ride in the afternoon."

I was glad for Stevie. "And Lila?"

"Lila's fine. We're going to stay with Lou until Wheat takes us to Gulfstream for the winter. Lila will go to school in Hallandale Beach."

"Excellent," I said.

I heard the click of boot heels in the hallway and Calixto walked in. His white shirt was pressed, his jeans perfectly creased, and his Lucchese boots polished to a mirror finish.

Becky Joe's eyes were all over him. "Ain't you something. I swear I have never seen a better lookin' man."

Stevie squirmed a bit, Gunny rolled his eyes, and I studied my hands on the bedsheet.

When I looked up, Calixto's expression hadn't changed, but there was a slight gleam in his eyes. "Fia, what are you doing tonight?"

"Oh, lordy," Becky Joe said. "Do you have to even ask?"